I0753367

MY PLANET
The Chronicles of Moe Revisited

MY PLANET

The Chronicles of Moe Revisited

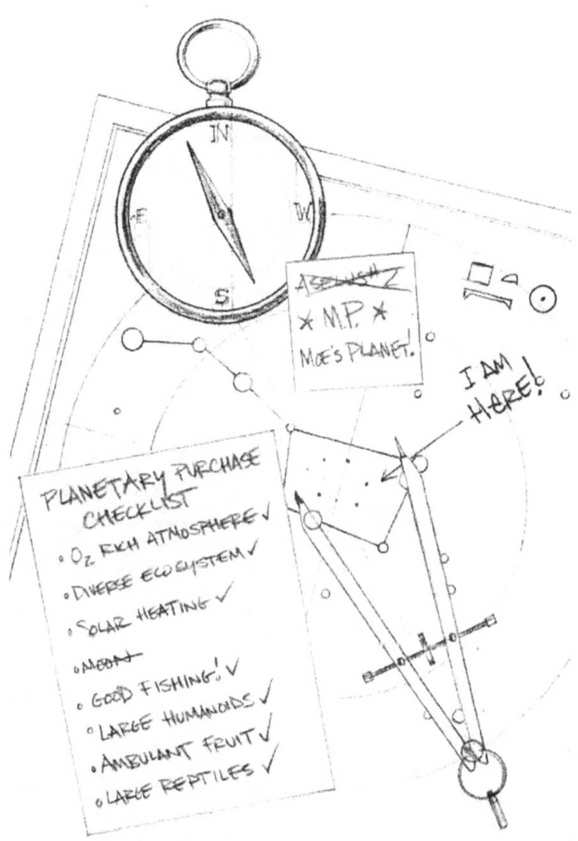

MARK MOELLER

Illustrated by Bill Ennis

MY PLANET: THE CHRONICLES OF MOE REVISITED

Author's disclaimer: This book is a work of fiction. All of the characters in this book are fictional and are not based on any particular individual. Any resemblance to actual events or individuals, living or dead, or from any other planet, is entirely coincidental. The stories in this book are based only on the author's imagination.

Illustrated by Bill Ennis. Please visit billennis.com
Cover and interior design by JamesMonroeDesign.com

ISBN 13: 979-8-9956985-0-0
Printed in the United States of America
First Edition 2008, Second Edition 2026
30 29 28 27 26 5 4 3 2 1

To order, or to contact the author, visit markmoellerauthor.com.

This book is dedicated to the proposition
that the future will be as funny and as creative
as our children want it to be.

CONTENTS

FOREWORD

Ecclesiastes 1:9 states, "There is nothing new under the sun." The verse refers to human nature, the cycles of life and history, and the fact that what we experience has been experienced by millions before us. This basic truth applies to storytelling as much as it does to the human experience. Every book or movie these days seems to be highly derivative of something else. Many lament that Hollywood and the literary world have "run out of ideas." So when you come across a story that is so unique it doesn't remind you of anything else, it is like striking gold.

Such is the case with *My Planet* by Mark Moeller. It's written like a letter from a good friend who just moved to an amazing new place that you're considering moving to as well, and he's trying to help you avoid the mistakes he made when he moved there—except this isn't just some new town, it's a new planet—one that he had towed into deep space by a corporation that sells them. The story he tells is so full of hilarious misadventures, you're not sure if he's trying to encourage you to make the same leap, or discourage you from doing so.

On his own planet, he is able to grow forests, have oceans installed, and stock it all with living creatures, some known, some created or altered in labs, including dinosaurs modified for domestic living. Think of it as a collision between *Jurassic Park, 2001: A Space Odyssey,* and *Gilligan's Island,* except this proud, new planet-owner is his own skipper and professor, and must decide every action alone. And as is usually the case when man starts tinkering with nature, the abominations and dangers that come with them is inevitable.

My Planet has been compared to *A Hitchhiker's Guide to the Galaxy,* and rightly so. If you have ever wondered what you would do if you had your own island—or world—you are in for a mind-bending adventure, and a lot of laughs!

—Mark Rickerby
Owner of Temple Gate Films
Contributor to over 30 *Chicken Soup for the Soul* titles

INTRODUCTION

To my friends, family and those who are bored to the point that reading this book is justified. My name is Moe, a name that has been handed down several generations from one of my ancestors who lived at the beginning of the 21st century. My first name is Mark, which in Latin means "warlike," a fact that for some reason, has always made sense to my mother. I had always planned to change my name to Tieberous J. Mcfudd, but my wife refuses to be Mrs. Mcfudd. I was born in December of 2210; I won't give you the day because it seems to obligate people to send lavish gifts, which many very popular and cool people have done in the past.

If you have a hard time understanding my Old American English, I apologize. The reason I'm writing in this form is for my parents, who I assume will eventually take the time to read my book. It would be great for them to know that the years of schooling, in which I minored in O.A. English, didn't go to waste. Some of you will have to refer to an American English Dictionary (1980 to 2030 edition) for some translations or your reading device will translate it for you to Modern Earth English minus the sarcasm. Many of you already know some of the information in my book and have heard some of the stories. I assure you that my rendition is the closest to the truth and the most entertaining version. A lot of authors will change individual's names to protect the innocent. The fact is, all my friends and family are guilty of something, so I left all the names the same. Sorry, Tripp. I can't say that I am completely innocent because I myself was once arrested for conspiracy to commit public nudity. You will be happy to know I was acquitted due to the lack of evidence against me.

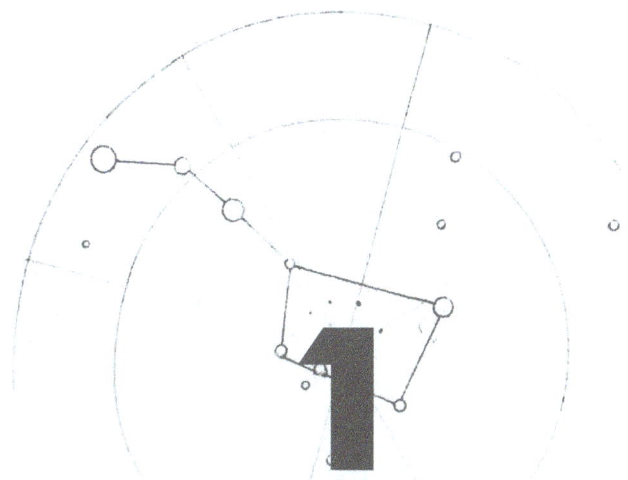

1 Welcome To My World

For those of you who don't know, a few years ago I bought my own planet. When I say "years," I'm referring to Earth years, having been raised on Earth by parents, who consider themselves to be Earthlings in every regard. In my book, I use Earth measurements in both time and distance. Luckily, in the year 2163, the combined governments of the Earth did away with the Metric System and shamed both the scientists and citizens that used it. Government officials found the metric system frustrating and the users of that system self-righteous. There was a small movement that attempted to show that the metric system was actually a far better system of measurement, but their outcries fell on deaf ears. You might ask yourself, why would I bring up something that happened hundreds of years ago? To tell the truth, I don't retain information very well, so when I do remember something, I like to share it. It's a feeble attempt to express intelligence.

The following stories and personal insights are based on journal entries that I make on my shuttle trips back and forth to my planet and other places in the galaxy where I travel for work. One of the nice things about being in space is that it is quiet. I mean, creepy quiet. Sound can't travel where there is no air, and trust me, there is no air out there. This does make space a good environment for deep thought and recollection.

I do not record the dates of my experiences, so there is no chronological order to my narrative. I find that if I put dates in my books, people spend too much time debating my timeline, and my friends seem justified in arguing that my information is all wrong. The reason I am writing this book is so it can be used as a guide to successful planet ownership and practical problem solving. I understand that not everyone can afford to buy or lease a planet, but for many of you, it might be one of your long-term goals. If it is, I hope you will find a lot of helpful hints in this book that are based on my experiences, both successful and unsuccessful.

Recently, I have seen a new trend; authors have started to print their work on paper again. I'm sure many of you have gone your entire lives and never read literature from an actual bound paper book. Most of you will probably think of it as Neanderthal and just one small step above cave painting as a way of sharing information. I thought it would be fun to print this book on paper with real ink. Yes, a digital audio and tri-digital 3D version will be made available as well.) To quote my friend, Tripp: "a book without pictures is not worth reading." It is this mentality among men that leads our wives and partners to treat us, as a group, like we're ten years old. If I do have pictures, they're going to have to be artistic renditions, because I can't afford holograms for my book. Another friend Chuck, mentioned that perhaps I should get someone a little more intelligent than myself to write my book for me. As much as I appreciate his opinion, I think he could be a little more positive with his feedback. If I lacked the intelligence to write a book, I'm sure someone would have told me before now.

So, I bought a planet. It isn't much of a planet as far as planets go, but it's right for me. Coming up with the funds was no small task. Part of the cash deposit was from a legal settlement from when I was blown up at the age of eighteen. The rest was a loan from my father. (By the way, "Thanks Dad.") My father is a clever man and very industrious. He has made a fortune by developing a way to remove R-7 gas from large asteroids. Fortunately for me, he thought it was more important for me to get an education than to work on a drill rig in space. This work is always in the middle of nowhere, and very dangerous. I would explain how his invention works, but as my father is famous for saying, "It's proprietary information," Besides, I don't know exactly how it works, I know it has something to do with the gases trapped inside the rock when the planet's explosion formed the asteroids. Anyway, my father sells the R-7 gas all over the galaxy to fuel suns and stars, both natural and engineered. R-7 gas is the only known substance that can be used to replace hydrogen as a sun's fuel source and still be cost effective. R-7 gas is also used in the manufacturing of Steelglass or Clearsteel, which is glass used for shuttles, ships, and general construction in space. The sand used to make this particular glass is from the planet Armerious Telron, and it requires extreme heat to melt it. The clear metal that is formed is twice as strong as steel and half the weight of aluminum per square inch.

I know . . . more pointless information. Back to my planet: I sometimes refer to it as MP1X or "Moe's Planet" because the name it came with was Aselus #2 and I thought it sounded dumb. The 1X doesn't stand for anything; it just sounded cool. Besides, it's my planet and I'll call it whatever I want. Yes, on an Area 5 Space DSPS Map or (Deep Space Positioning System), it's still labeled Aselus #2.

Before the purchase of MP1X, my father and I had a meeting in his office, and we discussed at great length the responsibilities involved in owning a planet. Well, we sort of discussed it—he did all the talking and I sat and did my best to act like a person who should oversee a whole planet. He wrapped it up with his "Living a Responsible and Useful Life" speech, which I could almost recite from memory. For him, I believe MP was an investment that he was putting in my charge, but he was also buying into the consequences of his investment. Since there aren't any colonies on MP, there are fewer things for me to be responsible for. I do my best work when there are three or less people watching me do it. I also promised to read the Planet Functions Manual before I changed anything that would affect a global outcome. Fortunately, the PF Manual is easy to reference on a tablet.I can just tap the screen and ask questions. It has twelve thousand chapters, and I am proud to say I have read six of them. I'm saving chapter 7 The Stabilization of Planet Rotation Momentum Equaling Gravitational Pull Monitoring Systems—for when I have time to really enjoy it. It sounds like a real page-turner.

MP is a type-B planet, and the original planet blank was built about 300years ago by the Do It Our Way Design Firm, one of the most notable planet engineering companies on record. After the planet was stabilized, its surface was designed by and finished for Lord Henry Pincey lll, who, fortunately, was from Earth. I say "fortunately" because, being from Earth myself, it already has a lot of the things I was looking for in a planet. It has similar weather, natural water, and air filtration systems like Earth. Or should I say, "like Earth *was*" since Earth has been upgraded. It seems that the Pincey family had to sell the planet for financial reasons, and that meant I got a good deal on it. It would have been worth more, but Lord Pincey lll did not have the planet appraised, probably because a proper appraisal takes up to twenty-two Earth years to complete. That includes surveys, geology, water content evaluation, quantity estimations, and mapping. It is possible to request all those things from the bureaucrats at O.W.D.S., but to get the answers from them takes about the same amount of time and money.

The natural gravity level of MP1X is seven because of the planet's size. As you know, the Earth is nine, so it did away with the need for me to lose that excess weight. The average adult human male on Earth is 160 pounds, so on MP, they would be about twenty pounds lighter. I'm a bit over average for being from Earth; not that I'm too chubby, but let's just say I've never ordered half a sandwich before. My love of food is one of the best reasons I have for getting up in the morning. The only time I lied to my wife was when we were dating, and I convinced her that I was into exercise and other athletic activities like hiking without robotic assistance. Trust me when I tell you the only time I have climbed a mountain is when the LT6 Hiker Service robot I rented carried me, which allowed me to enjoy the beautiful surroundings without all the heavy breathing, sweating, and occasional chest pains.

My planet is pretty much self-sufficient other than some gardening and pest control that I do myself. On MP, most of the lakes and rivers are naturally heated through sunlight and thermal pockets. The river near my cabin is the Lady Pincey River. It is called this only because I haven't thought of a clever name to replace it. The LP River runs from the mountains north of the cabin all the way south across the great plains and into The Great Blue Lake. I haven't renamed that one, either. The lake by my cabin, which I call Lake Moe, of course, has a fusion heater, so it can be heated for a comfortable swim in a few hours but the change in temperature tends to kill off my more sensitive fish.

The planet core is molten lava and is supposed to have a shelf life of ten thousand years. At least that's what the realtor said. (Cross your fingers.) The oxygen levels were a little higher than they are supposed to be because there isn't any pollution. The first week I was there, I walked around in a state of nirvana until my body adjusted to the "oxygen high." Luckily, my buddy Chuck found a buyer for some of my extra oxygen, and since then, we have brought the levels down to normal. Fortunately, planet-generated oxygen, or natural O2, is worth more than manufactured air on the open market. So, I made enough on the sale to make some of my planet's global improvements.

For those of you who are not familiar with the effect of time in relation to space travel, I can explain it this way. One day on My Planet is roughly three quarters of a day on Earth. Well, not a day as in sunrise to sunset, but a twenty-four-hour period. Time in relation to space changes a bit outside our local galaxy. It's not a concept that is easy to figure out but if you understand Einstein's E=MC squared you can probably figure it out. The first couple of times I left Earth on a trip when I got back, I had the bends something awful. Believe me when I tell you drinking Bearvenan Spiced Rum does not help at all, but a good piece of Bry chocolate does.

Back to time and space. My shuttle computer has my calendar and planner on it, and she keeps me on schedule. This is vital because you can only use the whole "time/space relation, equality" as an excuse for missing your mother's birthday party so many times before you are out of the will.

My home on MP1X is right next to Lake Moe. I call it a cabin due to the rustic setting. My lovely wife Tressa informed me that a home of that size, with so many modern devices, really isn't a cabin. I explained that a cabin is a place in the woods that you can go to get away for the weekend. Obviously, the whole conversation wasn't worth debating with her because she said I was right. Moe 1- Tressa 2,462!

My cabin and accessories are powered by growth generators. This is a human invention that was developed after scientists found that the solar panels that were being installed all over the Earth were the leading cause of global warming. The growth generators are built into trees and large plants around my house. I did have them removed from my fruit trees because the fruit I was growing only got to be half their normal size and wouldn't ripen. The rest of the plants and trees grow fast enough to give me plenty of power. By the way, the information on the solar panels may be just propaganda from my brother-in-law. There are very few solar generators still used on Earth, so you can decide for yourself. For a couple hundred years, Earth's engineers used tall wind turbines with massive blades to generate energy, but we sliced and diced many of Earth's large bird population to extinction in the name of pollution control. The new bladeless towers are more efficient and nature friendly.

My cabin was built by the Do It Our Way Design Firm and was paid for by the Pincey family as part of the closing expenses for the planet. If you are planning on having a home or resort built on your planet, it's important to have the cost, if possible, included in the closing costs of your new planet. The O.W.D.F. built my cabin, shed, and barn with the designs that I submitted to them. In fact, it took them less than a week to get it all done. When you have over a hundred workers, not including robots and automated construction machinery, you can really get crap done. I had flown out to MP1X to check on how it was going, and the whole project was done. The Relleom project manager handed me the code key to the front door lock, which was odd because I didn't plan on locking the doors. I believe it was more ceremonial than anything.

The cabin is beautiful. It was constructed of large lodge pole pines that came from a forest not far from where I had it built. I had to cut some of the trees down for fire management anyway. The whole setting looks like a picture out of an American Old West novel. Because much of the lumber was from MP, this cut way back on the cost of the whole project.

One of my favorite parts of my cabin is the big, wood burning fireplace. It's made from cut stone and has a rough texture on the outside edges. The stonework goes all the way up to where the chimney touches the vaulted ceiling. The fireplace is large enough that I can put almost any sized log in it. If you have never smelled the smoke from a good wood fire, you are really missing something special. I had a roasting spit and frame built in for cooking over the fire. A spit is a metal rod that is designed to hold food while it is being cooked. A small motor turns the spit so the food cooks evenly.

The first week I was in my cabin, I cooked a large bird over the fire. I won't tell you what kind of bird it was because it is now a protected species on Earth. Historically, it was one of the most consumed animals on Earth until the late 2180s. I can't tell you where I got this bird from, but I can tell you it was not the one that disappeared from the bird aviary at the ZooParc de Beauval in France last year. I took great care to cook this magnificent example of poultry in a traditional Earth style, covering it with garlic, sage, and other Earth spices. Unfortunately, I must have misread the recipe or used the wrong wood for the fire because it was quite possibly the worst thing I have ever tasted.

Above my fireplace is a big wooden mantel, and I planned to get a largemouth bass replica to go on top of it to represent my redneck heritage. Tressa was not happy about the fish idea, so instead, I found a projector that mounts flush to the top of the mantle and projects a large, three-dimensional bass that appears to be mounted, or it can swim back and forth along the length of the mantle. It can also project a talking moose head, a large marlin mount, or for Tressa, a large bouquet of colorful flowers that sway slightly to some unknown breeze. Tressa has mentioned that the moose head, which she has named Mortimer, is very entertaining, and his jokes, according to her, are "actually funny."

All the woodworking was laser cut to save on cost, but it's done to look like it was hand carved. To maintain the rustic appeal of my cabin and barn, I went without the N.R.S. on the interior and exterior, including the furniture. N.R.S. is Nanotechnology Repair Systems, which is a micro-thin layer applied when products are manufactured that allows the wood and paint to fix itself when it is damaged. This has given me the chance to fix any problems that come up. I do enjoy a good project. My LX shuttle has N.R.S., thank goodness, but it is just for the exterior and the inside upholstery. As you probably know, you can't leave items on your shuttle seats for more than a week or the N.R.S. will cause your upholstery to partially or completely absorb it.

MP1X and the others in my area share a sun that was built by the Light of Day Star Company. This company is run by Relleoms who subcontract a lot of work for Trillions—the group that discovered Earth. Fortunately, my father's company has a huge contract with Relleoms to supply them with R-7 Gas. So, after some serious negotiation on my part, I get to trade R-7 Gas for sunlight. (Thanks again Dad.) Believe me, it's much better to do business with a Relleom than a Trillion. For those of you who haven't met a Relleom or didn't know that they were, they are a friendly humanoid species who happen to make some of the best food in the galaxy. You can find them working as chefs in restaurants all over the galaxy except for Earth because of the E.R.T.W.A. or Earthling Right to Work Act. Even with a Blue Card, individuals from other planets cannot work on Earth in blue collar jobs. Oh, sure, they can be attorneys, college professors, and bankers, but they can't program your service robots or work in the food service industry. You have probably seen the anti-E.R.T.W.A. rallies and protests on the news.

None of the planet owners in my neighborhood wanted to put up the money for a moon. It would mostly be for decoration since none of the planets in my neighborhood need a moon for gravity or ocean tide control. It doesn't matter to me, but it would add some nice ambience to the nighttime. I recently found a small self-levitating moon in a catalog that has a circumference of about two miles. The company that manufactures them claims that installation is free, and it can be placed and maintained at any altitude the customer requires on low-to-medium gravity planets. They also advertise that they can manufacture it to look like any planet or moon in our solar system. The problem, other than the huge price tag, is the fact that it isn't lit, so it would be a big, black spot in the sky at night. Because of its size, it would have to be placed close to my planet so that the sun would not shine on it at night. They can light them, but the process would involve a radiation issue. At low levels, it isn't dangerous, but it would screw up my limited TV reception. Although I said it would improve our planet's value, my lovely wife said no. Actually, what she said was, "Not a chance in hell, Moe!" She is the responsible one in this relationship. It wasn't just the price; Tressa likes to watch her TV shows while she is on MP, so I didn't dare mess with that, either. The planet Aselus-1 is close enough to MP that it's like having a moon anyway. Aselus-1 is owned by the Do It Our Way Design Firm who built my planet. I think they keep it as a company retreat and/or a tax write off. They are closer to the sun than me, so I get quite a bit of reflected light at night unless it's cloudy. At night on MP1X, if you look at Aselus-1, it is bright enough that if you close your eyes, you can still see the image.

The weather on my planet is not something I can control. But I do have a calendar that gives me the forecast for the next ninety-six years. So, I know when it's going to rain or snow, give or take a minute or two. If I wanted to, I could spend the money and buy a climate control system for my planet. The problem is, I don't trust myself with the weather. If it was up to me, there wouldn't be any snow on MP at all. But snow is important to the climate and the water shed, according to my planet manual. I really enjoy the random nature of the weather, and it makes for a nice change from day to day. If the climate isn't going to be what I'm in the mood for, I just spend my weekend on another part of the planet. With my weather planner, I can schedule my fishing trips in advance to avoid being rained on. I do not fish in the rain. If it's raining at my cabin, I just hang out, drink hot chocolate, and read a good book in front of the fire. Yes, I have a sensitive side. Yes, I feel it's necessary to explain myself. Yes I may be struggling with who I really am. And yes, that may be the reason I shoot at things. You should stop being so judgmental.

2

Off Planet At Last

In the R-7 gas business, you need tankers. Subsolar gas tankers are huge container ships that are pulled through space from drilling and pump sights to storage lots, and then to customers by tugships, which are the tugboats of space. Most of you would have never seen a gas tanker because they are so large, they can't be on a planet with regular gravity levels or the tanks will collapse in on themselves under their own weight. The tugship's captains dock the tankers in space to allow these individuals to visit whatever planet they call home when they are off work. Sometimes, if the moon is full, you can see the outline of the docking station, if it's between the Earth and the moon. You can't see them during the day because the sun would have to reflect off the tankers, and trust me, there is nothing shiny on a gas tanker.

My father's company, Orion's Belt Mining, LLC, employs a couple dozen tugship captains. Every six months, all these pilots come to Earth for mandatory safety meetings and to review their shipping assignments. I was twelve years old when I went with my father to my first company meeting to meet all the captains. I had always wanted to go, but to be honest, this group of individuals were probably the roughest group of misfits a person could ever meet in the known universe. No one with any social skills or a desire to communicate with other individuals on a regular basis would ever aspire to be a tugship captain. My father was always hesitant to expose me to this rowdy bunch. One thing I have learned from being around them now for most of my life is that they are content with who they are. The fact that they are among a limited number of individuals who are good enough pilots to do their jobs well provides them a freedom that most people don't have. This gives them a feeling of camaraderie that most of us crave in our lives.

The annual company meetings are held in the company's conference center and usually last a couple of hours. Otus, the OBM safety specialist, oversees much of the meeting and reviews the space transportation regulations both the companies and the government require. After all the regulations are reviewed, my father gives a short speech that goes over any new company business, followed by a short motivational bit. When he is done, he always takes a minute and gives the captains a chance to ask any questions or share any complaints. This is usually the shortest part of the meeting because most captains really are the best there is at their jobs and don't need instructions on how to do it. They do take this opportunity to make sarcastic comments about each other and question everyone else's piloting abilities. This is, of course, done in good humor, and with my father present, usually done mostly in good taste. Before he was done, my father turned and gestured in my direction as I sat behind him in a large comfortable chair.

"This is my son, Marcus. Someday he will be running this place, so don't pick on him too much."

My dad winked at me when he said this, then turned back to the group and finished up. When the meeting was over, the majority of the twenty-some-odd tugship captains headed to a pub that happened to be across the street from the OBM's conference center. The Stray Cat Bar was usually empty in the early afternoon, so there was always room at the bar to fit the whole motley crew. For a couple of hours, these otherwise solitary individuals would relax and socialize. After a few drinks, they would tell stories and jokes about work or life without the restraints of my father's or anyone else's less than approving glances. Without the censorship of good taste or the obligation to tell the truth, their stories became legendary.

When the meeting adjourned, my dad stepped off the podium and made it a point to shake the pilots' hands, and a few of them even received one of my father's legendary slaps on the back. I always appreciated that my father showed so much respect to these captains, who are such an important part of the success of his company. I followed him down the line, shaking everyone's hands. I also received a hug from Captain Molly Grim, who I found to be nice in a very terrifying way. Captain Molly appeared to have once been an attractive woman who now seemed more ready for a bar fight than a girl's luncheon.

I was following my father back to his office when I saw all the tugships parked in the company's parking lot. We had arrived early, before the meeting, so my father could go over some things with Otis beforehand. The large ships arrived after we were in the soundproof building. The enormous tugships sat in a row. The one closest, just behind my father's shuttle, was the Space Slug, one of the more infamous tugships. The Space Slug was owned and piloted by Jasper Bazzelman, one of my father's oldest employees. He had told me stories about Jasper for years, and from the look of his beat-up ship, his reputation was well deserved. My father had another meeting to attend, so instead of sitting in his waiting room, I asked if I could check out the ships.

"That's fine, Markus, but don't go on the ships, and come back to the office when you are done looking," he said as I turned and headed that way. It was a long walk to the ships, and as I crossed the sunny pavement, some movement caught my attention. The group of pilots were leaving the conference building through a back door and making their way across the parking lot and street to the tavern. The captains all had flight jackets on with their names on their chest and the name of their ship across their backs. I recognized Jasper Bazzelman; he was the shortest and most stocky of the group, with a bushy beard and flat, matted hair. It looked like he had combed it that morning for the first-time in a long time. The group laughed loudly as they moved in a mass into the tavern. My curiosity got the best of me and I looked to see if I was out of view of my father's office windows. Seeing that I was in the clear, I diverted from my current path and headed in their direction.

As I crossed the street, the last of the pilots entered the Stray Cat, their laughter fading as the large, wooden door shut tight behind them. I walked to one of the tavern windows first and tried to peer in. The outside of the glass was dirty and the inside much darker than the sun-filled sidewalk I stood on, so watching from outside would be impossible. Feeling a little overconfident, I decided I would sneak in and try to blend into the crowd.

With great effort, I pulled open the heavy door and walked in. The door closed, pushing me forward into the room. The sound of loud conversation and laughter that filled the room suddenly went silent when I entered. “So much for a stealthy entrance,” I mumbled to myself.

As my eyes adjusted to the dim lights, I could see a room full of rough pilots staring right at me. Jasper stood at the bar and appeared to be in the middle of ordering a drink from a KT1S service robot that served as the tavern’s bartender.

Jasper smiled at me through his long mustache. “Well, Junior Bossman Markus, to what do we owe the pleasure of yer company?”

Jasper spoke Earth English very well, but there was always a hint of an accent with the heavy use of his Rs. I shrugged my shoulders, not prepared with a reasonable answer. He laughed out loud and motioned for me to come over and stand by him. As I approached, the rest of the group returned to their conversations. When I had crossed the room, Jasper was waiting. He put his rough hand on my shoulder and turned me to face the bar. Looking up at the six-foot four-inch robot, Jasper spoke loudly.

“Bartender, get this gentleman a drink! He is going to be the boss of this group someday and we want ‘im treated well.”

There was a roar of laughter and applause from the crowd. The very intimidating robot loomed over me, and as it looked down, a light turned on in his chest. The flat red beam started at my feet and scanned its way to the top of my head. After his quick analysis, the robot bartender spoke clearly toward the rough-looking tugship captain.

“This gentleman seems to be below the legal age allowed under law to be given any drink other than water, or perhaps a lemonade. Unless he is able to produce a form of identification proving otherwise, I must deny him service and must ask to have him removed from this tavern."

Jasper raised his hand and answered the robot.

"He has his I.D. right here." He dropped it outside, and I grabbed it for him. "He looks young," he continued, "so you lot harass him everywhere he goes."

Jasper looked down at me and winked. With his right hand, he pulled an identification card out of his pocket and held it in front of the robot. The KT1S robot's scanner fired up again, reading the card.

"According to your identification, you are Jaspeireous Bazzelman from the planet Kalon and you are two hundred and six Earth years old. Is that correct?"

I looked up at the robot, unsure of how to respond. And then, in a moment of sheer courage, I nodded my head and frowned, furrowing my eyebrows to show my serious side. "That's me," I replied in the deepest voice my pre-teen body could muster. There was another roar of laughter from the crowd, and in the midst of the loud cheers, a small light in the robot's chest turned green.

"Well, Mr. Bazzelman, what would you like to drink?" the robot asked in a more gracious and sociable voice. I panicked; at that moment, I think I would have preferred to have been thrown out of the bar than to be asked any more questions. My mind flashed back to a conversation my parents were having about ordering drinks. My father said something to the effect of, "The Jupiter Rum is so strong, only the tugship captains can handle it." It was the only drink I knew by name, so I blurted it out.

"I'll have a Jupiter Rum, please." Jasper looked at me, his

eyes wide open and his bushy eyebrows raised in surprise. He turned back to the bartender.

"I think I'll be having the same as Jasper here," he said, patting me on the back.

The robot turned, and with one of four arms, he reached the top shelf of the bar and retrieved a dark brown glass decanter filled with liquid. With another arm, he wiped off the antique container, and with a third arm, he pulled the cork out with a "pop!" His last arm lifted two small glasses from a lower shelf, and he poured the dark brown liquid into the small crystal glasses. The KT1S pushed the glasses forward on the bar till they sat within reach of us. Jasper grabbed both glasses and handed me one.

"Here you go, Captain. That will certainly put hair on yer chest!"

I took the glass and stared down at the thick brown liquid. I'm not sure, but it looked like the rum might have moved slightly on its own. The gruff old captain lifted his glass and touched it to mine, clinking them together. He raised his drink while he leaned his head back, emptying the goblet in one quick shot. When he spoke, he was slightly out of breath. "Oof, it's been a while. I may be getting too old fer Jupiter rum."

He inhaled a breath of air and blew it out as if he was trying to extinguish invisible flames burning in his mouth. Everything in my head said this was a bad idea, and that I should put the glass down and take the walk of shame out of the bar. Many of the pilots were watching me, and I seemed to be in this situation a bit too deep to just walk away. Jasper looked at me and smiled.

"You know, Captain, you do have to pilot your ship this evening. Maybe you should pass on the rum and we'll get ya something a bit less aggressive to drink."

Several of the other pilots, including Captain Molly, were watching and nodded in agreement. Molly had a somewhat concerned look on her face as she looked down the long bar at me.

"Yer gunna want to be careful with that rum. Too much can turn ya inside out!" she said, and the rest of the gritty bunch nodded in unison once again. The problem was that at my age, their concern for me came off as more of a dare than a deterrent. I stared down at my reflection in the gravy-colored liquid. Lacking the ability for sensible reasoning, I raised the glass to my lips and took a small sip of the warm brown potion, the strong-smelling vapors instantly clearing my sinuses. As the drink filled my mouth and ran down my throat to my stomach, I immediately began to regret my decision to drink it. My whole body felt like it was on fire while simultaneously freezing, then finally everything went numb. My stomach wanted to throw it up, but my throat and mouth refused to allow the liquid fire to pass their way again.

I looked up at Jasper and, as clearly as I could, said, "I should get back to the office before my father misses me."

Jasper nodded his head. "Good idea. I best walk you over there."

I turned awkwardly and started back toward the exit; walking was difficult because I couldn't feel my legs or feet. Jasper had his hand on my shoulder and kept me walking straight, which was difficult with the room tilting side to side. The other pilots that were close enough slapped me on the back as I passed, which accelerated my desire to throw up. The pair of us made it out of the tavern and across the road, stopping only long enough for me to "be sick" in a waste container in the parking lot. This was an opportunity to re-live the whole burning throat and mouth again. Jasper pulled a rag out of his pocket and handed it to me to wipe my face and mouth off. I leaned against his hand as he guided me through the doors of the office, sitting me in a big chair in the waiting room. My whole body was going from cold with chills to hot and sweaty within seconds of each other. Ms. Tracy, the receptionist, peered down at me from her desk.

"Wow, Moe, you don't look so good." She turned to Jasper. "This young man seems to be a bit green!"

"Well, Ms. Tracy, Captain Marcus here wandered into the Stray Cat and had a sip of something he probably shouldn't have," Jasper replied, shrugging his shoulders.

"Alright, his father is going to be a while. You better get back to the tavern before he comes out. I'll keep an eye on him," she said, using her nose to point at me. Jasper looked me over one more time.

"Well, Junior Bossman, you will be okay after a couple hour nap."

I smiled up at him, my vision still a little foggy. I went to say thanks for the help but when I opened my mouth, all that came out was a large belch. He smiled and patted my head, then turned and walked out of the door.

"Wow, is that Jupiter Rum? I can smell that burp all the way over here!" Ms. Tracy said as she waved her hand in front of her nose. I looked up at her but couldn't remember how to talk, so I managed to smile up at her with the side of my face that was still working.

"That's what I thought," she said as she shook her head back and forth in disapproval. I leaned back in the chair, hoping it would support my head that suddenly felt a hundred pounds heavier. Minutes later, my father walked into the room and saw me sitting in a chair.

"Hey, Marcus. I'm going to be a while longer. Are you okay to wait?"

I smiled and gave a thumbs up. I figured it was best not to try and speak at that moment.

"You look tired, maybe you should go out and take a nap in the shuttle till I'm done."

I smiled again with the half of my face that was working, and this time I did a double thumbs up. He stared at me suspiciously but turned and spoke to Ms. Tracy.

"Will you call cleaning services?" my father said to Ms. Tracy. "I think something in one of these trash cans has gone bad. They should come empty all of them."

Ms. Tracy nodded her head while shooting me an evil eye. My father turned and then walked back to his office. When he was gone, I looked over at his middle-aged secretary, who sat looking at me and shaking her head again.

"Do you think you can make it out to the shuttle by yourself, or do you need me to walk you out there?"

"I'm okay, I think," I managed to blurt out as I slowly got to my feet. The room was swaying a little as I walked toward the light coming from the large glass doors that led to the parking area. I misjudged the distance to the door, and before I could stop, smushed my head against the glass with a dull thud, leaving a faint impression of my face on the warm, clear surface. I pushed open the door, opening my eyes just far enough in the bright sunlight to get a bearing on my father's shuttle location, and then slowly made my way in that direction. This was the last thing I remember till I woke up in my bed sometime later.

As I opened my very heavy eyelids, I noticed it was dark in my room and there was an unusual sound coming through the bedroom walls. It was a faint buzzing sound, as if my father had left the shuttle running in the driveway. I thought it was weird because the sound dampening walls of our home usually kept outside sounds out. There was an odor that filled the room—a smell that was very similar to when I had worn shoes for a couple days without socks. I didn't know if the smell or the sounds were aftereffects of my first sip of Jupiter Rum. That would explain the taste in my mouth that can be compared to having eaten Rosson Black Cheese, which I took a bite of last month after losing a bet to Chuck. My head felt like absurdly heavy. It was dark and I assumed that I had slept through the afternoon and evening. With a hoarse voice I managed to growl to my bedroom system.

"Computer, lights on."

I heard a soft chime and a somewhat seductive woman's voice respond, "Yes, my Captain."

Suddenly, the room was brightly lit. It took a second to focus, but after blinking repeatedly, my surroundings came into focus and my heart sank into my stomach. It appeared that I was in a cabin on a ship, and it was one I had never seen. There were no windows, just a closet, a wall mounted computer display, and a handful of pictures on a digital display board. There was what seemed to be a small bathroom and a door I hoped was an exit. I looked down and noticed that I was still fully clothed, including my shoes. I slowly got up, my head still buzzing, and walked to the door, stopping for a second to look at the pictures on the dimly lit display. There were several pictures of sporty shuttles, and a couple shots of an attractive girl wearing a swimsuit. In one photo, the same girl was standing holding hands with someone who looked like a clean-shaven version of Jasper Bazzelman. On one edge of the picture was a date, 4/8/2122. I stared at it, trying to do some quick math in my foggy head and determined that it was apparently taken almost 100 years ago. I turned and walked to the door. As I depressed the handle, I heard a click and the door slid open automatically.

The hallway in front of me was lit by a warm red glow. I stuck my head out into the hallway, which had a solid wall on one side and a long continuous window on the other. The red glow came from the window. As I stepped across the hall and peered out into space, I could see an enormous, red planet below me passing slowly. The view was incredible, and my heart started beating faster as I stared down at what I can only assume was the planet Mars. It was incredible to see this close, with huge craters, jagged rock mountains, and swirling storm clouds of red dust and sand.

I had never been this far into outer space, and I stared out at the incredibly bright stars surrounded by intense darkness. To my surprise, my mind was immediately at peace. I had always expected that the vastness of space would terrify me, but that couldn't have been farther from the reality of being there. I have always found serenity in solitude. People have asked me if I am ever affected by being occasionally alone on my planet. To be honest, I have never been more comfortable than when I'm solo. (Don't tell my wife I said that. I love you, baby, and you're very pretty.)

The steel glass window felt cold to the touch and there was a slight vibration in the smooth surface, I guessed, from the ship's engines. I turned to my left and moved toward a door at the end of the narrow hallway. The closer I got to the end, the louder the buzzing sound became. I reached out, touching the button on the door, and it slid open, revealing a large engine room full of working machinery and wall computer panels displaying the current engine stats and ship functions.

As I turned to go back in the other direction, the door automatically slid shut and the sound of the equipment was once again muffled. I passed the bedroom compartment door that was now closed and walked toward the other end. The warm light from the large, red planet below was beginning to fade as the ship passed over it and left it behind. As I got close to the end of the passageway, my excitement and anxiety started to build. Just as I reached out to touch the access button, I could hear what sounded like muffled rock music playing from behind the door. I pushed the button, the door slid open, and I was instantly blasted by the sound of an electric guitar being played at a feverish pace. The loud music, combined with my serious hangover, made me pause momentarily. I was wondering if my head was going to explode, or if I was going to vomit, or both at the same time.

The dimly lit room was the bridge of a ship. Most of the wall space was covered by electronic control panels and monitors. The front was all windows, and in the center was a captain's chair facing away from the door. The light from the electronics showed the outline of someone sitting in the chair, his socked feet on the dash, and his arms moving frantically, following a sudden drum solo in the music.

I stepped forward, closing the distance between us and stopped just to the side of Captain Jasper Bazzelman. It was when Jasper extended his arm especially high to reach an invisible High Tom drum that he caught me out of the corner of his eye. His head turned sharply, and his body and swivel chair followed till he was facing me. His eyes were open to the point where it was most likely painful, and his mouth opened slightly. With his one hand, he reached up and touched a button on his console and the loud music stopped abruptly.

"What the . . ."

What followed was a very expressive use of Kalonian vocabulary that I have decided not to repeat in case you're tempted to translate it. Even though he described it quite specifically in his native tongue, the surprise he felt at my presence I can't in good taste repeat at this time. So, to sum up, I'm going to go with "Golly, this is unfortunate" and "How in the fresh pineapple did you get on my ship?" It became apparent to him that I was as surprised as he was as I stared back at him with my hands out, palms up, and shaking my head. He closed his eyes then opened them again slowly as if to reboot and restart the conversation.

"Okay, let's try this," he said, pointing a finger at nothing in particular. "What is the last thing you remember?"

I looked up at the ceiling hoping it would jog my memory, then I described standing up and going outside and how bright it was leaving the office. I told him that I could see my dad's shuttle, and I headed toward it. After that, I got nothing. Jasper lowered his eyebrows, showing he was thinking hard as he slowly turned his chair till it faced forward. He leaned forward and took a handful of shelled, salted peanuts out of a container in a cupholder by his armrest and threw them in his mouth. Chewing this salty treat appeared to be the process he used to help him think.

"I guess the first thing to do is get a message to your parents to make sure they know you're not dead or stolen. With a little luck, I won't get fired, and you won't be killed by your parents.

I left Earth—oh, sorry—*we* left Earth close to two hours ago, so the sooner I call, the better."

Jasper put on his headset and pushed a sequence of buttons on the instrument panel in front of him. The call must have gone through to my father because Jasper began talking in an apologetic voice.

"Yes, sir. This is Captain Bazzelman. I am about two hours off-planet and just discovered a stowaway on my ship. Yes, sir. He's okay. I believe he climbed aboard my ship by accident. He seems to be a little fuzzy on the details as to how he came to be in my company. I can return him right now or he can stay on board till tomorrow when I return with that empty tanker from the storage lot Jupiter 6. No, sir, it's no problem. I'll have him clean the galley to give him something to do. No problem, boss. I will see you tomorrow evening." Jasper took off his head set and put it back down on his instrument panel. "Well, it looks like you have a stay of execution till tomorrow," he said as he turned back to face me.

"Thank you. Did you want me to start cleaning the galley?"

"Nah, you don't have to do that. My mangy T-1 bot keeps the whole ship pretty much spotless. Why don't you take a seat on the couch over there and work on a good story to tell your father tomorrow." He gestured toward a small couch in the rear of the cabin. I looked out the big windshield of the ship.

"If it's okay with you, Captain, I would like to stand here and look at the view," I responded, then walked to the window and peered out.

"I can do you one better than that. You better take a step back," he said as he pushed a button on his panel. There was a mechanical sound as the floor in front of me opened and a second captain's chair came up through it, filling the space between Jasper and myself. "There you go, have a seat right there," he said with a self-satisfied grin.

I sat down in the soft captain's chair and stared out at the incredible view. Jasper chuckled at the starstruck look on my face. "Is this the first time you have been in deep space Mr. Markus?"

I looked over at him and nodded. "Yes, it is. It's the most amazing thing I have ever seen in my life. Oh, and you can call me Moe. Everyone except my father calls me Moe."

"Alright, Moe it is!" he said, smiling. I pointed at a large grey dot directly in front of us.

"What is that right there? I don't recognize that planet, or the stars around it."

Jasper leaned forward and hit another button on his panel and the whole view in front of us lit up with small blue lettering. Each star and planet that I could see had a name and location number next to it. The grey planet was titled Jupiter 3611 and it gave its distance from us, which was slowly clicking down. I stared at the names, and I must have still appeared to be puzzled because Jasper, still looking at the stars, chimed in.

"When you travel in deep space, all your perspectives change and it takes a bit to adjust your mind. It's kind of like looking at a large tree on Earth—if you look at it from one side and then walk around to the other side, most things that you remember about it have changed completely. Even the best pilots get turned around in space sometimes." I looked over at him.

"Have you ever been lost before?" He smiled.

"Nah, a ship's captain will never admit to having been lost; we refer to it as an unexpected detour from charted space," he said, winking in my direction. "The only thing I worry about is running out of salted Earth peanuts before I figure out where the hell I am!" he added as he casually pushed a button on the ship's console.

As I sat watching the view in front of me, I realized that the taste in my mouth had worsened. I was trying to clean the layer of slime off my front teeth with my tongue when I saw the captain staring at me. "Sorry," I said, realizing how annoying the sound from my mouth movements must have been. "My mouth tastes like I used my tongue to clean the floor in my brother's room."

Jasper laughed out loud and then reached down in his pants pocket and pulled out a small tin. He opened it and took out two blue lozenges that seemed to glow slightly.

"Try these," he said, handing me the two mints. "Only put one in your mouth at a time and let the first one dissolve before you put in the other."

I took one of the gummy tablets and put it in my mouth. When the mint hit the moisture of my tongue, it seemed to explode. I can only describe it as trying to take a sip of orange juice coming out of a high-pressure hose. It took me a moment to catch my breath, and when I did, I put the second blue pill in my mouth, feeling a similar sensation to the first. I opened my mouth a bit and exhaled, the sound of the air escaping sounded like a strong wind.

"Is that better, Mr. Moe?" Jasper said, looking my way and smirking. I just smiled and nodded my head, still looking forward as my lungs blew air through a small hole between my pinched lips, inflating my cheeks. "Good thing," he said, putting the tin back in his pocket. "Yer breath was starting to peel the finish off the upholstery!" He chuckled again.

For the next few hours, I just sat and stared out into space. Jasper put his music back on, turning the volume down to a more comfortable level as we cruised along. Just before we reached the tanker storage lot, we made a quick stop at the Worm Hole Café for dinner. Jasper explained that once we had the tanker in tow, it was difficult to stop anywhere for anything. I really liked the café, and Jasper introduced me to Tonya the cook-slash-waitress.

"Are you taking up half my parking lot with that stupid Space Slug of yours?" Tonya said as she stopped in front of our booth.

"Yes, ma'am, I am. I think it classes up the place!" Jasper answered, smiling brightly.

"Who is your sidekick here?"

"This young man is Moe; he is my boss's son, and he is on a ride-along today."

Tonya looked down at me through her reading glasses that were perched on the end of her nose and smiled.

"Well, it's nice to make your acquaintance, Moe. What would you like to eat?"

I was still suffering from my adventure at the Stray Cat, so I wasn't sure if I was ready to eat yet. In fact, the way my stomach felt, I wasn't sure if I was hungry or if I was going to never eat again. I stared at the menu tablet, unable to decide. Jasper finally took over.

"Moe here had a drink at lunch that didn't agree with him, so why don't you get him a number six to go and just bring him a piece of your Brie Chocolate Pie, and I'll have the same."

I looked up and nodded in agreement. I must admit that I felt much better after I ate my piece of pie, and the meatloaf sandwich I ate later was also delicious.

It took a couple of hours to reach the Jupiter #6 storage lot. As we approached, I could see the giant black tankers lined up next to a docking satellite station. Jasper checked in with the docking station chief, and after they finished their short exchange of greetings and a few off-color jokes, we were cleared to pick up tank #41A. Captain Bazzelman skillfully backed the Space Slug into position where several robotic arms attached it to the massive tanker. The sound of metal contacting metal rang through the ship, as well as the sound of latches locking down.

With the tanker now in tow, we headed back to Earth at a much slower pace. I stared at the display on the screen in front of me, where I could see a small blue dot labeled "Earth." The number next to it read "250,000 GMM." I looked over at Jasper.

"What is GMM next to these numbers?"

"That's Galactic Mile Measurement" he responded.

"It says that Earth is two hundred and fifty thousand GMM. How far is that in Earth miles?"

Jasper thought for a minute, working out the math in his head.

"It's close to five hundred million miles away." I looked at the screen, my eyes wide open. He smiled at me and nodded. "That's why it's better when you're human to think of it in GMM and not in Earth miles, so it doesn't freak you out so bad. At the speed we are going hauling this tanker, we should be back to Earth in about twelve hours."

We sat for a while as we slowly passed planets and I tried to take in all the magnificence that surrounded me. It was like the first time my parents took my family to see the desert on Earth. The vastness of the open plains of sand, sagebrush and red rocks topped with blue sky and a few white clouds towing their shadows across the sand made me want to live there forever. Space seemed to have the same effect on my mind. Jasper interrupted the silence.

"When you woke up from your bender, where were you on my ship?"

"I believe I was in your cabin, Captain," I answered hesitantly. Jasper turned to look at me.

"You didn't throw up in my room, did you?"

I responded quickly to assure him. "No, sir I did not throw up in your room, or on your ship that I can remember. After I barfed in the garbage can in the parking lot, I don't think I had anything left inside me to throw up!" He nodded in relief. I looked at him thoughtfully. "So, who is the lady in the pictures with you? She looked cute."

"That's my girlfriend, Kinsey," he said, smiling.

"How long have you two been dating?"

"Well, let's see. I was in my nineties, and she was seventy-five, so if I had to guess, we have been dating off and on for around 130 Earth years."

"If you have been dating that long, why haven't you two gotten married?" As a twelve-year-old, it seemed like a reasonable question.

"Well, we do love each other, but there didn't seem to be any reason to rush into any long-term commitment," he said, turning his head to wink at me.

The rest of the trip wasn't especially noteworthy. Much of it was spent staring out into space with an occasional question or two for Captain Bazzleman. He was nice enough to answer them, but I sensed it threw him off a bit to have someone aboard his ship that he felt obligated to communicate with.

I had taken a long nap and was awakened by the sound of the tanker being docked. The huge tank shook and groaned as the electromagnetic docking arms took hold of it. Jasper received a clearance call through his headset, and we pulled away from the dock leaving the enormous tanker in temporary storage.

"Yeah, I'll see you in about two hours," he said through his headset to whomever was running the docks that day, and then turned his attention to me. "So, Captain Moe, did you figure out what to say to your father?"

I thought about it for a second. "I think I'm going with something as close to the truth as I can. Like you said, that won't get you fired or myself murdered. I'm going to tell him that out of curiosity, I followed the group over to the Stray Cat and to fit in, I ordered a root beer. When the bartender put out the drinks, I accidentally picked up the wrong one and took a drink of it. You realized what happened and were good enough to walk me back to his office. The next thing I remember was waking up on your ship. That part is actually true."

Jasper looked at me for a moment, tilted his head a bit sideways, and nodded. "Okay, I'll give you my contact information, and you let me know how that went over. With a little luck, I will be a couple million miles away when you tell him that story," he said, chuckling to himself.

Half an hour later, we landed next to the OBM buildings. My father's shuttle was the only other vehicle in the large, brightly lit parking lot. As we landed, I could see my parents leaving my father's building and walking toward us. Jasper opened the side door on his shuttle, and as we climbed down, he put his hand on my shoulder and whispered over the hum of the cooling shuttle's twin ion engines. "Good luck, Moe!"

I didn't look up at him, but just nodded in response. When we reached my parents, my mom bent over and hugged me as my father put his hand on my head and mussed my hair. My father shook the pilot's hand.

"Thanks, Jasper, for bringing him home. I hope he wasn't too much trouble."

"No, Boss, he was fine. He got some firsthand experience at docking a tanker and navigating deep space, which is good to know if he is going to run this place someday." My mother smiled at Jasper and looked down at me.

"Maybe in a year or so when you're not grounded anymore, you can do another ride-along with Captain Bazzlman here."

Jasper responded by looking down at me and gave me a thumbs up. I smiled back in response. My father and Jasper turned at the same time toward the Space Slug and the two of them walked back in that direction together. They chatted for a minute out of earshot of my mother and myself, and their conversation ended with both of them laughing. My father patted his oldest employee on the back as he climbed aboard his ship, then turned and walked back to us, still laughing to himself and shaking his head.

"Well, Markus, Captain Bazzlman says that you have a good story that explains all of this. Perhaps you should share it with your mother and I as we fly home."

I swallowed hard and turned to get in the shuttle. I'm not sure if my parents believed my story, but I figured enough time had passed to come clean. Jasper had retired last year so I assumed it was too late for him to get fired.

Over the years, my parents have allowed me to go on several long hauls with Captain Jasper. I have acquired a large portion of my knowledge of deep space navigation and, of course, great off-planet dining from him. Having traveled the galaxy for work and vacation, Jasper was a great mentor to me. One of the hardest things for Earthlings to accept is that the rules we live by on Earth aren't always the same as those of an alien race. Most non-Earth populations are more advanced than us, so they tend to be more tolerant of our ignorance. If you irritate an alien, he will probably ignore you. If you aggravate an alien, you're going to find out what it's like to be genetically reincarnated from a restoration file. That's if anyone bothers to bring you back. I have always been fascinated with other life forms and enjoy their company.

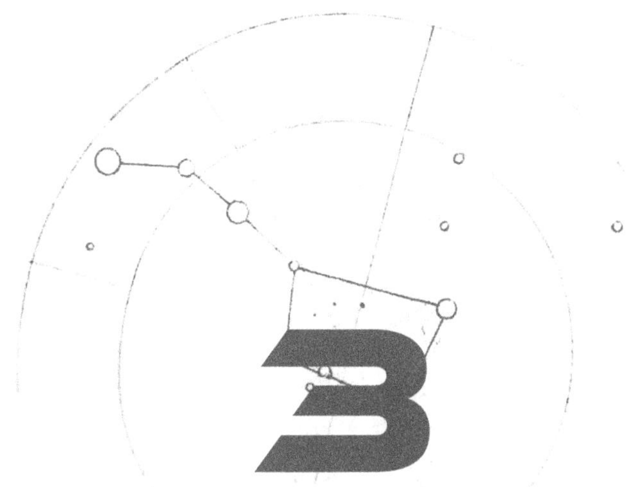

3 Pets and/or Food

Unfortunately, Lord Henry Pincey III did not take the time to keep the wildlife on my planet up to date. From what I can tell, "Lord Pinhead"—as I refer to him—had bought an African Wildlife Package from Earth. The problem is, it's difficult to keep the balance between predator and prey. I have found that in my rainforest, there are still some exotic birds left, but there doesn't seem to be any living large animals or reptiles. Because of this, I decided to go a different way and purchase some engineered animals. Luckily, my friend Chuck works for NTEG (Non-Traditional Earth Genetics, Inc.) He really is a genius, and is famous around NTEG for the work he did on the unicorns that were designed for the New York City Zoo. Both unicorns were put down after they gored two teen girls to death, but it really wasn't Chuck's or NTEG's fault. There was a huge sign that read:

1. DO NOT PET THE UNICORNS.

2. NO, THESE UNICORNS DO NOT HAVE MAGICAL POWERS.
3. DO NOT ATTEMPT TO RUB THEIR HORNS OR RIDE THEM.

So, the liability and/or blame falls on the zoo-going public.

For my planet, Chuck and I came up with the idea of a Utah Velociraptor. The raptor was a cool prehistoric dinosaur that lived on Earth during the Cretaceous period. With a big cash deposit, NTEG was willing to re-engineer them for me. One of the problems was that the raptors were carnivores, and I didn't want to be a snack for my own pets. The ability to supply them with enough meat to sustain them was also a concern. So, I had the idea to engineer them as vegetarians. This worked great at first, but because of their genetic makeup, my Veggie-Raptors wouldn't eat the fruit or vegetables that I put out for them—I assume because they couldn't chase them. They are hunters by design and it's in their DNA to stock their game. I solved this problem, temporarily, by rolling round-shaped vegetables in front of them so they could chase them and pounce on the unexpecting fruit with their large, sharp claws extended, then devour the remains of the smashed fruit with their razor-sharp teeth. My long-term solution was to purchase trees that have Redna fruit. This is a large, high-protein fruit with legs that allow the fruit, when ripe, to run to a new location to re-seed itself. I call them rappels because they look like large, running apples. These trees produce fruit year-round. I've eaten one of the rappels and they aren't too bad. A word of warning, though—you must eat them off the tree. When they fall to the ground and start running, they use their natural sugar for energy, and the further they run, the more bitter they become. Plus, eating them after they grow legs is creepy. Fortunately, the raptors don't care about the taste; they're in it for the chase.

I also wanted the raptors to come in a black color. They look awesome with their black, shiny scales. The problem is, I had to make them cold-blooded, so they don't overheat. This means I must keep them in a warm, dry climate. This was good news to me because my cabin and lake are in a high desert area of my planet. According to NTEG, the raptors can procreate and are safe to eat for humans, which was one of the reasons I could justify the cost. Not that I could ever eat one. They're too expensive.

It will be nice to have baby raptors, but I'll leave it up to them to decide when they are ready to be parents. I don't want to impose roles on them, and I respect their privacy. My barn has individual stalls in it to allow the raptors to sleep inside. Unfortunately, my raptors like to sleep outside, grouped together to stay warm. They do come in when it rains or snows, but they like to pack together in one stall, which is impressive because the stalls are only ten feet by twelve feet in size and my raptors are thirteen feet long from nose to tail tip, seven feet tall, and weigh 200 pounds fully grown.

The raptors have also developed a protective instinct for Tressa. Whenever she is walking around the property by herself, the raptors will surround her and walk alongside her till she gets back to the cabin. I thought it was kind of cute because, to tell the truth, I don't think those stupid lizards care if I live or die. She thought it was cute too, but walking everywhere surrounded by big reptiles with bad breath and a tendency to growl at every sound or unexpected smell gets old fast.

Most of the fruit and vegetables are from the original planet design and are Earth-based. I installed a food processing system in my cabin. Some of you have eaten this food and know how bad it can be. For those of you who haven't, I'll explain. A food processing system is a machine that uses a large protein cube to convert into food. The machine will create food based on the program recipe you put in it. It was developed in 2045 to feed the poorer parts of the Earth due to famine or drought. After tasting the food, some humans were quoted as saying they would rather starve. Personally, I don't think it's that bad with the right recipe, but I only use it when it's necessary. There is something about eating a meal that was scraped from a big, black protein cube that takes away my appetite.

One thing that my food processing system does do well is hot chocolate. If any of you want the recipe for the perfect cup of hot cocoa, give me a call. It has taken years to get it just right.

The best fruit on my planet is, without a doubt, the Carrieack cherries. These are similar to the fruit called Bing cherries on Earth except that this dark red fruit is about two pounds apiece and are a little more difficult to pick. The Carrieack cherry tree is a little larger than my rapple trees, and it's mobile. These trees' roots are used to bring nutrients from the soil into the plant, but when the tree feels the vibration of something approaching its location, it uses its roots as tentacles to lift the tree and run away. They're not really fast, but a human would not be able to catch one on foot. I have only about a half dozen of these trees on MP and they all have maturing fruit at different times of the year, so I can pick cherries almost year-round. The key is figuring out how to restrain the tree to pick the ripe fruit without damaging the branches or thin bark of the tree.

One of my good friends, who shall remain nameless, was able to acquire for me a set of police assault jaws. The "grabbers" as most humans refer to them, are hydraulic jaws police can quickly extend out from the front of their cruisers. These large pinchers clamp on and secure any particular shuttle whose occupants the police want to restrain instead of blasting them out of the air, which does happen on occasion, especially with Air Patrol.

With grabbers mounted on my shuttle, I can catch and hold even a fully grown Carrieack cherry tree without doing any damage to the tree trunk or my shuttle. By putting a little downward pressure on the tree, the roots become immobile, and after a few seconds, they dig themselves into the ground and hold on. I think this is a natural response to keep the tree from being blown over in a strong wind. After it digs in, it's easy to get out of the shuttle and pick all the cherries that you want off the lower branches. A few more words of warning, though—eating more than one of these delicious fruits at one sitting can really "clean you out," if you know what I mean. Also, if you are out in the open and caught in the path of a retreating Carrieack tree, stomp on the ground as hard as you can, and hopefully the tree will sense the vibration and stop. Being run over by a two-thousand-pound tree is probably something you won't survive, or would even want to survive.

These trees became a favorite target of my raptors, so I was forced to move all of them out of the raptors' normal range. The raptors have grown fond of running after the trees and jumping up to snag fruit off even the upper branches. Several of my cherry trees have deep gouges in the trunks where the raptors have used their sharp claws to slow their accent. Using my grabbers, I carefully hauled all the trees a safe distance from my cabin with my shuttle. What I was afraid of was that the raptors would chase the Carrieack trees until they died of exhaustion—the raptors, not the trees—and most of all I didn't want those stupid lizards eating my cherries.

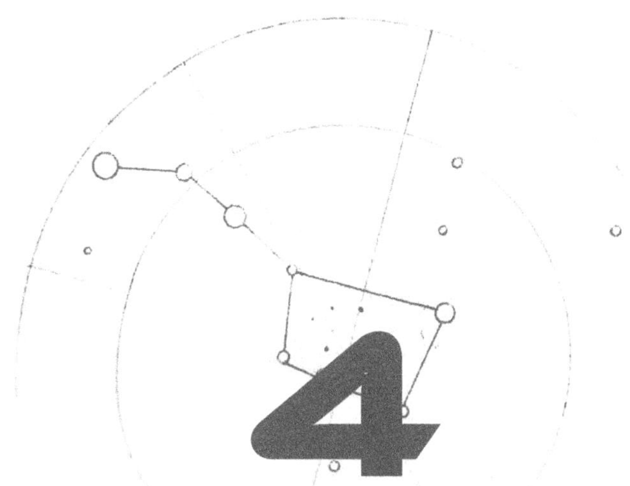

4 Fishing and Genetic Reincarnation

Growing up on Earth, one of my favorite things to do was to go fishing. This is an old Earth tradition that involves using what is called a "pole and a reel" to catch fish. I'm sure that any of you who have spent time with me will have seen my collection of antique fishing poles and lures, which are used to deceive the fish into biting. On Earth, you have to catch and release fish unless you have a commercial fishing license. I have different regulations on MP; I practice catch-and-release-in-hot-oil. Remember—my planet, my fish.

Soon after the purchase of MP1X was complete, I thought it would be cool to bring a collection of freshwater fish, then grow my own—mostly because I love to eat fish and it's so expensive on Earth. This leads me to one of my favorite stories about my buddy Chuck, and how he became a Genetic-3 instead of a G-2. A bunch of my friends were coming to My Planet for a weekend of fishing. To get ready for these guys, and to show off, I had used a super-grow formula on my trout. A little head's-up on this—you should really read the warning labels on a box of Fish-Grow.

When we went out fishing the first day, we only found one large fish on the radar instead of the two thousand I had planted. Instead of giving up, we decided to focus on this one fish. Unfortunately, we could not get him to bite, probably since he had eaten everything else in the lake. After an hour or so, we became bored and a little high on oxygen. Someone, who shall remain nameless (Tripp) pushed Chuck into the water. Within a mere second of falling in, Chuck was being attacked and eaten by this monster fish, which had amazingly large teeth for a trout. That's another warning they should put on the box.

I don't think the fish was hungry, so it might have been a territory thing. We all got a good laugh out of it, and then went about trying to find a big piece of Chuck. Obviously, the bigger the piece, the better for GR. Most humans from Earth don't have a problem with genetic reincarnation, which is the process of re-engineering a body from remaining tissue. Now, you can reanimate someone from a file code, but the problem lies in the fact that all the memories they have had since their code was filed are lost. If you use a big enough piece of them, then all of their memories are saved up to the moment they died. Frankly, I feel this is better, because if you can recall how you died, it will help you avoid that situation in the future.

The problem with GR is that humans have a tendency to deteriorate a little from each copy that is made. I am a G-2 because, as most of you remember, I crashed my first shuttle when I was 18 years old. It was a Cobra 248, and it was fast and really cool—and a great way to pick up girls. The problem was it had a faulty fuselage, and on my way back to college, the outer shell cracked and the decompression splattered me all over the walls of my ship. Luckily, my parents found enough of me under the back seat to reengineer me. That was a relief because the memory loss would have caused me to repeat my freshman year. Anyway, that was the lawsuit that I was talking about in chapter 1.

The money I got from the manufacturers of my Cobra paid for the rest of school and the deposit on my planet. Thank you, Cobra, Inc. Remember that any modification on your shuttle or ship should be made by the dealership to protect your warranties. The only sad part about my death was that it was pretty anticlimactic; for me, anyway. I always pictured death as a bright light at the end of a tunnel or a moment of clarity when all the questions in my life would be answered. Nope. Just a large crack and then total blackness until my father opened the door on my uncle's GR machine and I walked out naked, in front of the whole family and a few neighbors.

Some religions don't allow members to be genetically reincarnated. They think it's an offense to God. Luckily, my religion doesn't feel that way. Besides, it's not something you want to happen to you. It doesn't necessarily make your natural life span any longer, because you begin where you left off. Don't get me wrong, it's a great way to get a second chance if you die accidentally. Trust me, I would rather be a G-2 than a dead #1.

After about an hour, we found Chuck's big toe floating on the surface of the water. When he came out of the GR machine, he was pretty upset. Chuck was not too happy about being a Genetic 3. How he had become a G-2 was never explained to us and we didn't ask. Frankly, Chuck is far more intelligent as a G3 than any of our motley crew. As I understand it, if he was ever genetically reincarnated, we were supposed to make him six feet tall so he could be taller than his wife, Ashell. I didn't feel bad for him because Tressa is taller than me. Besides, I can't do upgrades on my GR machine, so we would have had to take his toe back to Earth and he would have missed the whole weekend. After a year, Chuck still whines about it. I am reminded of a quote from Mao Zedong, the leader of the Chinese Communist Regime, who said, "Dude, shut up and fish."

To help Chuck feel better, I took him out on the lake with a box full of Argilelion compressed air grenades. I keep some around the cabin to help remove tree stumps. It didn't take long, and Chuck had the monster fish thoroughly disposed of. It's always fun to hear him tell the story of how he was eaten by a giant trout. The sad part of the whole experience is that Chuck is still a lot more intelligent than the rest of us, even as a G-3. I think the person who should have been upset is Ashell. I'm sure there were some modifications she wanted to make to her husband.

Tripp had suggested that I put mermaids in the lake. Supposedly, they are fun to catch on light tackle and put up a real fight. I think Tripp just has it bad for mermaids. Besides, the thought of trying to get a hook out of one of their mouth's creeps me out, and a mature mermaid can eat their body weight in fish in less than a week. So, I told Tripp to get a girlfriend or spend his own money on a mermaid. If I can't afford my own herd of woolly mammoths, I'm not going to spend my savings on a school of mermaids. By the way, Tressa believes that I have misquoted Mao Zedong. In my defense, it's difficult to translate Mandarin Chinese, but I think I'm close.

Along with fishing, I spend a lot of my time hunting on MP. There is an insect I have discovered on my planet called the Black Bug. The best way to describe this insect is that it looks like a five-foot long, 150-pound grasshopper or cricket from Earth. I have no idea which planet it originally came from, but it can mow down one to two acres of vegetation in a day. They are also quite the breeders. I am not sure how often they lay eggs, but I have found nests that had two to three hundred fist-sized eggs. According to my planet manual, which I haven't finished reading yet, the eggs of the Black Bug are poisonous. However, the legs of a mature bug are edible. (Black Bug—the other green meat). It would be interesting to figure out who it was in our galaxy that figured out that Black Bug legs were edible; probably not anyone from Earth. Earth residents are well known in the galaxy for being less than adventurous when it comes to what they will eat. Don't get me wrong—Earthlings will eat anything. We just don't want to be the first to try it. I believe it comes from our subconscious need for self-preservation. I, however, will try anything once—if you put ketchup on it.

One of my older brothers, Kyle, stayed on MP with me for a week, and we must have bagged close to 400 of the ugly bugs. The key to a successful bug hunt is to remember that Black Bugs are cannibals, so if you shoot one and leave it, other bugs will come to feed on the carcass. We found this out one day while Kyle and I were flying in my shuttle, and I decided to lean out the door and shoot a big Black Bug that was about 100 feet below us. This was no small task since the shuttle was moving, and the Black Bug was also flying. I did, however, make a great shot and the huge insect crashed in an open field, causing a large cloud of dust to rise into the sky. When we flew back over the area almost an hour later, there were close to fifteen Black Bugs eating their fallen comrade.

Kyle and I cut some large bushes and hid behind them on the outside of some tall grass that the Black Bugs love to graze in. Typically, they will eat until dark and then start where they left off the next morning. By the time we got set up, we could hear the bugs flying toward us. Their green and black wings make a clicking sound when they fly. A large group of them sounds like pouring a bucket of marbles down a flight of wooden stairs. When there isn't any wind, you can hear them coming from miles away.

It wasn't long before we were shooting up a storm. Kyle has a Tella 6 rifle, which is a bigger caliber than my Tella 7, but it doesn't have the range mine has. However, his does have more knock-down power up close than mine does. The Tella rifle was developed as a non-lethal way for the American military to protect bases and military checkpoints during the 2040s. The Tella rifle was most useful against terrorists who used civilians as human shields. This gun shoots a bolt, or slug of energy, that can be adjusted in size to either stun or have lethal force on a person or animal, depending on the operator's needs. This is the same technology that is used to power satellites, vehicles, and other electronics without a direct connection, or what used to be referred to as cordless. The larger the bolt, the longer it takes to recharge the weapon's power supply. We found that to kill a Black Bug takes a small charge, so Kyle and I could shoot them all day without recharging. By the time we were done shooting, the ceramic barrels of our rifles glowed with the heat.

I would like to apologize to those of you who don't approve of hunting and the killing of any creatures. Actually, Tressa would like to apologize. I, however, am in charge of the Black Bug population since they have no natural enemies. If I killed a grasshopper on Earth, no one would care, and it shouldn't make an difference just because a Black Bug is bigger. I made a good living as a child having people pay me to eat bugs. So don't write to me. I can't stand hate mail. Some of you might say Black Bugs are defenseless. The truth is, if I filled my shirt and pants pockets with green grass and lay in a field, those bugs would eat me alive.

We cooked up several hundred pounds of bug legs using Kyle's favorite barbecue recipe. The best way to describe the taste would be like eating large snow crab legs on Earth. So, the taste is great, but it's the fact that the meat is green that throws me off. Kyle, however, loves them and ended up taking home about 300 pounds of Black Bug legs. My guess is that he violated about twenty Earth import regulations, but since my name was not on any of it, I didn't care. Not to mention the fact that Kyle and his four boys ate all the evidence.

Black Bugs have six legs but only the back legs have enough meat to make them worth eating. I believe these are the legs they use for hopping and to jump in the air to start flight. I have seen them jump over a hundred yards at a time without the use of their wings. They also have this black sticky substance that comes out of their mouths when they're eating. When I was inspecting one we had shot, I got some on my hands and it took me days to get it cleaned off. Trust me, Black Bug saliva doesn't come off. In fact, I am thinking of marketing it as a form of glue or sealant. I think "Moe's All-Natural, Not From Concentrate Bug Glue" has a nice ring to it.

5 Family: Friend or Foe?

I thought I would take a minute and introduce my family to you. If you know my family, I'm sorry, but I will update you. My parents are human, and as I said before, they are Earthlings. This fact they take seriously, as most of you know. They don't travel on vacation off-planet very often. My dad does travel a bit with his work, but only when he must, and only when he's going to be gone for less than a day. My mother has been as far as Mars, but she complained the entire time. She wasn't big on spending two days on a cruise shuttle just to sit under a glass dome and look at large red rocks. I tried to explain that the resort there has the best food anywhere in the galaxy, but she was on her way home by the second day. The famous Earth entertainer, Frank Sinatra, once asked in a song, "Let me see what spring is like on Jupiter and Mars." If Mr. Sinatra asked my mom that question, it would be that it sucks any time of year on Mars. Well, my mother is too good of a person to say that Mars "sucks." She would, however, say that she has not yet learned to appreciate Mars. She can't say that about Jupiter because it's owned by a private corporation and is private property. If it doesn't come from Earth, my mother really isn't interested. It did help a bit that when she was outside the gravity-controlled areas on Mars, she weighed only around forty pounds.

My parents are both in their sixties, and for being middle-aged, they are very active. My grandmother on my mom's side is my only living grandparent. Grandma Fisher, or Granny as we lovingly refer to her, is 110 years old and still active enough to drive us all crazy. None of my other grandparents wanted to extend their lives through genetic reincarnation. I think they wanted to give up the ghost and take their chances at the afterlife. This is common with humans with strong religious beliefs. Not me. If Death wants me, he'll have to take me kicking and screaming. When I get to be a senior citizen, I might feel different.

I have two brothers and one sister. I have been the closest to Kyle, whether we are hunting or fishing, or working on his shuttle. My brother Toss is always off-planet and always self-absorbed. I don't think I would have to worry about offending him because reading a book I wrote would be the last thing he would do. My younger sister is Kinsey. I call her Zap. As a child, she was playing with an old electrical lamp in the family room of my parents' house when the cover fell off of the power supply capsule and she touched the exposed crystals. She took enough volts to make the tips of her hair smoke a little. She's okay, though. Or I assume she's okay because she has tested in the top one percent of the students in her school. Go, Zap! I told Kinsey that when she graduated, she could bring all her friends and camp for the weekend on the beach of one of the MP's islands. No boys, Zap.

Besides, it's a good chunk of her inheritance that I am spending on my planet. Love you, Zap!

My wife is Tressa, and I must admit, she is the most wonderful person on the planet Earth. She and I met in college, where Tressa was a tutor for my economics class, which I was failing. She has a laugh that makes me melt on the inside. Trust me on this, she laughed a lot at my economics homework. She is six feet tall, which is about two inches taller than myself, and no, I don't have a problem with that. Her hair is long and black, and she grew it herself. Not that transplanted hair isn't nice—I just think it's cool that hers is natural. The first time I saw her in the school library, I wanted to run to her, throw myself at her feet, and pledge my every waking hour to her happiness. What I did say was, "Please, please, please, be my economics tutor." She unsympathetically agreed to help me, for a small fee, of course. After a long courtship, I convinced her that I was smarter and more charming than I had let on, and she agreed to be my wife. "Oh, what a tangled web we weave when first we practice to deceive."

Tressa is now the head of her department at BYN, my alma mater. Go, Wolverines! According to her co-workers, Tressa always puts in a hard day's work. I'll have to take their word for that since I'm not sure what a hard day's work consists of. Tressa is the kind of professor that makes all the male students pray that they'll get to be in her class, until they take her first test—then they pray they will pass. Although she has spent weekends on MP, she is not fond of the remote location. To me, this works out perfectly because I really like the alone time. Yes, I count time with my friends as alone time. I'm sure it wouldn't be long before she would be changing things anyway. (Just kidding.) Because she got a better grade in Old American English than I did, I'm sure she is going to have to proofread this book. I plan on blaming Tressa for any misspelled words, inappropriate language, and misuse of commas in my book. Not to mention the fact that Tressa's vocabulary is way gooder than mine.

Tressa and I don't have any kids yet, but who knows? I am kind of tired of not getting any gifts on Father's Day. We both have a lot going on in our lives, and since we're still in our thirties, there really isn't any reason to be in a hurry. My parents have some grandchildren from my brother Kyle and his wife Shantell, so they haven't put the screws to us quite yet. However, my mother is fond of saying, "Grandchildren are our reward for not killing all of you when you were teenagers." I'm hoping she was kidding. After all, I do have my own planet, so having enough room is not a problem. Getting my parents to let me take their grandchildren and live in another galaxy would be a problem.

Some of you have met my buddy, Tripp. He has never learned Old American English, so unless he uses a device that translates this manuscript, he won't understand it. If someone is reading this to Tripp, please skip this chapter.

Tripp and I met in school when we were kids. My best guess is that he is a clone. Most clones have the same look that Tripp has. He is tan with perfect teeth, hair, and weight. He has always been smart and athletic, which poses the question—"Why am I a friend of his?" If you have lived on Earth, you know that for the past twenty years, clones have been treated as second-class citizens and are the brunt of many jokes and racial remarks. Cloning has always been a controversial science at best. The whole industry is always under investigation for questionable practices and ethics. Many politicians run for election on platforms either for or against cloning. Most clones are children of humans who could not have kids of their own due to physical problems or sexual orientation. I am not judging Tripp, or his moms. I would hope that someday humans would evolve past being so judgmental about other, more perfect people. There are plenty of other intelligent life forms in the universe that we could hate. Tripp is also my only close friend that is still single. He has come close esto marriage a few times, but has always fallen back on his bachelor ways. I think that lifestyle will get old soon; at least I hope it does. I grow tired of the constant flow of beautiful, yet noncommittal, women he constantly parades in front of us married guys. If you are a woman looking for a man to settle down with, let me know. I have all of his contact information.

Tripp is one of my best friends, and even though he cost me a fortune when I had to buy 400 acres of fire bushes, I love him. Many of you have heard Tripp tell this story. Unfortunately, he leaves out many key parts of it. I will remedy this. A while back, Tripp and I were racing dune buggies in the northern desert on MP. A dune buggy is a vehicle from Earth with big tires and an electric motor that allows you to travel across sand dunes at speeds up to 240 miles an hour. Now, if you crash at that speed, there won't even be a big toe to copy. So, we keep it around a hundred miles per hour. Yes, it's true I did say that my buggies have tires. If you are from Earth, you have probably never been in a vehicle that has wheels. To tell the truth, I like the feel of wheels more than the low-impact, magnetic levitation systems that are mandatory on Earth. How can you run things over if you are using a nonimpact levitation system? It's true that you can't go as fast when you use wheels, but to me, the feel of the terrain is an exciting part of the experience. I don't mind leaving tracks; in fact, it really helps to be able to backtrack if you get lost.

We had stopped so we could check out a mature crop of fire bushes that I had planted. It's always a good idea to check on automated water systems when you plant in a desert. A few days in hundred-degree temperatures without water and all that would be left of a crop is sand. A fire bush is a big plant that looks a lot like a tumbleweed from Earth. When a fire bush senses danger, the bushes will self-combust, the flames changing colors randomly from red and green to purple and silver. This is beautiful to see at night, but what Tripp didn't know was that they also will roll away from a predator—like a Black Bug, or another ignited fire bush.

When we stopped, during our afternoon ride, Tripp thought it would be a good time to relieve himself. Obviously, the fire bush that he had picked for his target did not like being peed on, so it rolled away. Not knowing a fire bush could move, Tripp let out a loud yell. This, in turn, scared the fire bush and caused it to ignite while still in motion. As you have probably heard, or figured out, this caused a domino effect with the other bushes, and in a matter of five minutes, my crop of four thousand plants was reduced to 400 acres of ash. I heard later that you could see the beautiful fire from Aselus #1. It also melted both of the dune buggies and we ended up walking back, which took two days. Luckily, we had a nice layer of soot on us to protect us from the sun. Nice one Tripp. Besides, what are third-degree burns among friends? Fortunately, we had tire tracks that could lead us back so we didn't get lost. Things always look different when you are walking than when you're flying in a shuttle, and it's easy to get turned around. To quote my favorite mountain man, Jeremiah Johnson, "I've never been lost—just fearsome confused for a month or two."

To add insult to injury, my fire bush plantation was not covered under my planet's insurance policy. I guess "due to their unstable nature," the fire bush is on the list of plants that are not covered. I've really got to start reading the fine print on these things. Luckily, my insurance adjuster took pity on me and paid for the dune buggies. Thank goodness my adjuster, Ms. Tischner, was a human from Earth that works for a Trillion corporation. There are almost seven billion Earthlings. Many are working off-planet, and we tend to stick together. Go, Blue Planet!

My buddy Chuck is married to Tressa's friend, Shantell. This makes hanging out for a weekend much more convenient. Tripp is usually a third wheel, but an entertaining third wheel. Until I got married, Shantell really didn't approve of Chuck and I hanging out and fishing together. Of course, when I got married and Tressa and Shantell became good friends, this allowed Chuck and myself the freedom to do whatever we wanted. I guess the single guy is always going to be considered morally questionable—"A Moral Black Hole," or as Tressa puts it, "A Moral Swamp" to a married man. I have never thought of myself as a bad influence, but it's always up for debate.

I think the only flaw that Chuck has is his love of a game called golf. For those of you who are not from Earth, golf is a game that is played with a variety of clubs and a small ball that golfers attempt to hit into a hole. Not a big hole, mind you, but one just big enough for the ball to fit into. The game was invented in the 17th century, and in the thousands of years that it has been played, they have failed to make the game interesting enough for me to want to participate. But if the golf bag was filled with different caliber rifles and the balls moved on their own, attempting to escape their doom, now that would be a game. A true golfer will tell you that it's the difficulty of the game that makes it great. I think those people should play blindfolded and make the game even greater. Honestly, I think golf was invented in an attempt by the Scottish people to screw with the rest of the planet. Luckily for me, Chuck plays golf with his coworkers from NTEG, so I don't have to play golf to maintain our friendship.

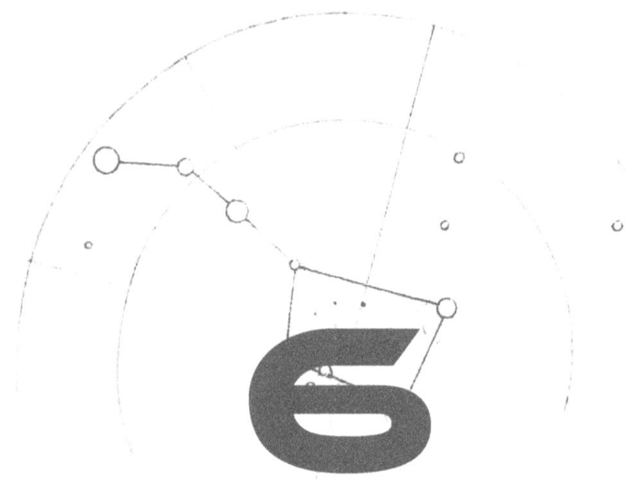

6
Why Buy a Planet?

When asked that question, I can't help but answer; "Why not?," or "Because it was on sale." The truth is, I have always wanted a planet and this one was available. It's difficult to find a planet that is designed like the Earth and isn't a serious fixer-upper. When I saw the listing and the price they were asking, I had to work it out. When Tressa saw the price, she told me she expected it to be a large chunk of cold, black rock out in space and probably in orbit around a sun that is about to go supernova. We were both surprised, and the Pincey's family was apparently trying to keep the sale of Aselus #2 quiet. My guess is that they had to sell or foreclose on the planet. It's not good for your reputation as part of a royal family if you need to sell your planet for financial reasons.

The "Do It Our Way" design firm that built MP is owned by the Trillions, the group that discovered Earth. As humans, most thought it was pretty demeaning to have been considered to have been "discovered." I'm sure that the American Indians felt the same way when Columbus "discovered" ancient America. For thousands of years, Earth humans were terrified that some more advanced group was on its way to attack and take over our planet. The truth is that the Earth is smaller than most space shuttle stops, and definitely the smallest human-inhabited planet in our galaxy. So capturing Earth and taking all of its riches isn't a big score for most alien races. For non-Earth cultures, the thought of attacking us would be like kicking over an ant hill just to watch the ants run around. Luckily, the ones with the power to take over the Earth are the ones who wouldn't go to the trouble.

According to the records I have read, at first, the Trillions had tried to pass themselves off as Gods to the inhabitants of Earth. But I believe their special effects weren't that great so their big production failed. After that, they admitted to being venture capitalists who thought the Earth would make a great resort planet. Unfortunately, the Trillions found that we Earthlings had pretty much used up all of our natural resources. Our water and air was unhealthy, and we had way overpopulated our small planet. Most of the information that the Trillions had on Earth was from our satellite transmissions. Unfortunately, most of the transmissions were hundreds of years old and had just been floating around in space. Our old TV shows and radio broadcasts painted a better picture of Earth than its current state.

So, instead of flooding the Earth with vacationing aliens, they decided to allow Earthlings to buy into projects they had going in other parts of the galaxy. Earth's inhabitants, they found, made great workers and did a fine job of cleaning up messes the Trillions themselves had made in other galaxies. Trillions, as most of you are aware, always think of themselves as upper management, if you get my drift. In return, they gave us affordable space travel and great medical and dental innovations, most of which, I am sure, they had stolen from other humanoid planets. Having contact with the Trillions made it possible for Earthlings to venture out into the galaxy. This worked out well, especially with the medical advancements. These medical upgrades have given us a life expectancy that is now well over 100 years, which would have led to even more catastrophic overpopulation of Earth if not for all the people who have migrated off planet. All this information is from my eighth grade Earth History teacher, Margin Snail. Thank you, Ms. Snail. Personally, I think most humans were relieved to find out that they weren't the most intelligent creatures in the universe. It took away a lot of the responsibility. The Trillions had humans to push around, and humans had the opportunity to blame their mistakes on poor leadership.

I should advise you to never tell a Trillion what you are thinking, or share any idea that you might have with them. Since the human race is less than a million years old, Trillions believe that no matter what you can conceive, it really isn't worth hearing about. In fact, they suppose that we, as Earthlings, should consider ourselves fortunate that we have survived our own biological timeline. To them, it is as if we, as Earthlings, had "won the evolutionary lottery." When you consider all of the devices that we have developed to defend ourselves from ourselves over the last thousand years, it's amazing we haven't blown the planet and our species to tiny bits.

Back to my planet. Most people that invest in planets or time-share property away from the Earth do it for the freedom and the no-holds-barred lifestyle. There are some humans from Earth that save up their whole lives so they can retire to some exotic planet. On your own planet, you can pretty much do whatever you want. I think it's just time for me to be alone. To swim in the ocean by myself, to walk through the deserts, climb large mountains, or just sit on my thinking rock and play my flute. Originally, I thought it would give me a sense of accomplishment to walk where no human had walked and to see things that no human had seen. The problem is that, of course, no one had done it or seen it because it was my planet. I think I was looking for that sense of accomplishment that ancient man was searching for by crossing uncharted oceans, going to the moon, or climbing Mt. Everest. But after all our new innovations, these things are no longer a challenge. In fact, I took my nephew for his thirteenth birthday to that restaurant on Everest last summer. It was okay, but it has a trendy, teen kind of theme. There are a lot of old street signs and old pictures in antique frames of people that had climbed Mt. Everest. Of course, this is before you could just drive a shuttle there for lunch. I have to say that there is a great view of Tibet and Nepal through the restaurant's big dining room windows. To get a good table with the best view, tell the receptionist that Moe recommended their place. As a food critic, the food at the Mt. Everest place was not worth the price, so go for the view and not for the food.

Most of the things I enjoy are simple accomplishments, like my herd of raptors and my growing fish population. There is a lot of pressure to make things work, and work together. You must think ahead so that you don't put things together that should never be together. I won't go into details. Having your own planet has great rewards. I love looking forward to seeing how my trees and plants that I designed have grown. I think I do a good job of picking animals and also controlling the populations of the tastier critters. I'm sorry, but I don't think humans fought their way up the food chain to be vegetarians. Besides, I have seen manatees at the zoo eating just salad, and I think they are grossly overweight.

I think the desert is my favorite climate on my planet because I love the warm, dry environment. I can hike or ride dune buggies for days out there. A few months ago, Tripp and I took a couple of my raptors out to the western desert. I assumed the dry air would be good for them. I have a trailer that attaches to the back of my shuttle that I can't take into space, but it does allow me to transport pets and other stuff around my planet. To check how the raptors would adjust to the hot temperatures, we took two of them with us. The hardest part of this experiment was deciding how to get two full-grown raptors into a trailer. Tripp thought we could lasso them one at a time with a rope and drag them in. I told him that if he wanted to hold the rope that is attached to 200 pounds of muscle and teeth, then he was welcome to give it a shot. We settled on rolling Carrieack cherries into the trailer and when the raptors gave chase, we just closed the door.

Tripp and I parked the shuttle on top of a small plateau made of volcanic rock. Unloading my raptors was a lot less work. We just opened the door and out they came. Using their tails for balance, the raptors were jumping from boulder to boulder, having a great time on the rocky hillside. The tragedy happened when there was a rockslide, and Bosephus, my largest raptor, started chasing rocks down the steep slope. Before we could catch him, he had caught and eaten at least three big rocks. I never said that velociraptors were the smartest pets you could own. Bosephus died shortly after his lunch from what we could only assume was digestive distress. No, we did not eat him, even though Tripp suggested it. (He can be a cold-hearted bugger.)

One of the things that I have found to be necessary in successful planet ownership is good communication. It's important to know the designers, the engineers, the previous owners, and the people who provide your utilities. You should have a detailed list of everyone involved so you can get any questions answered. Or, more importantly, you should always have someone to blame when something goes wrong. When it comes to warranties, the Trillions can be very vague. Take, for instance, the three thousand halibut I had delivered to my planet for fishing near MP's north pole, along with two tons of live herring to feed them. While they were in transit, I was informed by the fish farm that I needed to bring the minimum water temperature up thirteen degrees. This should not have been a problem. According to my planet manual, my fusion heater could raise the saltwater ocean up that much in about twelve hours. So, I set the thermostat and didn't worry any more about it.

The week after the fish were delivered, thought it would be fun to try some deep sea fishing. I was dying for some fish sticks, an Earth delicacy. When I was flying over, I noticed that several of my large glaciers were gone and most, if not all, of my fish were lying on the shore. Come to find out that my state-of-the-art fusion heater had raised the temperature to 113° and I now had almost 60,000 pounds of poached Halibut—that, by the way, the raptors wouldn't eat. After reading my manual, I found out that the warranty would cover the ice shelf and glaciers, but wouldn't cover the fish because they weren't native to the planet. Of course they weren't native to the planet! It's engineered. It would be 300 years before they were considered native. As for the ice shelf and the glaciers, I can make my own damn ice.

Where is MP1X? Good question. I'm not going to tell you. Having any of you showing up whenever you want would not be cool. Just kidding. I'll tell you where it is, but I won't give you the landing codes. MP is in a group of stars that are referred to as "The Meatball." Its actual name is Picturesque Galaxy South, which I'm sure was named by the realtors firm that covers that galaxy. It got this nickname Meatball because it's a round group of engineered planets that is in the middle of what is referred to as the Big Dipper. As seen from Earth, the Big Dipper is part of a bigger constellation of stars called Big Bear or Ursa Major. The Big Dipper is more well-known due to the fact it's easier to see from Earth. Thank you, Miss Cornell, my college astronomy teacher.

I happened to see Miss Cornell the other day when I went to pick up Tressa after work. She would really like to take a group of students on a field trip to MP. Since it was too late to go back and fix the grade she gave me my junior year, I told her it wouldn't be possible. The planets in the "Meatball" are all in my POA, or Planet Owners Association. Lucky for me, the association only meets every twenty-three years. Their last meeting was three years ago and lasted twenty-eight hours. During that time, they approved Lord Pincey's request to put MP1X up for sale. As I understand it, if the owner of a planet wants to sell, he or she or it must inform the POA of their intentions first so they can have the first right of refusal. The good news is that no one in the group wanted to buy it so it was made available to me.

To get to MP takes about eight hours in a quick shuttle. It's approximately fifty-three light years from Earth. Of course, I have a fast shuttle. I usually sleep or take time to write in my journal, which is how I retain all this useless yet, I hope, entertaining information. In a commercial shuttle, it would take about ten hours, but there isn't a place on MP to park one. Those of you who thought it would be fun to bring your mobile homes out to MP for a weekend, sorry, there is no large landing pad. Trespassers will be shot on sight—well, maybe yelled at on sight. Or I could spray you with rapple juice and let you play with my pet Raptors. So, if you want me to sign your copy of my book *My Planet—The Chronicles of Moe*, or my last one *Dude, Don't Eat That*, which is a food guide for off-planet dining, you'll have to catch me on Earth. It was originally titled *Eat It Before It Eats You* but my publicist said it might scare people away from some off-planet diners and pubs.

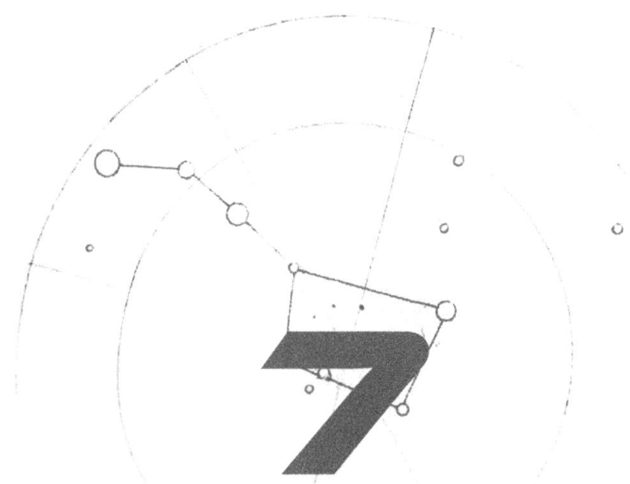

Please give to the Mammoth Fund

There are several things that MP really needs, and I thought this would be a good time to share my list with you in case anyone is looking for a planet warming gift like, say, for my birthday, Christmas, Earth Day, or just for fun.

The top of the list is a woolly mammoth. NTEG has told me that they have all the research and genetic material to make this happen. Unfortunately, they plan to charge me per pound to recreate a mammoth. So I was thinking that if anyone wanted to donate to the "Create A Woolly Mammoth" fund, that would be great. And if a group of you wanted to put in for a whole herd, that would be even better. I have no plans to hunt them—I promise. NTEG has warned me that because they would be genetic creations, they wouldn't be able to shed their coats during the warm season. I would either have to keep them from migrating in the spring or pay someone to shear off their extra hair once a season. I think it would be worth the extra work and expense. If any of you want to help, let me know. I assume finding someone to shear a mammoth won't be easy. No, I don't want elephants. Everyone who is anyone has elephants. A woolly mammoth is bigger and does better in colder climates. Besides, the thought of riding a woolly mammoth through ten feet of snow, knocking over trees and stepping on black bugs would be more fun than I can imagine. I smile every time I think about it. It's true that a mammoth is more of a "want" than a "need."

What I really need is a good set of satellites. At night, it's difficult to get a call out to Earth because of the rotation of Planet Moe. If I had a good set of satellites and a transmission booster, I could call home any time . . . Mom. It would also allow me to pick up old Earth television shows and football games. Yes, the shows would be hundreds of years old, but it would help me with my Old American English to watch these old TV reruns that are still floating around in space. What the Trillions call pollution, I call entertainment. The system that I have now only allows for a limited reception time to receive and download shows. The majority of this reception is dedicated to Tressa's shows, which is fine because she needs a distraction while I'm fixing stuff, and being on MP is her chance to relax.

I did find, or should I say Tripp found, the remnants of a satellite while walking back to the cabin from the fire bush incident. It was an older model, and we figured it was shot down by some vandals probably a hundred years ago. It was popular at that time for college students on spring or summer break to harass other systems and shoot down satellites for fun. They would often hang parts of the satellite in their dorm rooms for all to admire. The Trillions put an end to this by increasing the fine and confiscating shuttles, which were usually owned by the student's very unhappy parents.

The other thing I really need is about 130 billion gallons of water. Now that sounds like a lot of water, but the Earth has around 350 million trillion gallons of water on it, so you guys have got to know someone who is willing to sell me some. Let me explain why I need all this water. In the Western Desert on MP, there is a large red rock canyon. It's very similar to the Grand Canyon on Earth. From what I can tell, the iron ore that the rock is made of has caused it to oxidize into its red color. If I am wrong, please don't write and explain it to me. In the canyon, there isn't any rain so no streams or rivers flow through the canyon. Because of this, the canyons are only red. The Trillions are really into mono-chromatic colors. This means it all kind of blurs together. My idea is to flood the canyon with the water. As the water evaporates, it will leave a discoloration on the red rock walls. As the water level goes down, I'm going to add other organically safe metals to it to give the layers of rock different colors. I am hoping to get the same effect as the Painted Desert on Earth. I think this would really improve the resale of MP if I ever decided I could part with it. My father has told me that if I could find the water, he would be willing to haul it in a couple of his gas-tanker shuttles. It will probably cost me a birthday present or two in the future, if I haven't already spent them.

One option would be to harvest some large ice chunks from either a passing comet or even get one from Saturn's rings. Comets aren't the cleanest and tend to have unusual and dangerous DNA in them when they melt. I really don't want something unidentified growing in one of my lakes! It's been said that Kcap7, a small planet in Sector 11, harvested a comet, and when it thawed out, something grew out of it that ended up consuming every life form on the planet. I can't verify that but I do know the whole planet has been under quarantine for fifty years and no correspondence has been sent from the inhabitants. If anyone reading this book had any relatives or friends who were residents of Kcap7, I don't mean to make light of their unfortunate and suspicious disappearance. As I understand it, Saturn's rings have mostly been picked clean of clean ice, and even if you find some, the scavenger permits are expensive.

I know that these items are not the easiest to come up with, and it's possible that they are all a bit expensive. There is, however, a gift that I need that wouldn't cost an arm and a leg, but because it's no longer in production, it has been hard to find an M-Series tree trimmer which is made by A.R.T. (Alpine Robotics Technologies). I found out why the series was discontinued when the M-S robot that I had on MP suffered a sort of a breakdown. My M-S was set up to trim my bushes and hedges around my cabin and garden. The problem occurred when the artistic program it was running caused it to sculpt all of my bushes and trees into quite obscene figures. As A.R.T. described it in their recall letter, a former disgruntled employee had programmed the M-Series robots to trim any plant it could find into what can only be described as pornographic shapes. The recall letter, of course, came almost two weeks after this incident.

Tressa, Chuck, Ashell and I had gone out to MP for Chuck's birthday, and as we came in for a landing, Chuck, who was looking out the side window, began laughing hysterically as he was pointing toward the garden behind my cabin. Without warning, Tressa whacked me on the back of my head while giving me "The Look." It wasn't till I had landed my shuttle on the driveway pad and had a clear view of the closest bush that I realized why I was in so much trouble. In my defense, that eight-foot bush trimmed to represent a well-endowed woman was not part of the programming I made for my M-Series trimmer robot. The rapple trees were even worse, or better, depending on your point of view. My Carrieack cherry trees seemed to be untouched, and it's possible that the M-Series robot couldn't get one to sit still and gave up. The hardest part of this situation was convincing Chuck that I hadn't done this whole thing in honor of his birthday.

In a moment of desperation, I ran to my cabin, got my Tella 7 rifle, and went looking for my robot. We found the robot working on a pine tree at the far end of the garden. I don't feel comfortable describing the form my thirty-foot tree now represented but it was outstanding work on the robot's part. I had Tressa hold my rifle as I endeavored to coax the small, round, hovering robot down out of the tree. He would not respond and kept trimming at a feverish pace; it was obvious that he had a vision for that tree and his small shears would not be stopped. While leaving the cabin, I had set my rifle on the lowest setting, thinking I could short out my trimmer without destroying it, and when it fell, I could catch it because my M-Series only weighs about two pounds. My hope was to have it reprogrammed so it could fix the big mess that I now had. When I pointed my Tella 7 Rifle at it and pulled the trigger, the poor, misunderstood robot exploded into tiny, shiny bits. Holding my rifle up to where I could see the control panel, I discovered that the rifle was now set on magnum, which is powerful enough to drop an Earth elephant on its backside. When I turned back to look at Tressa, who was the last person to hold my rifle, she gave me a look like she had never seen the rifle before in her life.

So, I'm looking for an M-Series robot that I can have reprogrammed to fix the very realistically sculpted plants on MP. Please let me know if any of you can get your hands on one. If I can't find one, it will be at least another year before I can take my parents out to MP to stay at my cabin. I did try and fix some of the plants myself, but it just made them look worse.

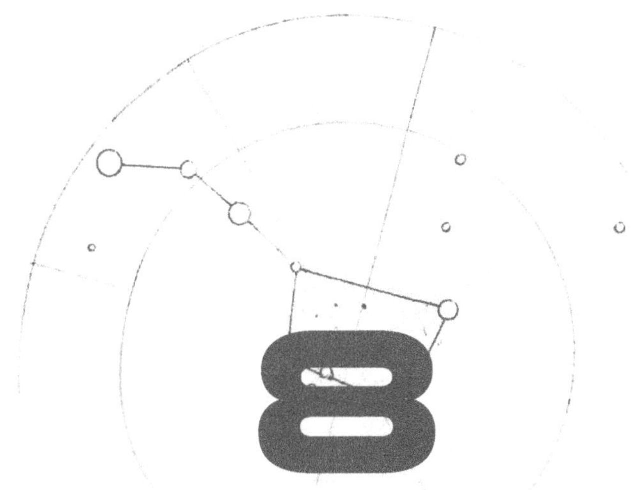

8

Don't Lean On The Redwoods:

There are two keys to a great redwood forest—redwood saplings and a lot of time. On Earth, redwoods grow between three to ten feet a year. When I saw there was a redwood forest on the map of MP, I got very excited. The visions of a cool, multi-level tree house and a redwood deck on my house on Earth danced in my head. When I took Tressa out to have a picnic in our beautiful forest, we found ourselves somewhat disappointed. Instead of sitting in the shade and enjoying a nice meal, we sat in the front seat of my shuttle and looked at approximately forty square miles of six-foot redwood saplings.

Now, a less creative person would have given up, but I had a vision, and I knew that science could help. The Trillion nursery that sold me my fire bushes had a great fertilizer that was supposed to do miracles. A miracle was what I got …kind of. It took two days and three tankers of SFF546 fertilizer to cover my forest. In less than nine months, I had the most beautiful eighty-foot redwood forest that anyone has ever seen. Tressa was so excited that she took a group of friends out to show it off. They took the FB shuttle that we use to get around the planet because it is too slow to fly in space. Its real name is TRS-XL transport. Most of you probably have or had this model to get your family around Earth. It's slow but it's big and comfortable. I lovingly call it FB or Flying Brick.

Chuck's mother-in-law just so happens to be the president of the United Arbor Foundation on Earth. Ashell thinks I have a real chance to be awarded the Arbor Day Pioneer award. If nothing else, this would impress my mother, who thinks of herself as having a green thumb. The group didn't land in the shuttle because the area still smelled quite a bit from the fertilizer.

After about a month of planning, I had the perfect design for a tree house. For those of you who are not from Earth, this is a home or just a hangout that is up in a tree. The tree house is usually supported by the lower branches of the tree, which are often eight feet or more from the ground. Children on Earth often build their own tree house or "fort" by themselves, which is both fun and dangerous. Because of how high off the ground it is, you have a great view of the area around the tree; and when the ladder or stairs are pulled up, no one can bother you. Yes, I know on my own planet there isn't anyone to bother me, but that's not the point. Everyone should have a tree house.

After flying over the forest for about an hour, I found a great clearing on a hill surrounded by very tall trees that seemed like it would be perfect for my tree house. The problem with my forest became apparent when I landed. As I got out of my shuttle, I could hear a cracking sound followed by several crashes. Over the roof of my shuttle, I could see the top of some of my trees leaning away from my landing spot. When I rushed around the shuttle, I noticed ten or fifteen trees had blown over from what I could only assume was my shuttle exhaust. This was confusing because my Tanner LX Shuttle has a planet-friendly, low-impact exhaust system on it that I purchased just weeks before. If I might quote myself, "Necessity is the mother of shopping the New LX Shuttle Catalog." On closer inspection, I found that my redwood trees were hollow in the middle. With a running start, I was able to knock over a seventy-foot tree by tackling it. Other than making me feel more manly than I have ever felt, it put a damper on the tree house plans. No, there wasn't a warning label on the fertilizer. I hope this doesn't affect my Pioneer Award. I'm willing to split fifty/fifty any award money that I get with a person who finds a practical application for a 100-foot, hollow redwood tree.

The nursery only came up with one solution. They have a form of bamboo that was developed for the planet Rosson. Rosson is in my neighborhood, galactically speaking. It only gets an hour of sun a day, and only on its southernmost pole. This bamboo is very strong and tall and will grow to fifty feet, I hope, with no sunlight at all. I bought 200 plants and planted them in the inside cavity of my trees by way of small holes I drilled in the sides. As the bamboo grows, it should fill the void and support the tree. I should know if this works in about two months. Wish me luck. Fortunately, there's no wind scheduled in that area for another eight months.

This also put a damper on my elk planting. To go along with my redwood forest, I was hoping to import some Rocky Mountain elk. This is a large deer from Earth. The problem is, they grow large antlers that they rub against trees and bushes to remove a protective felt covering. I am sure the elk would easily knock over a lot of my trees and/or punch them full of holes, so I'll have to wait. On Earth, the elk are protected, but I understand they used to be hunted and eaten quite regularly by humans. Yes, I do have every intention to hunt them. I don't see the problem in this. There aren't a lot of vegetarians in the human race, most of them having died off. So if you buy your meat at the store, or if you have ever worn or used leather, please don't write and give me a hard time. I am man—hear me roar. Plus, my Tella 7 rifle only stuns them anyway, and the animals and/or friends wake up feeling pretty good. After looking at the prices in the catalogue, I think they're too expensive to eat anyway. The elk are not my friends. Once again, my planet, my elk. Or soon to be my elk.

The same farm that has the elk also has a smaller species called mule deer. I believe they got their name from their large, mule-like ears. If I buy the elk, then I can get a two-for-one on the deer. Without a natural predator on MP, not including me, they think the deer will do well on my planet. I'm going to take Chuck to go look at them next week. I was also considering some bighorn sheep, but with their massive horns, and their knack for charging into things, nothing on MP would be left standing.

9
What's With The Holes?

It's kind of odd that I would buy a planet that has at least a quarter covered in snow when I really don't like snow. I understand it is all part of the balance of nature—blah, blah, blah. Now, if I liked skiing or jet boarding, then it would be different. All of my clothes are self-adjusting so the cold really doesn't bother me. I think I'm just a desert kind of a person, so I don't spend a lot of time in the Arctic. Last year, though, I took Chuck, Tripp, Tressa, and Ashell up for a day of skiing. My job was to drop them off on the top of the mountain and then wait for them at the bottom. They like to ski and I took the opportunity to scout for a good location to put my potential mammoth herd.

While landing at the bottom of Mount Moe, I noticed the large clearing I had picked had odd pock marks in the snow. Remember, when you land a shuttle on the snow it is a good idea to check the depth first. There is nothing worse than stepping out of a shuttle into waist high powder. The spot I picked to land had a good hard crust on top of the deep snow, so it was safe to walk on. If it can hold up my shuttle, it can hold up me. As I approached the field, I found the entire area was full of holes. Since I am always up for a good mystery, I began to inspect the perfectly round tunnels in the snow. They were about a foot and a half wide, but I had no way to determine how deep they were. Some of the holes were full of snow, as if they had been there a while. The "fresh" ones had sides that were smooth, as if something warm had melted the snow as it passed through it recently. My first guess, which wasn't a very good one, was that it was from small asteroids. After a moment of contemplation, I remembered that all asteroids had been cleaned out of our galaxy while MP was being built. Plus, the holes were smooth, perfectly round, uniform in size, and had some sort of silver particles that lined the hole. Asteroids would leave a crater instead of a smooth hole, and would have been surrounded by debris from the impact.

While working this problem out, the group showed up, ready for another run to the top. I wish these guys would learn how to jet board, then they could ski down and jet board back up without my taxi service. After looking at the holes, Ashell ruined a good mystery by solving it. "They were worm holes," she said with great confidence. I decided to argue this point. I have seen worms on Earth and even cut up a few in school. Well, I ran a simulator in biology class. I know that earthworms are small and sensitive to cold, and according to the simulation, they live in soil, which they eat.

Ashell was good enough to let me finish while looking at me like I was a slow learning three-year-old.

"These are Possel worms, and are probably from the planet Rosson."

The worms, as she described them, are designed to live and take on nutrients from the snow. They can grow up to fifteen feet in length and weigh about 240 pounds. They have a silver-colored mucus layer on their skin that keeps them from freezing to the sides of their holes. Ashell said she had done a paper on them in college. She also told us that she had a lot of pictures of them back on Earth that she was happy to show me. The holes are where the worms come to the surface to breathe and mate, which they do every night. She informed us that the worms are hermaphrodites. This means they have both male and female organs. This makes me wonder why they have to mate at all. Because I can't possibly know the age of all my potential readers, I'm going to abandon this train of thought.

I didn't know if she was right or not since I haven't finished my planet manual yet. I really should read it on one of my trips home instead of writing in my journals. One thing I did know is that I wasn't waiting to get back to Earth to see what one of these things looked like. So, as I waited for the group to finish another run down the mountain, I came up with a plan. Actually, I had two plans—one that worked and one that really had no chance of working.

Plan 1: The Worm Snare

A snare is about as primitive a trap as a human can devise. I think that's what I liked about Plan 1. I realize that most of you have no idea what I'm talking about, so I'll explain it a little better. To make a snare, you take a piece of rope or cable and make a loop in it with a knot that would allow the loop to tighten around whatever you are trying to catch. In primitive times, this would more than likely kill the animal or reptile you were trying to catch.

I had several hundred yards of shuttle cable that I used for tying off while in space port. I thought it would be perfect for a worm snare. At first, the girls wanted me to take them back to the house but then decided that this was something they had to see. Men putting their life in danger for no good reason seemed to be a great form of entertainment. The two of them took up a position in the front of the shuttle to watch as we three idiots went about setting our snare.

According to Ashell, the worms should come to the surface as soon as it's dark. As the sun went down, we picked the closest and what seemed to be the most traveled hole, and put the cable around the opening. Then we backed up about fifty yards and hid ourselves in the snow, the idea being that when the worms surfaced, we could pull the cable, which would tighten around the worm, and the three of us could pull it out for a better look.

After about an hour, we started to feel vibrations in the snow that seemed to grow in intensity. In the light from Aselus 1, we could see several large, bullet-shaped heads emerge from the snow. They were a shiny silver color—almost metallic. The cable we were holding started to take up slack. I assumed the worm was carrying it with him as it rose out of the snow.

This is the part of the story when Chuck tells everyone that it was my idea to wrap the cable around our gloved hands so we could hold it better. I don't remember, but if that's true, Chuck was the only one dumb enough to do it. (Sorry, Chuck.) The snow worm, as I have dubbed them, must have felt the tension from the cable and decided to retreat back into its hole. At this point, Tripp and I had both decided that seeing a Possel worm up close wasn't that important. By wrapping the cable around his hand, Chuck had given up the option of changing his mind. The cable suddenly tightened, cutting a deep line in the snow. Chuck then went from lying still in the snow to about twenty-five miles per hour in less than a second, leaving Tripp and I staring at each other.

Chuck looked like a human bobsled gliding smoothly across the snow. Jumping to our feet, Tripp and I ran as fast as we could follow the trail in the snow. Luckily, Chuck is big enough that his size didn't allow him to fit in the worm hole. When we caught up to him, he looked like a mannequin that had been turned upside down and stuck headfirst in the snow. We pulled him out and took turns brushing off the snow and ice. I couldn't believe that a person with a broken hand and a separated shoulder could laugh so hard. I think he liked it better than skiing. We could also hear the applause and cheers from the front of the shuttle. I carefully unwrapped the cable from Chuck's hand and pulled it out of the hole. It was empty at the end so either we had decapitated the worm, or it had slipped off. Since there was no blood or goo on the cable, we assumed he or she, or both, had gotten away undamaged.

Plan 2: Tube Tided

We took Chuck back to the cabin, and after rendering some first aid, he was all set to make another attempt at worm catching. You have to love Chuck; he has the mind of a doctor and the attitude of a grizzly bear. He's the perfect friend. I think that Chuck and I share the same brain; he just got the smart half. Ashell informed us that worms have a thick layer of skin followed by a layer of blubber that protects them from the cold. They don't have any nerve endings, so my Tella 7 rifle won't work even when it's set on magnum stun. Tripp thought we could blow one up, which sounded like fun but really didn't make a lot of sense, so I laid out the plans for our next attempt. I promised Tripp we could blow something up next time.

It just so happened that the exit pipe on my fusion heater is about the same size as a tunnel made by the snow worms. I had some excess pipe left over from some repairs I had done recently. I thought that if we cut a piece off, about fifteen feet long, it would work. So, while everyone skied the north face of Mount Moe II the next day, I strapped a piece of pipe to the shuttle and dropped it off to the newly named Worm Town. After picking them up from their last run, we went back for another attempt at the evasive snow worm.

Tressa and Ashell sat in the climate-controlled shuttle and drank hot chocolate, ready to watch what they lovingly referred to as "The Worm Hunt Fiasco Part II." The guys and me carried the piece of pipe to the edge of a new worm hole and stood it up vertically. We used the cable to hold it in position over the hole, thus extending the hole another fifteen feet. We each held a piece of the cable and tied one end to the pipe, then Chuck and Tripp tied theirs to a nearby pine tree. I held my end of the cable, tied around a stick as a handle. The pipe now extended the hole another fifteen feet above the surface of the snow like a small black smokestack. The three mighty hunters then took up positions nearby and laid in the soft snow surrounding the trap.

It was almost an hour later when we started to feel the vibrations of the worms moving through their snowy tunnels. Small chunks of ice danced on the surface of the snow. Before we were quite ready, the pipe began to vibrate, then suddenly stopped. I thought later that the worm must have sensed the change in its surroundings. Just when we thought our plans had failed again, the pipe began to vibrate once more. The support cables started making a humming sound from the vibration, almost like a plucked guitar string. In a matter of seconds, the worm's head poked out of the end of the pipe. As planned, I yelled "go" and let go of the cable at the same time. The worm trap fell to the ground. The worm-filled pipe hit the ground with a thud, sending up a cloud of powdered snow. Chuck reached the trap first, and with all of his strength, pushed the bottom end of the pipe away from the hole.

We watched for what seemed like an eternity, not knowing which end of the pipe to come out of. Suddenly, it made its move, exiting from the bottom end of the pipe and making its way across the snow, tapping its head on the icy surface, searching for a hole or soft spot to dive into. My adrenaline took over and I yelled, "Get him!" We launched ourselves on top of the giant worm. We landed face down, the three of us straddling the giant silver worm as it twisted back and forth. Tripp was on the far end and was thrown into the air as the worm lifted, by what I assumed was his tail end, landing on his back in the soft snow several feet from his last position. Before we could ask if he was okay, he had rolled over to his knees, and we could hear him laughing, which sounded a lot like a growl. Instead of attempting to stand, he crawled quickly the ten feet and threw himself back on the worm's slippery, silver back. I don't know if worms can think or if they just respond to instincts, but after a minute, it stopped struggling and lay still, seemingly playing dead while working on another strategy for escape. A half a minute passed without any movement, I yelled out, "Hey! Do you think we killed it?"

Tripp, who was now facing Chuck and I, looked up as if to

respond, but before he had a chance to answer, the huge worm started to vibrate. The rapid motion was so intense that it sent little ripples through the powdery snow around us. This seemed to be an effective plan on its part because the snow slowly gave way and all four of us started to sink in the cold powder. When it got to the point that we, the motley tribe of worm hunters, no longer had our footing, the worm easily slipped out from under us and into the deep snow.

Chuck had sunken so deep in the snow that when I looked over, I couldn't even see his brightly-colored snow suit. The girls turned on the bright shuttle headlights and stepped out into the cold night air.

Ashell called out, "Hey, are you morons OK?"

The sound of our uncontrolled laughter must have eased their minds. With a great deal of effort on our part, we climbed out of our holes and struggled to get to our feet. It was difficult to move since we were so out of breath from laughter. The front of our winter suits and gloves were covered in a silver layer of slime that shined in the shuttle lights. The girls, who had been thoroughly entertained, were good enough to pull us out of our holes. Even Ashell had to admit that the snow worm trap was a success.

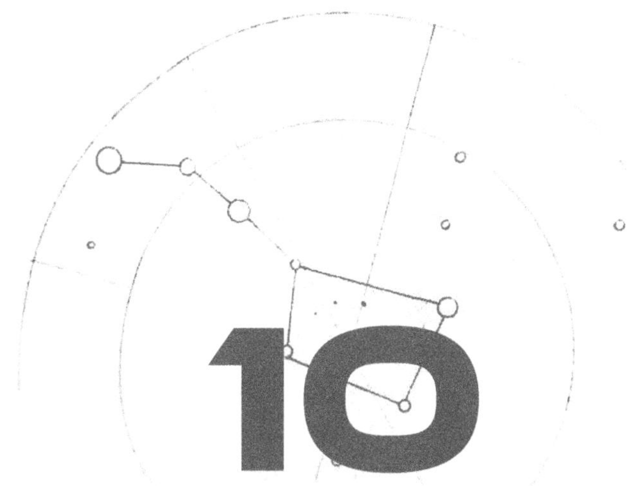

10
Home Again—Home Again

Even though it gets harder and harder to leave MP, I still consider Earth my home. I have said in the past that our planet is overcrowded. However, I think there is a comfort that comes from being around people. Not that I don't enjoy my alone time. I do. But even though the ability to leave everyone and everything behind me is always enticing, there's something to be said for just being one in a crowd. I think that is what draws people to live in big cities like Old New York and Moscow. Most of these people could live anywhere in the galaxy, but they insist on living in small homes close to each other, walking in crowds and eating in groups.

My parents love Earth. I think it was my mom who coined the phrase, "Making our planet a home." They still live in the home where I grew up in Central North America. Their home is near the shore of the Great Salt Lake. The lake, when it was discovered by the original settlers, had such high salt levels that even salt water fish couldn't live in it. Because of the salt harvesting over eight or nine hundred years, the salt levels were down so far that fish farmers could plant sea life from the ocean in the lake. In fact, that's where the fish farm is that I bought my halibut from; which in turn became expensive fertilizer. The Great Salt Lake is now the largest producer of shrimp and lobster on Earth. Yes, I know, more useless information.

It's a great place to grow up—surrounded by the Rocky Mountains and wonderful deserts. Tressa likes to visit just for the skiing. I enjoy the fishing, both on the lake and the rivers that come out of the Rocky Mountain range. There is a lake north of my parent's home that is hidden up in the Teton mountain range. It's one of my favorite places on Earth. The lake is so secluded, we have to park our shuttles at least a mile away and hike to the campground.

It's a small lake surrounded by lodge pole pines that seem to be fighting to be the closest to the water. The property managers only allow a small number of fishermen on the lake at one time to avoid crowding. I make my reservations a year in advance. The fishing is awesome and the surroundings epic. It's also a protected air space area, so there aren't any large billboards floating around advertising local restaurants and hotels. Nothing bothers me more than trying to fish with a billboard floating ten feet above me telling me it's two for one night at the Jackson Hole Casino and Lodge.

Chuck swears he saw a black bear on one of our trips. I think black bears are extinct, but if there are any still alive in the wild, that's where they would live. I'm guessing Chuck saw something else. It was probably a wild boar, or knowing Chuck, a big rock. I have spent days in my shuttle scouring the mountainsides of

MP, trying to find a place that could come close to Hidden Lake. Nothing yet.

Even though most of you will disagree with me, I do have a job. I am now a mapmaker for my father's company. Thank goodness for nepotism. I map out routes for R-7 gas transportation. Yes, I know, anyone can draw a straight line on a star map. It's actually more complicated than that. I have to know all the transportation and speed regulations around certain planets, and I have to acquire all of the customs declaration forms from each byway station. I've put a lot of miles on my LX Shuttle, but I did get the company to pay for it. I'm not quite as dumb as my college professors thought I was. I got the LX model because it runs on R-7 gas and it's the fastest personal shuttle on the market. It's a limited edition, which means that the Tanner Company can only build about four million of them. When you look at it that way, it doesn't seem like such an exclusive group of shuttle owners. There's also a new boost system that is available only for that model. The problem is, it would make my LX faster than my FSS—or Flight Sensor System—could detect things that I don't want to crash into in space like asteroids, satellites, other shuttles, and so on. Tressa said that she would miss my shuttle if it got destroyed.

Back to my work. I don't really need the income, but I love my job and it keeps me busy. Most of you remember my more destructive phase. Well, it wasn't really destructive, but it wasn't productive, either. I spent time looking for companies to work for. When I found a company with potential, I would go to work for them as a low-level employee. After a few weeks, I would figure out who in the company was the biggest jerk. I mean, the person who treated everyone like scum. Then I would buy the company and personally fire that person or persons myself. Once I had weeded out all of the people that ticked me off, and advanced everyone who really did the work, I would sell the company. Unfortunately, after a while, business owners started to recognize me and everyone treated me very well as an employee. This took the fun right out of it, so I quit and went to work for dear old dad.

My father gave me a really small and crappy office so the other employees in the company wouldn't complain. Luckily, I don't spend a lot of time there. Besides, I'm really good at my job, so no one complains too much. Well, except Miss Tower, my dad's secretary. I think she dislikes me. I also think that she secretly runs the company. (Love you, Miss Tower.) Tressa thinks my job is a smokescreen for my trips to MP. I have got to find that tracking device on my shuttle. Besides, MP is on the way, or way back, from a lot of the places I have to travel to. So, if I must stop there for lunch and feed my raptors, I don't think it's the company's business. I am not paid by the hour or the mile, so just leave me alone. My motto has always been "Never work when you can be eating, never eat when you can be fishing, and never fish when you can be hunting." My father made me take the plaque with my motto on it down off my office wall. Maybe I can get it on a bumper sticker for my shuttle.

The company headquarters are on Earth, really close to where my parents live, so I often get visits from Zap when she's home from school. Luckily, my brother Toss rarely visits my parents' house, and he never comes to the office. I think the sight of people working really bothers him. Toss and I do not spend time together. In fact, I'm not sure what he's doing for a living. He's probably living off his inheritance. Frankly, I don't care.

Growing up, he and I didn't get along. I'm sure it was just the differences in our personalities, or it could be that he is basically a self-righteous dork. Truth be told, I think the conflict between us can be traced back to just a few years ago. I had bought the company that Toss's current girlfriend was working for. She was a Trillion, or at least part Trillion, and had the personality of an empty cereal box. I'm not sure what Toss saw in her. To make a short story a little longer, I fired her. I think she might have taken it personally, especially when I replaced her with a T-2 robot. It's sad when a robot has more personality than a human. She dropped Toss that very day, and he hasn't quite gotten over it. The funny thing is, she's the one who hired me in the first place. Talk about irony!

There are few Earth-made products anymore. It's so much easier and less expensive to buy products from other planets. I have even caught my mom with imported stuff. She just puts a "Made on Earth" sticker on them. She must have a whole roll of those stickers stashed in their house. If my shuttle wasn't Earth-made, or at least assembled on Earth, I don't think my father would have let the company pay for it.

The majority of things that humans enjoy are available for a cheaper price somewhere else in the galaxy. When you have a planet like Parcelus that is about forty percent diamond, it's hard to pay what they want for one on Earth. The food is a whole other story. Many of you have accompanied me to that bistro on Mars. I realize a person wouldn't fly all the way to Mars for dinner, but if you're going by there, you've got to stop in. Tell Tyson the chef that Moe from Earth sent you. Tyson is a Rellom and a real crack-up to be around.

One thing that Earth is still famous for is their nuts. You

can use a handful of peanuts as currency anywhere in our galaxy. I got Tressa and myself a whole week's stay at a space station resort for a can of pecans that my mom gave me to feed to my raptors. If you can get your hands on good Earth walnuts, the galaxy is yours for the trading. I keep a few cans of mixed nuts in the back of my shuttle in case I get in trouble off-planet.

To those of you who are reading my book and haven't been off-planet, always ask if the food you are going to eat is EHC-approved. Remember that the Earth Health Counsel is trying to keep you alive and healthy. One of Zap's friends was on vacation with her family, and she decided to have some Beronean spice drink. It is a very popular drink at many off-planet resorts, but BSD is not approved by the EHC for humans. You would think that the logo that represents a pile of dead humans on the label should be a sufficient warning. When her parents found her the next morning, there was nothing left of her but an empty shell. The sad part is that the only file on her for the GR machine was five years old. Her parents were not happy to have a teenager again. I guess her and Zap don't hang out anymore because of the age difference; that and she had no idea who Zap was.

Most restaurants, markets, and space station vending machines have a human menu. I do not mean "human" *on* the menu. If you see "Human" or "Earthling" on a menu, you are in the wrong place and should pay for your drinks and get out of there. If anyone stops you, tell them you are a Trillion. There is nothing in our galaxy that can stomach the thought of eating a Trillion.

After church every Sunday, my family always goes to a restaurant right by our home. They have a recipe for lobster bisque that has been handed down for ten generations and it's awesome.

The lobster comes fresh from the Salt Lake. Most places will try to pawn Black Bugs off on you. Remember, "If it's black, send it back." Yes Black Bug meat is green, but "if it's green" doesn't rhyme with "send it back," which makes it easier to remember. They also have these little crackers they serve with their soups that are to die for. I won't give you the name of the place because they're not going to pay for the advertising, and I prefer that it stays "not so busy." I do give their complete menu in my book *Dude, Don't Eat That*, in the chapter on Earth's best soup. Just the thought of that lobster bisque has gotten me through many hours of church.

I realize that I don't talk about religion, but it's important to my family. Many humans left their religions when the Trillions came to Earth. I guess they thought that if the Trillions weren't Gods, then there must not be one. My ancestors continued their religion and passed it on to my family. I think the biggest disappointment to humanity was that the Trillions couldn't tell them what religion was true. Earth has had a long history of fighting with itself over our religious beliefs. I always thought it was odd that Jesus Christ, while on Earth, taught us to love one another, and then the religions spent hundreds of years killing each other over how He said it. I'm not pointing any fingers, but you know who you are.

Because my family and a lot of my friends live on Earth, I think I will always call it home. If I ever get a chance to live on MP full time, I would still visit Earth for holidays and Sundays for the lobster bisque. I don't think Tressa would live on MP full time because she really enjoys her work and her friends. It's possible that we could get a clone made of her that could live on MP and clean the cabin. But for some reason, I think she would consider that inappropriate. When Tressa #1 came with me for the weekend, it would probably be awkward to have both in the house. At the turn of the century, there was a law passed that made it illegal to clone someone without their permission. I guess the problem was that humans started cloning movie stars, models, etc. Of course, when I say humans, I mostly mean the human males. I found it entertaining to see socially awkward men with a beautiful and voluptuous female that looks very similar to a famous movie star. It became such a problem that the governments on Earth had to step in and start regulating cloning.

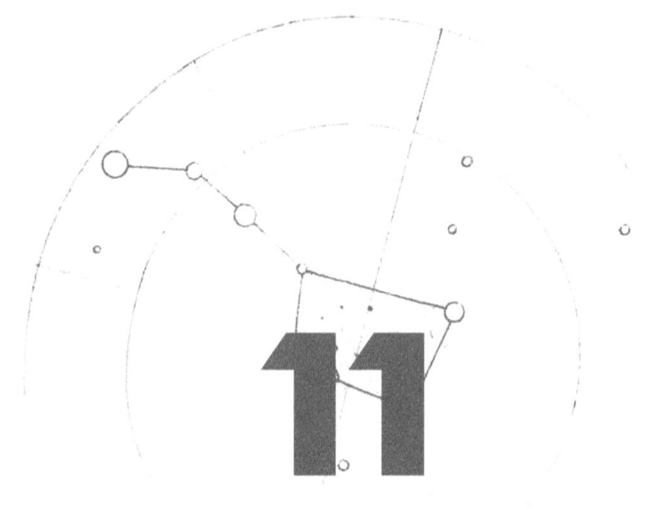

11 Castle Moe

One thing I have discovered is that owning a designer planet leaves few surprises. Most parts of the landscape and plants are exactly what you would expect. Having grown up on Earth, and because I haven't spent a lot of time on other planets, I'm always surprised to see things on my planet that I don't recognize.

On one of my last trips to MP, Chuck and I used up a whole tank of fuel in the FBS flying around the other side of my planet. When I say, "the other side," I mean the opposite side of my planet from my cabin and Lake Moe. On the side of one of the mountains, in the Grizzly Bear Mountains range, we made an unusual discovery. Perched near the top of a rocky ridge was the most unusual clump of trees I had ever seen. They were very tall and unusually big around. They were covered in moss and vines. We flew over them again to get a better look. The trees seemed to have ornate carvings in them that completely covered the top section, which was tapered to a point. The trees had been planted around what looked like some sort of structure. Because of the overgrown foliage, it was hard to pick out details. In the center of the grove, there was a smooth, flat space. This appeared to be a perfect landing spot for my shuttle. Before we landed, I checked my maps to see if there was any indication of what this place was. There wasn't.

I'll tell you, there is nothing more surprising than to land in a clearing and find yourself in the courtyard of what we came to discover was a medieval castle. The odd-shaped trees, as you might have guessed, are very beautiful towers. Having been ignored for some time, the towers and the battlements that they surround are heavily overgrown with vines and moss that was woven into the stone. There was a beautiful but also overgrown garden with rock walls surrounding what appeared to be large lawns now covered with bushes. The courtyard was cut cobblestone, decorated with a beautiful stone fountain that I'm sure would run if it had water pressure. At the far end of the courtyard, Chuck noticed a large, beautifully carved wooden door. Over the door, cut in stone, was a large coat of arms. The stone tablet was intricately sculpted and included a shield held up by two lions. The name "Ludwig" was carved beneath it.

On the opposite wall, to the side of the large doors, was a metal plaque that had been set into the stone. I didn't write the inscription down, but in general, it said that the castle was a gift given to Lord and Lady Pincey from the president of the United British States in honor of his leadership abilities in uniting the country during the controversy that broke out while accepting the French into the Union.

This fortress is a replica of the Neuschwanstein castle. Obviously, I copied that name down. I'm not sure what language that is, and my translator watch didn't know, either. I have to assume that the original castle design is from Earth, and probably from somewhere in the British States. The masonry work on the courtyard and walls was incredible. The stone from the original on Earth was more than likely cut by hand by master masons, while this copy was probably scanned then laser cut to match the original.

The castle is huge. I don't know if it's bigger or smaller than the original, but from the outside, it's big. The anticipation was building to see what was on the inside. The doors were a little stiff and it took a minute for the two of us to get them open. Eventually, they gave way to our determined pulls on the large metal handles, the hinges squeaking with the weight of the heavy wood doors. Chuck stood to one side, bowing slightly. His hand motioned politely toward the open doorway, allowing me to enter first. I stepped through the entrance into the shady interior. There was a bit of dust that hung in the air, visible where light shined through the large windows. Chuck followed me in, and we found ourselves standing on ornate rugs that covered a beautiful wood floor.

Once inside, we found rooms and corridors exquisitely decorated from floor to ceiling in gold and fine wood and long, spacious corridors filled with large paintings. Chuck ran from room to room, trying to decide which one to officially call his own. The floors that were not wood are polished stone that was a little slippery because of a thin layer of dust. The walls are painted beautifully and the sparse furniture in the castle is finely crafted. Other than needing a good dusting, everything in the place seems to be new. Well, *new* is relative. I mean it's *unused*. It doesn't seem that Lord Pincey lll or his family spent any time there at all.

The windows are small and seem to be made of sunglass. They obviously still have a charge because even though the outside is covered in vines, the inside is bright and warm. That must be the reason that the moss and vines have grown so fast. Most plant life is attracted to the artificial sunlight the glass gives off. The stained glass windows are all dark and dreary. Chuck informed me that sunglass is hard to color and really hard to laser-cut into shapes for stained-glass style windows. There is one large, decorative window in the banquet hall with great detail and colors that depict Lord Pincey standing victoriously over a slain dragon while holding a hefty sword with muscular arms. A depiction of Lady Pincey kneels at his feet with her arms around the leg of her powerful guardian. The commemorative inscription below it read, "Lord Henry Pincey the Dragon Slayer." What it should say is "Tacky." Chuck said that he thinks the whole window is figurative and it more than likely represented some great achievement that Lord Pincey had made. This made more sense because, based on what I have read about Lord Pincey, he would not be able to lift the sword he was holding in the window.

I am surprised that the Pincey family didn't list the castle as an asset to the planet. At least I didn't see it listed under homes or dwellings. I did find it later in my Planet Function Manual, in Chapter 614 titled *Home And Dwellings*. Next time any of you are on MP, remind me to take you to the castle. It's the coolest fort ever. Tressa hasn't seen it yet, but I'm guessing she would be willing to stay on-planet for an extended time if we slept in Castle Moe. It's not often you can stay in a place that has a throne room.

While looking around, I found a master bedroom with a really cool, big bed. The poles that hold the bed up are carved to look like towers. The master bathroom has a sink with a sculpted swan as a faucet. A swan is a large waterfowl from Earth. The water seems to work fine in the bathrooms and the huge kitchen.

There are many different sculptures in the castle, and I noticed that they all have very similar faces carved into them. My guess is that they were all done to resemble Lady Pincey. There are several large paintings of Christ and his Apostles. I don't know if they're replicas of paintings from the original castle, or if Lord Pincey was big into Christianity. This would make sense because the castle has its own chapel in it. In the hallways and rooms, there are ornate candle holders and chandeliers made from gold and ivory and encrusted with jewels. All of the lights that we tried worked.

Between two of the rooms, we found a hallway that looks just like a cave. According to Chuck, my human dictionary, it's referred to as a grotto. As we walked down the hallway, torches that hung on the walls automatically started to light, their yellow and orange flames dancing on the rock walls. I'm not sure what purpose a grotto has in the castle, but it was my favorite room, with rock walls and a table and chair made from some kind of twisted wood. Built into one of the walls is a waterfall with different kinds of plants arranged artistically around it to make it all look natural. The whole room looks like it's from a Shakespearean play. The cave-like surroundings, the waterfall, furniture, and lighting made me want to quote from Shakespeare's King Lear, or sing a good Gregorian chant.

In between the grotto and the kitchen, we found the pantry/laundry. The door to this room was closed and creaked a bit when we pushed it open. Along the facing wall, we could see a line of high-capacity washing machines and dryers. Chuck estimated that we could do the laundry for an entire village with all of them running at once. To our left, there was a row of cabinets, which ended up being full of cleaning items. The last four cabinets were deeper and wider than the first, and when I opened them I jumped back, startling Chuck. We both stared at the body of an older human male standing in the cabinet, slightly slumped and covered in dust. He had gray and black hair, and a thick mustache to match. He was wearing an antique black tuxedo and black bowtie. Stepping back in surprise gave me a clear view of his entire body. His lower half had no legs but was instead a cloth-covered cone that tapered down from the waist to a single ball that replaced his feet. Chuck laughed, and pointing at the figure, stated, "It's a butlerbot!"

I looked at him, still confused. He looked at me, still pointing at it.

"It's a butlerbot! Remember the movie *Death at the Baskerville Castle* we saw with the girls last year that took place in that castle in Old England?"

"Oh, yeah, I remember. You're right. He looks just like the butler robot that ended up being the murderer. Now I'm *really* creeped out," I said nervously.

Chuck laughed again. "Aw, they're harmless to humans."

"Really? Tell that to the Baskerville family!"

We looked at each other and laughed. Chuck stepped forward and pulled the robot's tuxedo jacket open to reveal a small green light in the side of its chest.

"Well, it looks like he has a full charge. Should I turn him on?"

I took one step back and nervously said, "Okay, give it a shot."

Chuck reached up behind its left ear and pushed the power

button. The butler robot's eyes blinked, and he straightened his slumped body. He turned his head slowly and looked at Chuck, and then me.

"Pardon me," he said with a low voice and a thick British accent. "Are the two of you maintenance?"

We both shook our heads no.

"Are you guests of Lord and Lady Pincey?"

We both shook our heads again.

"I am Moe, and this is my friend, Chuck," I replied. "I recently purchased this planet from the Pincey family."

He nodded, his head slightly acknowledging my explanation.

"I am Humphrey, the butler, and I am here at your service, Lord Moe and friend Chuck. Welcome to Pincey Castle. I do, however, need to see your identification code and your copy of the planet's deed."

I looked at Chuck and back to Humphrey.

"I have a copy of the deed and confirmation code for the sale back at my other residence. I would be happy to bring it back and show it to you on my next trip."

He nodded again. "That would be fine, Lord Moe," the antique robot continued. "If you would turn me off until your return, I would appreciate it. I would be humiliated if Lady Pincey found out I was tricked by two common thieves."

We looked at each other, surprised by his cheek until we remembered he was a robot.

Please do not take items from the castle," he continued. "Please do not instruct the staff. I will give them instructions based on your wishes. Please do not enter the armory, or remove items from the armory. Please do not consume food items from the kitchen or pantry due to possible expiration issues. Please leave the restroom doors open after use."

With his list of instructions complete, he nodded at Chuck and closed his eyes. Chuck stepped forward again and reached up to flip the switch, but paused to ask a question of the robot.

"Would it be okay if I called you Humpy?"

The robot turned his head toward Chuck and responded politely.

"You can call me anything you want, sir, but if you want me to respond, please call me Humphrey."

Chuck smiled and turned him off, then turned and looked at me with a devious grin. "You know Moe, I could reprogram Chuckles here and turn him into a real party animal."

I thought about it for a second and concluded that in this case, his arrogance served a purpose. I don't think running an entire castle and grounds is a job for a butler/frat boy party animal.

He shrugged and closed the cabinet. We opened the three other cabinets and found robots dressed in maid uniforms. They were all the same design as Humphrey, but they were women, and all three had different colored hair. Chuck thought they were attractive, especially the redhead. I had to threaten him to keep him from turning her on.

Chuck and I didn't take the time to count how many rooms there are in the castle, but it's a lot. When I get a chance to get Humphrey and staff to work cleaning up, we are going to have a serious party in that place. You are all invited if I can find somewhere to park all the shuttles. We may have to carpool. I've been thinking about it, and I think if I stun a couple of Black Bugs and let them go outside of the castle, they could clean it up. There is no place for them to go on the side of the mountain. When they get the outside cleaned up, we could all go up for a Black Bug barbecue. Yes, my bugs, my castle, my planet, and Kyle's barbecue recipe.

In the basement of the castle, we found a door marked Armory. The armory is the place in a castle or fortress where all of the weapons are stored. There is a whole collection of armor, swords, spears, flintlock guns and everything we could need to protect the castle from unknown attackers. The fact that Humphrey had forbidden us to enter the room made it impossible for us to pass it over. The huge, thick oak door creaked and moaned as we pushed it open. As we entered the room, motion sensors automatically lit torches on the walls. We stood and stared at row after row of medieval weaponry. I glanced at Chuck. His eyes were sparkling with excitement. He looked back at me, and when our eyes met, we knew we were of one mind and purpose. Chuck laughed cynically.

In the harsh light of the midday sun, two warriors stand with the points of their heavy broadswords resting on the worn cobblestone floor of the castle courtyard, their helmet-covered heads bowed in a show of respect to their adversary standing only a few small steps away. Their armor shines, reflecting the rays of sunlight dancing on the smooth, impenetrable stone walls of the mighty fortress. The knight clad in black armor is the first to raise his sword. Sir Moe can no longer restrain his primeval desire to strike down his lifelong enemy. With his blade extended in front of him, he lunges forward like an armor-covered bull. Chuck the Destroyer stands monumentally, his mind clear and his patience to his advantage. Sir Moe, unable to slow his attack, barely grazes the shiny silver armor of his opponent. The silver knight swings his sword flat side down and spanks the stumbling black knight on his chainmail-covered backside. The battle that follows is one that legends are made of. The sound of bone-crushing metal-on-metal rings through the halls of the castle. The battle continues for what seems like a lifetime. Finally both great champions collapse in total exhaustion and no longer have the strength to lift their respective weapons. The victory went to neither man, with both lying on their backs on the stone ground, bruised, bleeding, and laughing hysterically. Two broken fingers, two sets of bruised ribs, one possible concussion, and a ringing in my ears that lasted a week.

Victory to none, but a good time was had by all.

It was worth the hour it took to put all that stuff on and almost that long to take it off and put it all away. I didn't want to be in trouble with my butlerbot. I imagined he would be upset with our abuse of the antique and possibly historically important weaponry. I hope he knows how to get blood out of chainmail!

Tressa ended up shooting down the Black Bug clean-up idea. When I came back to get Humphry straightened out, he informed us that there were a handful of M-Series landscaping robots in an outside storage shed. It took Chuck about thirty minutes to get all five of the M-S2 robots updated and working on cleaning up the yard.

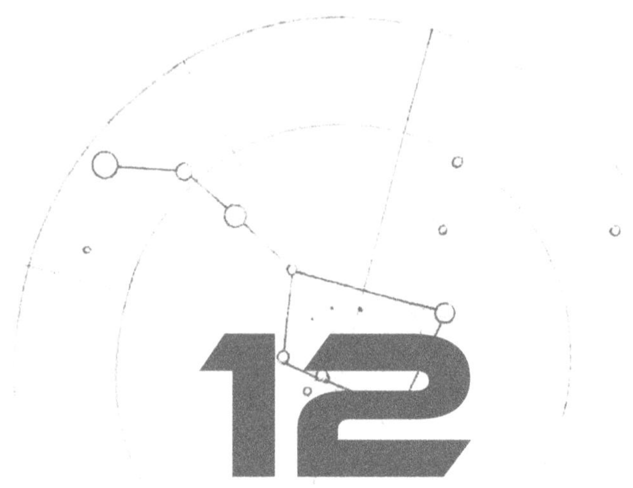

12
Farewell to Rednecks, Racing, & Rye Whiskey

One thing I enjoy on my long shuttle rides for work or to visit MP, is to read. This is a great way for me to work on my Old American English. One of my favorite authors is Dr. R. Peirce. He is a doctor of American History. One of his favorite subjects is the American redneck. No, it's not a bird. The American redneck was a group of humans that originated in the Southern United States.

I first heard Dr. Peirce at a seminar he gave at my college my Freshman year. I was hooked. I can't tell you how many times I have read his two books on the subject. *Redneck Mythology* and *A History of the American Redneck*. Professor Peirce is just one of a handful of historians who can read and translate old Southern English. I have read some of it and didn't understand a word of it.

The redneck was an offshoot of the American cowboy. According to Dr. Peirce's research, the redneck culture originated in the southern states after the Civil War. After the Confederates lost the war, in the minds of the rednecks, the Confederacy became immortal. There are many monuments that still stand today in the southern states that represent famous Confederate leaders. In my opinion, it's celebrating second place. This group seemed to embrace the past instead of looking toward the future. In an attempt to change the country's history, or just to hide it, some of the statues and monuments were destroyed or removed around 2020 or 2021. Because this action didn't actually change history they were replaced not long after. The name redneck comes from farmers having sunburns on their necks from working the fields. This, of course, was before farms were completely automated. The rednecks were usually referred to as the "working class" or "lower class." I'm not talking bad about them. I'm just telling you what I have read.

There are a few things that the rednecks invented that have lasted over the centuries. One of my personal favorites is barbecue. This is an official Earth original recipe for cooking meat. In the late 1800's, cowboys or rednecks began cooking meat in outdoor fires or pits, which gave the meat an amazing taste and texture. I have heard residents from other planets talk about Earth barbecues as far away as the Horse Head Nebula. Another thing I've adopted is the pleasure that rednecks derived from shooting holes in things. Several of my antique Earth pistols were originally owned by rednecks; at least that's what the gun dealer claimed. One thing I really love about the rednecks are their personal names. I have taken the time to research and have given all my raptors redneck names like Hank, Bobbi Sue, Leroy, Cletus, Ruby, Bubba, and Bosephus, who sadly passed away. Tressa, bless her heart, shot down the idea of naming our first child Bud (girl or boy).

According to Dr. Peirce's research, rednecks seem to worship car racing. Many of the race car drivers were given almost God-like status. At the height of popularity, drivers were more well known by their car numbers than their names. Numbers eight, twenty four, six, and three are some of the numbers that will forever have a place in redneck history. The sport of stock-car racing was born from rednecks souping up their cars so they could avoid being caught by police when they were running moonshine. At this time in Earth's history, it was against the law to make and sell alcohol, and as history has shown, the surest way to get a redneck to excel at something is to make it illegal. There are still great memorials that were erected for drivers that died while racing.

The only remaining redneck temple is referred to as The Grand Ole Opry, and there are many different artifacts on display there. After a hundred years or so of racing, there were so many advancements in the race cars themselves that safety was no longer an issue. In the latter part of the 2040's, they had eliminated car accidents, and along with that, injuries and deaths. This, Dr. Peirce believes, brought the popularity of racing to an all-time low and many alcohol and other racing-related businesses died off or focused on other sports. According to the book "Redneck Mythology", without the unity that racing brought to the rednecks, they quickly separated into clans, and after only a couple of generations, died off completely. I think this is an assumption on Dr. Peirce's part.

When the Trillions made contact with Earth, they brought with them Hansel, or what humans refer to as spice. Spice is a powder that is mixed with drinks or food. The reason I bring this up is that this spice replaced alcohol. Trillion spice has all the great effects of alcohol without the ramifications on the human body. With spice, you can have a good time without losing your ability to control yourself. Trillions soon found that there was a huge spice market with humans who had the tendency to use almost anything to make themselves feel better about being themselves. This probably aided in the demise of the rednecks, who used huge amounts of alcohol in order to enjoy endless hours of car racing and fishing where nothing seemed to happen.

Dr. R. Peirce also believes that rednecks may have fled Earth to their own planet. As far as I know, there is only one planet where you can still find alcohol. In fact, the planet Bosephus II is the only place you can find a Kentucky whiskey that is made from an original Earth recipe.

Another part of the redneck mythology that I enjoy is the fact that they revolutionized hunting. Up until the evolution of the rednecks, humans had hunted animals for food and clothes. Rednecks, however, made it a lifestyle. At that time on Earth, there was really no need to hunt. In fact, it cost more to hunt animals than it did to buy the same amount of food at a store or market. However, rednecks would not be denied their right to shoot things. I think it kept them from shooting each other. Rednecks chose to shoot bigger animals with larger antlers even though the taste was worse and the meat tougher. This may be the reason that barbequing their meat was a common practice. God bless the redneck mentality and their offensive mud flaps. By the way, Bosephus II has the largest population of white-tail deer in the galaxy. I know, I tried to buy some for my planet, but they do not export deer. The residents of Bosephus II view the white-tail deer as a form of deity and consider them holy. I think they just don't want to share.

For my next birthday, I would like to go see the temple in Nashville and visit all of the monuments. Chuck and Ashell have recently been there and said that the Rosco P. Coletrane Memorial is very interesting, and the Hank Williams Monument will bring tears to your eyes. I hope Tressa will enjoy the trip as much as I hope to. With her love of spicy chili, I'm sure she'll find something to do. Personally, I'm looking for a fifty-five-gallon barrel of George Jones's Original Southern Barbeque Sauce.

According to the brochure that Ashell gave me, there are a lot of restaurants and interesting stores in Nashville. They sell country-style food and clothes. There is a store there that is supposed to have 478 versions of camouflage clothes. I have some camo that I ordered from a catalogue, but when I wore it to MP, I kept getting run over by my raptors. They don't have very good vision. Chuck wears a cowboy hat that he bought in Nashville. It's made of straw, is very beat up, and looks worn out already. He claims it was that way already when he bought it and that it has what is referred to as Hat-i-tude; to me, it looks like he lost a bet. What Chuck really wanted was a hat that held two old-fashioned beer cans on the side and a straw that would allow him to drink out of both cans at once. He said it was too expensive, but to me, it doesn't sound very practical. Chuck did bring me back a sticker that he put on the back of my shuttle when I wasn't looking. The caption read "Save a Horse, Ride a Cowboy." Luckily, the sticker burned off on reentry to Earth.

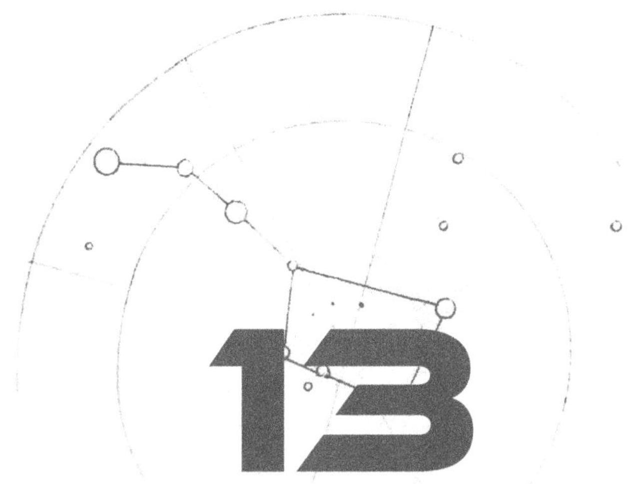

13
From Trash to Treasure

To save money on MP, I have cut back on a few things. One convenience I decided to live without was garbage removal. Since I have a whole planet, I thought I could figure out what to do with a little bit of garbage. But it didn't take very long before my trash condenser was full and I was forced into action.

After a fun weekend on MP, Chuck and I decided on a plan. We attached my shuttle cable to the large block of garbage. The idea was to haul it about 2500 miles away to one of my islands that has an active volcano. Using the shuttle and the cable, we would lower the garbage into the volcano and let the lava burn it off. We did it this way because if we were to just drop it, we could miss the opening of the volcano and cover the outside slope with trash. I do like to keep my planet clean.

Everything went as planned, which we thought was unusual. There is always something that goes wrong due to a lack of attention to detail in our plans. The only problem that arose was when

Chuck, who was running the cable winch, couldn't get the cable to pull all the way in. Not being able to work on it while flying, we decided to leave the excess cable hanging behind us and fly back to the house. While landing, I came in at an angle so the cable would fall behind the shuttle instead of underneath it. This was a fortunate decision, because the cable had been coated with metal and might have punched a hole in the shuttle if we had landed horizontally. In fact, the cable was so heavy that it left a three-inch-wide and six-inch-deep trench from where the shuttle had dragged it during our landing.

I figured that the light-duty saw in my toolbox would cut through the cable, and then I could reattach a new end. After cutting through the metal on the outside of my cable, I noticed that the shavings from the metal coating were a very shiny color. The outside was a black color, but the now exposed inside was a very cool gold color. With a rag and some polish I use for my shuttle, I was able to polish the coated cable until it shone like my grandmother's jewelry. The cable with the metal coated on the outside looked like a large gold candle with the cable as the wick. I am not sure what the molten metal is in the volcano, but it looks a lot like gold. This gave me a great idea, and from the look in Chuck's eyes, he had similar plans. The biggest question was, what did we have that we could coat in "gold" that wouldn't burn up or melt before we got it cooled off?

Chuck's first idea was a raptor. I didn't think this was funny. I don't think he likes my raptors. It may be the long scratch on his leg that caused his disgruntled opinion. I told him that raptors do not like to be teased. Chuck should know—he helped design the stupid raptors at NTEG. We settled on one of my rapple trees that had died. We tied the cable around the trunk of the tree and took it for a quick dunk in the volcano. This worked great. To cool it off, we dragged it through the ocean on the way back. The salt water was very efficient at cleaning off the black soot on the outside. I'll tell you, if you want a cool decoration for your yard, a twenty-foot gold tree is the way to go. Chuck and I could make a fortune selling gold-plated pine trees for Christmas. Not for the gold content, because gold is quite cheap on Earth due to the import of precious metals from other planets. The moon that orbits the planet Esined 4 is eighty-four-percent gold. It used to be that Earth gold was more valuable, but it was just a trend. Now you can have your driveway paved with the stuff.

After a couple of hours of hard work, we had dipped and polished most of the statues in the courtyard of Castle Moe—even the big one of Venus de Milo that had the face of Lady Pinsey carved in it. It's possible that by covering them with gold, we may have destroyed the historic value, but I'm inclined not to care. Unfortunately, we did destroy the first statue we tried to dip. Something about putting cold stone carvings in molten metal made it blow up. I finally figured out we could dip the statues if we hovered over the volcano for a few minutes and let the statue warm up slowly. I was never strong in science, but I do have a knack for practical problem solving.

I promised Chuck that if I ever had a raptor die of natural causes, he could dip it and put it in his yard on Earth. The only problem I see is that if the metal coating ever gets a leak in it, you'll be able to smell that cooked raptor from outer space.

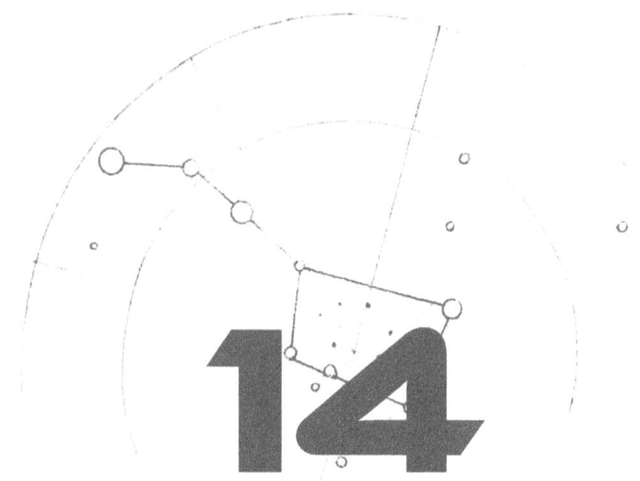

14

Don't Trust Free food

According to my Earth history book, during the two-thousand-twenties, Earth scientists developed a product called "Green Algae Derivative." Because this name didn't sound very appetizing, everyone just called it "Free." Many of you have asked me why I refer so much to Earth history. It's because most of my friends and co-workers that are not from Earth are always wondering why Earthlings are the way they are. I refer to our history to explain, or to use as an excuse, for the way we act.

Back to "Free." Within a year, the product "Gad" or "Free" was being used in hundreds of food products. The reason it's referred to as "Free" is because it has no calories or fat. In fact, it has no nutritional value at all. It's produced in many forms and can be a substitute for almost any food base like flour, meat, dairy, etc. At the time, this product was considered one of the greatest developments in food production. Humans have a tendency to overdo things in general. Eating is one of those things.

After the development of "Gad," a person could sit down and eat a plate of biscuits and gravy and a stack of pancakes without the issue of putting on a single pound of body fat. The problem was, there was no nutritional value, either. It was like eating a hologram.

Two years after its introduction, humans were in the best shape they had ever been in. Not since the Neanderthal time, when man ran everywhere and killed things with a spear, had we been in such good physical condition. Unfortunately, the health organizations had to start regulating the use of "Free." The two groups that seemed the most concerned about their weight—teenage girls and gay men—started dying off in huge numbers from starvation. This was a surprise to their friends and relatives, who always knew them to eat three square meals a day and show every indication of being healthy, then suddenly die of malnutrition.

"Gad" or "Free" did find a place in the market as a replacement for extreme fatty foods. There were Free hamburgers, Free butter, Free cream, and Free chocolate. It was more expensive for these products, but when you could put a big spoonful of butter on your mashed potatoes without any extra fat or cholesterol, it was worth the price.

The French scientists that developed "Gad" made a fortune and also received the Nobel Peace Prize in science. At the same time, they rejuvenated the market on French food, which had suffered for many years due to high fat and cholesterol content.

Many of you are asking yourself what this has to do with anything, and why would I take the time to tell you about this. The truth is, I love to eat food, and enjoy studying about its history on Earth. I don't think of it as just a fuel source. Not to mention, this is my book, and I'll write about whatever I want. I love to visit other planets and sample human-safe food. On occasion I've trusted a waitress and eaten something not approved and suffered the consequences. On the planet Bry, they have a form of pasta that you can't get anywhere else. Bry, by the way, is an abbreviation of the planet's name. To spell it in Old American English would take up this whole page, and I would more than likely spell it wrong. This pasta is one of the best dishes I have ever encountered. I call it pasta because it looks and tastes similar to Earth's spaghetti. It's actually some kind of living creature that is kept alive in a sort of green slime until it's cooked in hot liquid. It may sound disgusting, but once you have tasted it, you will be on your way home to grow Bry Worm Pasta in green slime. Remember to tell them to cook it thoroughly because if it can live in green slime it can live inside a human. A good trick I use is to let your food sit in front of you for a few minutes. If it doesn't move or change color, you're good to go. This is a good idea for almost everything you eat or drink off-planet.

Another of the foods that Planet Bry is famous for is chocolate. I mean chocolate in its true form. Not "Free" chocolate or "Mars" chocolate, I mean the way that chocolate was on Earth supposedly 300 years ago. The Bry chocolate chefs do not really make a lot of recipes out of their chocolate. They do not have chocolate cakes or creams or desserts; they just make small chocolate wafers. The last time I ate some, I truly believe that I felt the purest form of love. I also smelled fresh bread, felt a warm breeze on my face, and the tumblers in my mind finally locked into place and I briefly saw the future. Yes, it's possible that the Bry chocolate may be a mild hallucinogen. Personal results may vary.

There is an amazing amount of food that is available in

our galaxy for humans, and several good guide books available to help you eat off-planet. One that is a personal bible to me is *Where to Go When You're on the Go or Best Shuttle Stops—A Traveler's Guide to Good Food.* "Best Shuttle Stops" is a digital book and gives star map locations and hologram descriptions. This helps a lot because it's sometimes difficult to tell the difference between some food at shuttle stops. One sandwich can be the best that you have ever eaten and another can reverse your physical evolution back to the ape. Some humans do not believe in evolution, but after a bad sandwich, they will. Both of these books were written by a friend of mine, Brian Shadowfax. Brian and I met one day at the Worm Hole Café where he was writing an article on pies for one of his books, and we became quick friends. I have found it's easy to make friends when you are both enjoying good pie.

It was in my copy of *Where to Go When You're on The Go* that I found that great bistro on Mars. They have 258 different cheeses there. Tressa loves what is called squeaky cheese. She bought some on our first visit to Mars, and now I have to bring some back to her whenever I go past there. I haven't asked the chef what the cheese is made from because why ruin a good thing? If you happen to know what Mars squeaky cheese is made from, don't tell me, because I don't want to know. Personally, I prefer the gaslight cheese. If you can muscle your way past the gag reflex caused by the smell, it's some good eating cheese.

I find it difficult to find human-safe vegetables in space. That is why I grow a big variety on MP. I have leafy vegetables for salads and different kinds of peppers that I like to cook with. Tressa has the ability to eat the hot ones right off the plant. I have to clean out the seeds and an inside layer of skin on the peppers called the pith before I eat them. Plus, it's fun to say, "Clean the pith out of them!" just to irritate Tressa. It's not that I'm a wuss; I just have a more sensitive palate than she does. Not to be rude, but when she eats raw peppers, it makes an eight-hour shuttle ride home with her less than pleasurable.

I put up a rock wall alongside my garden. It doesn't keep the raptors out, but it does stop the wind from making my vegetables move. If they don't move, they're safe from the raptors.

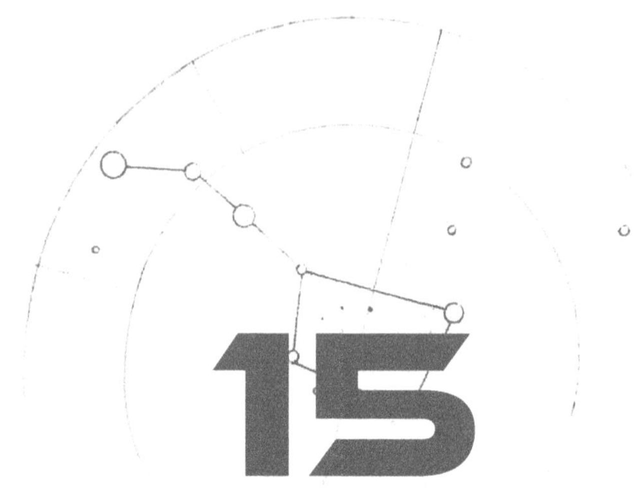

15 Bass Fishing and Dragon Racing

As far as I know, there is only one place on MP to find Largemouth Bass—a fish species from Earth that just so happens to be an integral part of the American redneck mythology. In fact, Dr. Peirce wrote several chapters on the Micropterus Salmoides Floridanus, or the Black bass. The rednecks lovingly refer to them as "large mouth Bass" or sometimes lunkers, a hawg, toad or a big 'un. Fishing for them was a big deal in their culture. It wasn't necessarily for the food or the trophy, because they were more commonly released. Large fishing tournaments were held, and some fishermen made a living off fishing for bass and demonstrating products used to catch bass. Dr. Peirce says they also spent a lot of time catching catfish, both by hand or using tackle, but it didn't have the following that bass fishing did.

It isn't easy to raise big bass to be lunkers. First the bass must have good genetics, so not all bass will get big. It's kind of like raising horses with the proper bloodline. You need to have a good environment for them and a lot of space. Bass like to have cover, so you need logs and grass for them to hide in. In the deeper parts of my ponds, I have strategically placed crashed satellites I have found, if they're not leaking radiation or dark matter. They sit on the muddy bottom and give the bass cover. Their metal frame is also handy because I can see it on my fish finder sonar screen easily. With the bass, there are several species of smaller fish like Bluegill, two kinds of shad and a large population of Crawfish. I have automatic feeders that feed this smaller population of fish that I have to refill with small brown pellets once a month. On occasion, I will trap a bucket full of crawfish and cook them in a traditional Earth boil. I won't go into the process, but I got the recipe from *Redneck Mythology*, chapter 8, titled *Fixin to Eat*.

Approximately 400 miles east of the west desert on MP is a swamp area that is very similar to the Everglades on Earth. Surrounding these everglades are large ponds and canals that move the water back and forth to keep the wetlands saturated. These ponds, I have found, are the perfect environment for Largemouth Bass. The bass that are there were originally planted by Lord Pincey. He managed to get the bass from an area on Earth known as Florida. I knew there was something that I liked about him. The water temperature is around 70° and doesn't seem to flow very fast in any one spot. The bass have only one natural predator besides me, and it's the Ezam dragonfly. It's bigger than the insects on Earth. This species is about the size of a large Earth bird and can grow to be four feet long with a six-foot wingspan. They will skim the surface of the water and will grab any fish that happens to be close to the surface like a bird of prey from Earth does. Because of their size and the speed of their wings, the dragonflies make a real cool humming sound as they fly through the swamps. It's kind of a creepy sound if you are out fishing for bass in the middle of the night.

On one of our "Guys Only" weekends to MP, we decided to do some bass fishing. Tripp, Chuck, Kyle and myself set out determined to catch a new MP bass record. We had also brought with us our college buddy, JT. The more people we have, the less each of us has to pay for fuel for each fishing trip. Now JT isn't much of a fisherman. In fact, he gets bored very quickly and constantly complains, but we bring him along to absorb all the bad luck. You have to understand that JT couldn't catch a bass with an Argilelion grenade, but the rest of us always have good luck fishing when he's with us. I can't explain it; I'm just telling you about it.

My twenty-foot fishing boat anchors to the underside of my shuttle, which allows me to put it wherever I want to fish. I installed a release lever in my shuttle so I can drop or pick up my boat without having to get out. I usually put my boat on the shore, then park my shuttle on dry ground. It uses up too much fuel to leave my shuttle in "hover" mode. We took the time to put all our gear in the boat before we took off so we didn't have to carry it down to the shore. If it wasn't for the fact that my friends would leave me when I put them in the water, I would just let them all ride in the boat on the way to the lake. Yes, they have done it before, and no, they won't get the chance to do it again. To be honest, they probably wouldn't because the last time they did, I left them, went hunting Black Bugs, and came back two days later. They didn't think that was funny at all, and I ended up paying for all the fuel that trip.

My boat has a shuttle-style air displacement engine on it that allows me to go across the water without scaring the sometimes skittish fish. JT loves to hydro-slide, which is a form of jet sledding, across the water. In Earth history, they used to do it behind a boat and called it water skiing. Because the hydro slide is propelled by a very noisy engine, we told him he couldn't bring it because it would scare the fish for twenty square miles.

After pulling in several large bass, Kyle hooked what was sure to be the biggest fish of the day. When the bass hit the surface, just seeing its tail in the air was enough to get us all excited. With all the yelling and commotion in an attempt to help Kyle land his fish, we didn't hear the hum of a large dragonfly behind us. When the trophy bass hit the surface again, the hungry dragonfly dove down and grabbed it. In less than a second, Kyle went from fishing, to fighting a large dragonfly. In a moment of inspiration, I grabbed my Tella 7 rifle and stunned the dragonfly. Who says mounting a rifle rack in my bass boat was a dumb thing to do? I think I have some rednecks in my family history.

Kyle pulled the dragonfly and his now stunned bass to the boat. Other than a few scratches on its side, the winning bass was in okay shape. Tripp and I took a scan of the bass so that Kyle could have a replica made later for his home. His wife will be so happy. At the same time, JT carried the dragonfly to the front of the boat. Being more of a pacifist, JT thought he could revive the dragonfly and let it go. Holding it by the legs, JT moved the dripping wet dragonfly up and down in the air.

At this time, I would like to explain that none of us had ever caught or shot a dragonfly before, and we knew very little about them. One thing JT found out was that to help them catch their prey, the legs of the Ezam dragonfly are very sticky, which allows them to hold even a slippery fish. His realization of this fact and the reviving of the dragonfly were almost simultaneous. At the moment that Kyle, already suffering from separation anxiety, was releasing his bass, JT, who is one of the skinniest people I know, took flight. Well, "flight" is not really the word. JT was being dragged across the water like a boat that had left out its anchor. We couldn't see him through the spray of the water until he hit the beach. I thought about grabbing my rifle but was afraid I might hit JT if I tried to stun the dragonfly, so all we could do was watch. When they hit the beach, JT started running, which kept him from being dragged through the mud. As the two of them approached what looked like some really nasty bushes, the dragonfly suddenly turned and headed back toward the water. JT had just enough time to get his feet in front of him and lean back. When he hit the water, it was like watching a professional hydro-skier skim across the surface of the pond. JT had figured out that by pulling on one leg or the other, the dragonfly would compensate by going the opposite direction. He mastered this in an attempt to save his life, and then he continued just for fun. JT skied across the lake in a large figure-eight pattern.

His biggest problem was that there was no way to stop the dragonfly and he didn't know what would happen when the large insect got tired. JT lined up on the boat and came in on a final approach. We could hear him yell at us to catch him. Both the dragonfly and his passenger were obviously getting tired because they began to slow down. When they reached the boat, JT was so tired, he couldn't lift his legs high enough to clear the railing of the boat, so he gracefully slammed into the side. This action had just enough torque to pull his hands free from the dragonfly's legs. The dragonfly flew away leaving his passenger flattened against the side of my bass boat. I can close my eyes today and still see the whole picture. Not even a shuttle full of Terean little people could be that funny.

JT is now determined to make dragonfly racing an Olympic sport. I agree. He just needs to work on a way to stop, or at least a safer form of landing. Kyle's bass replica looks great over his banister in his family room, and is a great tribute to his fishing abilities. My sister-in-law says he has a great view of it from the couch he now sleeps on.

16 Adopted a Town

It wasn't long after I had bought my planet that the news had spread to most of my family, friends, and even Tressa's coworkers at the college. At a dinner party Tressa and I attended, we were approached by one of the professors from the sociality department.

Dr. Waddell works as a Professor of Sociology and Human Behavior at the college, and as I came to find out, is in charge of an off-campus group called N.H.H., or New Human Habitat. What I understand about the group is that they find host planets that are human-compatible and then move whole communities there. Dr. Waddell made it sound like a humanitarian group. To me, it sounded like a large-scale sociology experiment. The N.H.H. group would like to place a community on MP and allow them to settle a small piece of land. In return, I would get a tax write-off and a moral boost to my fragile ego. I told Dr. Waddell, or Barbra as she has asked me to call her,, that I would do some research and get back to her. She has invited me to meet the leader of one of these groups who would like to be transplanted to my planet. Seeing the look of panic on my face, Tressa told Barbra that I would have to get back to her after I had a chance to do some research on the subject. This is the way a professor tells someone the answer is "No."

To be honest, I don't think I'm ready to be a landlord. There would be a lot that I would have to give up if I allowed a group to have access to my planet. For the first year or so, the settlers would have to be able to receive supplies. This means that transport shuttles, freight carriers, and, no doubt, relatives, would have to have the landing codes for MP. This would be like giving 100 people the key to your house and then in a year trying to get them all back. Anyone could land on my planet without permission or invitation.

I'm not sure if this group can govern themselves. If they're left unsupervised, heaven only knows what could happen. On one hand, they could be pioneers working hard to be successful, or they could be a group of spice-drinking slackers. To tell the truth, I don't want to be a big brother to 400 humans and spend my weekends checking up on them. Not to mention that Tressa told me it would be unethical for me to hunt them even if I only stunned them.

I believe it would not take long before they considered it their home, their land, and their planet. Not to sound too possessive, but I think it's human nature to want to own land without the possibility of being kicked off of it. If the day ever comes that I decide to sell MP, I think it would complicate things and decrease the asking price if there was a human settlement on it. It would also affect the bass to fisherman ratio. Out of 400 humans, there has to be a certain number that are fishermen. Denying a fisherman the right to fish is considered incredibly cruel to sportsmen like myself. It's probably better not to risk it.

The upside to having this group on-planet is that I could trade rent for some good janitorial work. I could get them to clean my cabin, prune my rapple trees, feed my raptors, and shave my woolly mammoths, (which I could pay for with their rent money). So, I guess the question is whether it's worth the hassle and foreseeable complaints to have low cost labor on MP.

Tressa asked me if I thought I could handle the long list of possible complaints such as:

"Can you make it rain more?"

"It's too cold."

"Where is all the good bass fishing?"

"The raptors ate our crops."

"Can we eat the elk?"

"Can my in-laws have the landing codes?"

"Why can't we live in your castle?"

"A dragonfly carried off our baby."

"Our parents are coming for the weekend. Can they stay in your cabin?"

"Why do we work so hard and you don't?"

"Why do you shoot at us when we complain?"

"Why does our leader always tell us what to do?"

"Can we have more land to start our own group?"

"Will you take us to that bistro on Mars?"

"Can you turn up the oxygen?"

"Can we ski on your mountain?"

"It's warm today. Do you have a problem with global warming?"

"Can we make alcohol out of the rapples?"

"Can I tell my friends that it's my planet?"

I think I have talked myself out of this whole deal. There are a lot of planets that the N.H.H. can relocate people to. I'm pretty sure the Trillions would donate a planet if there was a tax write-off in it for them. Besides, humans are still considered endangered in our galaxy, so the Trillions would probably set up a refuge on one of their planets if the N.H.H. would submit the right paperwork. The Trillions started the Human Preservation Group that forced restaurants in our galaxy to stop serving humans on their menus. This was no small task since humans are easy to catch, grow fast, and have no problem breeding in captivity. Humans also are very tasty, from what I've heard. One fast food chain of restaurants called The Purple Star went out of business when the Trillions started enforcing the ban. If something says "Man-Made," it's not what you are thinking. After a while, some off-planet restaurants and markets found that they made more money feeding humans than eating them. Remember to follow the dining guide in *Where To Go When You're On The Go*, Chapter 6. It could save your life. There are still planets that you want to avoid. Better safe than swallowed.

The Human Preservation Group has saved the lives of millions of humans, but they were infamous on Earth for a long time due to their testing on humans. My personal belief is that the Trillions consider humans to be just a few generations past dragging our knuckles on the ground and living in trees. My friend and I found this out our senior year when we went on spring break to the West Coast. I was just stepping out of my shuttle on the beach when I felt a pain in my backside, then the lights went out. When I woke up, I was lying on the beach next to my friends. We had all been fitted with ear tags and had tracking collars. It's very difficult to pick up on women when you are wearing a collar that makes different sounds every time you eat, walk more than ten yards, or show interest in the opposite sex. All four of us had to go to a medical clinic to get the science stuff removed. Unfortunately, it was a Trillion doctor that we ended up seeing and it took us a while to convince him that we knew we had collars on and tags in our ears. For all I know, it could have been his staff that had tagged us in the first place. When all was said and done, he was willing to remove them for free. The collar wasn't too bad, but the ear tag hurt like crazy. I still use the hole in my ear to wear an earring every once in a while, just to bother Tressa.

I was also approached by the Argilion Ambassador who asked me about the possibility of their government leasing MP for one week out of the year. He was somewhat vague about what they planned to do while they were there. I think that with the amount of cash they were offering me for the week, I wouldn't care what was going on. What I forgot to mention to the Ambassador was that I was familiar with their practice of leasing planets to use for testing new weapons. I have met planet owners who were foolish enough to rent to the Argilions and made the mistake of signing a waiver. All of them had damage that took years to repair. In fact, the Our-Way-Design firm refuses to sell the Argilions any manufactured planets for any price. To them, it's like selling artwork just to have it destroyed by the buyer. I decided to tell the Ambassador that the bank I used to get my planet loan would not allow me to sublease to any other government, which might actually be true if I took the time to read all the paperwork from my loan.

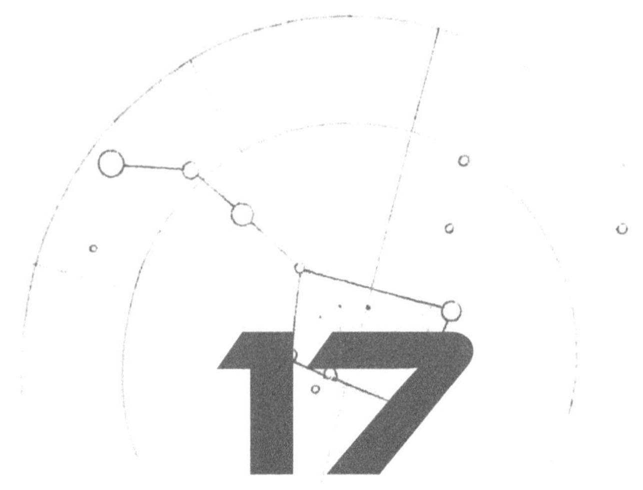

My Planet. Well, Mostly My Planet

Not far from my cabin on MP is one of the best fishing spots in the galaxy called Trout Creek. The area I love to fish is in a forest similar to Yellowstone Park on Earth. It is heavily wooded, with small clearings covered in grass. The Grizzly Bear Mountains surrounding the area have snow on the tops that last most of the year. The stream I love to fish is in the bottom of a large canyon filled with pine trees. The water is deep and clear and full of an Earth species of fish called Brook Trout. It must have been one of Lord Pincey's favorite places to fish because of the references to this location on my topical maps. I can't tell you where on MP this is, and I'll explain later. "Stay Tuned." I'm also not sure where the mountain's name came from because as far as I know, there aren't any bears on my planet.

On my last fishing trip out to Trout Creek, I decided to take a fly fishing pole. A fly pole is a specialized fishing pole/torture device. This rod is longer than a normal fishing pole and is designed to, with some very complicated arm movements, cast an artificial fly or grub to coax fish into biting. To tell the truth, I find fly fishing a sick form of exercise. It takes a lot of work and finesse to get the fly where you need it on the water to get the fish to bite. Some say that is the challenge of fly fishing they enjoy. Whatever.

This particular stream is less difficult for me to fish with a fly rod because I am able to reach over the water without scaring the fish. If I get bored, I just put on a worm or some floating bait over my Dry Fly. Rumer has it that I have been known to blow finicky fish out of the water with a large handgun. Yes, it's true, but in my defense, my planet, my fish.

On this trip, I had an unusual experience. I am not much for hiking, but on this day, I found myself farther up this canyon then I had walked before. Being a true fisherman, not counting my sidearm, I am always looking for that perfect fishing hole. The kind of hole where the water is so deep you can't see the bottom and there are places to stand and cast where the fish can't see you. After hiking for an hour or so, I came around a bend and found what I was looking for. The stream had a small waterfall that fell into a large pool and was surrounded by tall trees and thick bushes. As I approached the water, I noticed what appeared to be a large rock across the stream from me that had numbers written on the face of it. I thought this was out of place because even the Our Way Design Firm usually doesn't put ID numbers on their rocks, none that I had seen anyway. I thought it might be a survey marker from the map makers of MP. It wasn't.

As I approached the rock, I discovered that it was not a rock at all, but an older model personal shuttle with the ID numbers exposed though the foliage. The numbers were reflective and should have been visible from a great distance but were obscured by the shade of the trees and the thick underbrush. The front and the back of the shuttle had been wedged between two large trees and surrounded by some nasty looking bushes. The crashed shuttle was a good example of N.R.S., or Nanotechnology Repair Systems, being a problem instead of a benefit. Where the exterior of the shuttle was mashed up against the rock and trees, the N.R.S. had attempted to repair the damage, and not being able to separate itself, it was forced into including the rock and wood into the repair. So now this shuttle was permanently attached on the front and rear to some large, not easily removed, objects.

As I paced back and forth in front of the vehicle, I found there was no way to walk around either end, back or front, so I could not see the other side. The shuttle windows were tinted and impossible to see through, and the airlock side door was sealed from the inside. I decided that the only way to investigate any further would be to climb the built-in access ladder that runs on both sides of the craft. I was thinking that if I was confronted by someone, it would be an advantage for me to have the high ground.

My mind was going a million miles an hour, debating the origins of this ship. The first thing I thought of was that pirates trying to escape the Trillion Space Patrols had crashed here and their really cool-looking skeletons were inside, still grasping the shuttle controls. I thought it might also be a getaway shuttle from a big robbery and the cargo hold might be full of money, jewels, and salted Earth peanuts. My final thought before I climbed the ladder was that Lord Pincey had crashed here and didn't want to go to the expense of having the shuttle towed back to Earth or a space station to have it repaired.

Without more thought, I put down my fishing pole and started up the side of the shuttle, and with great effort, I might add, pulled myself up onto the leaf-covered roof. The first thing I noticed on top of the shuttle was the Pincey royal seal, partially covered by sticks and other debris. I think they put the insignia there to help avoid being searched at shuttle checkpoints. Once on my feet, I walked a few steps across the top, hoping the noise of the waterfall would drown out the sound the unstable shuttle made as it rubbed against the bark of the trees that held it in place.

When I got to the point where I could look over the air-fin that runs the length of the roof, I stopped. Next to the shuttle was a small clearing in the trees, which was covered with well-manicured grass. In the middle of the small meadow was a solar generator with several power cords running in different directions. All of the stuff that was originally in the shuttle was arranged outside like a large outdoor living room. There was a small table with a plate and a set of utensils arranged on it, and a clear glass container of what appeared to be water. Stretched across the length of the clearing was a thin wire with several pieces of clothing drying in the sun.

On the far side of the clearing, in the shade of a large pine tree, were two of the shuttle seats set on the grass-covered ground. One of the seats was in a reclining position, and lying on top of it was a barefooted gentleman reading a book. I assume he was alive because his foot moved to a musical beat only he could hear. So much for getting to see a cool skeleton. This person had a beard and long hair, which made it difficult for me to estimate his age. He was wearing a pair of cordless headphones, which may explain why he didn't hear me ascend the shuttle ladder. As stealthily as possible, I crossed the grassy clearing, and as I approached this individual, I pulled my 454 Casule Revolver out of its holster. I carry my antique revolver for fishing emergencies, but not knowing who I was dealing with, I thought it an appropriate move. I walked as close as I dared, and being so far undetected, I tapped the trespasser on his bare foot. He stopped reading and slowly lowered his worn copy of Tom Sawyer, exposing his somewhat bewildered blue eyes that peered through his overgrown hair. With one hand, he removed his headphones, the unrestrained music now loud enough for me to hear, and with the other hand, he placed his book on his lap then raised it in the air in a universal sign of surrender. I gave him a quick inspection. Finding him less of a threat, and to avoid any difficulty in our budding relationship, I holstered my hand cannon.

I believe that my first words to him were, "Who the hell are you and what the hell are you doing on my planet?"

To which, with great self-assurance, he replied, "I am Prince Justin Pincey and my grandfather, Lord Pincey the Third, owns this planet."

"Okay, well, I am Moe, and I bought the planet from your family about two years ago."

His eyes squinted and then blinked several times as he processed this information. Justin nodded his head as a sign he now understood.

"Oh, sorry. We haven't been able to keep up with family affairs of late since my communication and tracking relay were mounted in the front of my shuttle and were pretty much screwed when I hit that tree. Oh, I should mention it's a bad idea to put your shuttle on manual to land if a bottle of Brearenan

Spiced Rum is involved. I was feeling a bit overconfident," he said, winking one eye.

"I told him he shouldn't be driving when he's impaired!" a feminine voice said from the shadows inside the shuttle.

"I already stated that I was spiced and overconfident, or didn't you hear me?" the prince replied in the direction of the shuttle's open door. "Plus, you didn't offer to drive."

"I *did* hear you; I just wanted it to be on the record that I had done my part to avoid this situation. And besides, you won't let me drive."

As I turned to look at the shuttle, a beautiful woman emerged, walking toward the reclining Prince Justin and myself.

The woman was tall and had long red hair pulled back in a braid. She was casually dressed in a t-shirt and cut-off denim jeans. Her makeup and overall appearance showed no signs that she had been roughing it in the woods for an extended amount of time. On the contrary, she appeared to be almost perfect except for the pair of soft gloves she wore on her hands that seemed out of place for the warm temperature. For a brief second, I could have sworn she looked very familiar to me. She walked past me, and when she got close enough to Justin, she turned and sat down in the plush shuttle seat next to him. Looking over at the prince, then back at me, then back at the prince again, she raised her eyebrows.

"Oh, sorry! Where are my manners?" Justin said, in the way of an apology. He stood up quickly. "This is Moe," he stated, pointing his hand in my direction. Then he turned casually and motioned toward the woman. "This fare damsel is Caroline." She smiled at me with a mouth full of perfect teeth and responded with, "It's a pleasure to meet you, Mr. Moe."

I smiled back. "The pleasure is mine, Caroline." The memory hit me like a ton of bricks, and I realized it was the way she said "Mr. Moe." Without hesitation, or proper thought of her feelings, I blurted out. "You're a CARI?"

She smiled again. "Yes, Mr. Moe. I am a CARI, a Contemporary Artificial Robotic Intelligence—a model 10, if you were wondering."

"I'm sorry," I said. "It was improper for me to ask you like that."

Justin, who had sat back down, was moving his head back and forth, dragging his bushy beard across his chest, watching us. He looked at her then back at me, and chimed in, "How did you know she was artificial intelligence?"

Caroline responded first. "You seemed to be bothered by my confession. Do you have issues with A.I. individuals?

I looked at her thoughtfully and responded. "No, ma'am. I don't. To answer Justin's question, it was the way you said Mr. Moe that made it easier to figure out. Growing up, my nanny was a Cari model 8, and she would refer to me as Mr. Moe. When you said it, the resemblance was extraordinary."

Caroline, still smiling, replied, "I hope the two of you got along well."

I grinned and nodded my head. "Most of my happy childhood memories are from the time I spent with her."

"That's..." Caroline froze in place, her mouth still partially open, her clear blue eyes staring forward, unblinking. I stared at her, waiting for her to continue. I noticed that her hair had changed from a dark red to almost a strawberry blonde.

"Oh, sorry!" Justin said, realizing what was happening. "She has frozen up. She'll be back in a moment when she can reboot her mind. She hasn't had an update download since we crashed here," Justin said in response to a question I hadn't asked yet. I turned to him and continued with my questions. "How long have you been here?"

Justin looked up and sat for a minute as if he was counting. "It's been close to three years," he answered. His face seemed to show surprise to his own response.

"I am curious about how you have spent your time, being stranded in this spot for that long."

Justin smiled thoughtfully. "I spend most of my time reading books and listening to my old-fashioned digital recorder with classical Earth music on it. Caroline also has a few thousand songs in her files, and she can sing the entire scores from most well-known Earth musicals. She also has audio versions of around four thousand novels, and she's pretty good at doing the different voices and sound effects. She can even make Shakespeare seem interesting, which is no easy task when it comes to my attention span." Justin was looking at her with great fondness.

"We sleep in the shuttle, and the rest of the time we spend outside. I used to fish in this area with my father and was planning on spending the weekend here when we crashed." Justin leaned forward so he could visually check on his companion's progress before continuing. "Luckily, I brought my camping stuff, including the solar generator," he said, pointing at the box at the end of the wires. "The shuttle has a food processor in it but I think the protein cube has gone bad because my food has recently started tasting odd." He made a yuck face with one eye closed and his tongue sticking out. "I have caught a lot of fish from the stream, and I also found some bushes that grew berries that looked delicious. Caroline told me she recognized them from her picture files and said they were safe to eat, but she didn't seem sure about it. The good news is they didn't kill me!"

Even with his rough exterior, I was amazed to find him so articulate and well-spoken, which gave him an air of aristocracy. I think being a member of a royal family, Justin probably had the best education that money could buy. The prince was a bit taller than me—well over six feet. His long hair was bleached in strips from prolonged exposure to the sun. He had tan skin, and with his long hair and shaggy beard, it gave him the look of a beach bum from one of the tropical islands on Earth. I guessed his age to be around forty, maybe forty-two years old, which would make him just a year or two older than myself. He had an air of distinction about him, which I believe comes from his royal upbringing.

After our brief conversation, Prince Justin stood up, slapping his hands on his knees as he rose. "Well, if you give me a little time, we can pack up our stuff and get out of here. Since my family doesn't own the planet anymore, we are trespassing. I would be happy to pay for a lift back to Earth."

I put my hands up palms forward. "Since I'm the sole owner of the planet—well, me and the United Bank of Earth, Inc.—I have no problem if you want to stay for as long as you feel comfortable."

He smiled. "That's very hospitable of you, Moe."

Suddenly, Caroline began to speak, starting from where she had left off.

"Wonderful. I'm glad you two had a good relationship." She paused, looking at both of us and then directly at Justin, an embarrassed expression growing on her face. "How long did I glitch?"

Justin looked down at her with a comforting expression. "Just a few minutes, gorgeous."

I could see that her hair had gone back to dark red. Not wanting her to dwell on it, Justin continued, "Moe has offered to let us stay for as long as we would like. What do you think?"

She smiled at him. "If you would like to stay, Justin, I would like that as well. We do need some supplies, but other than that, I am quite content."

"I will be happy to bring you anything you guys need that I can get a hold of." I looked over at Caroline. "Just for reference, Caroline, who is your maker?"

She looked at me curiously. "I am from the Earth's division of Refined Robotics, a subsidiary of NTEG. Why do you ask?"

I smiled. "It just so happens I have a buddy who is a big fish at NTEG, and I believe he can get you any new updates and downloads you need."

She smiled. "That would be appreciated," she said in a soft voice. Justin looked at her and then me, remembering something.

"How about replacement hands?" he said eagerly. I looked over at Caroline's embarrassed face and then down at her hands. She raised them up off her lap and pulled one of the soft gloves off. Her hands were without skin, and the metal and ceramic skeleton of her fingers were charred black. She looked down at her hands sadly, turning them back to front. Justin looked at her, almost tearing up. "We had one of our power cables overheat a couple weeks back and it was burning its way toward the power relay, so Caroline grabbed it and pulled it out to save the generator."

"Good work!" I said,smiling at her. She nodded slightly and smiled back. "I have some supplies in my shuttle if the two of you would like to come down the trail with me,"

"Why don't you go with Justin? I need to charge, and I feel a bit out of sorts from my glitch," Caroline said as she reached for a cable next to her chair. Without looking down, she lifted the bottom of her shirt, showing the tan skin of her stomach, then plugged the end into a small hidden port on her side.

"Good idea, beautiful. I will be back soon," Justin said, smiling at her. Within seconds of plugging in, Caroline's hair changed again; starting from her scalp, the dark red hair slowly turned white. She looked at me and seemed amused by my stare.

"Justin was good enough to get me the new RTH, or Renew Transformative Hair, as an anniversary gift," Caroline said, smiling lovingly at the prince.

"Well," Justin said, winking at her, "it's a great way to tell what kind of mood she's in."

Caroline looked back at me. "You look like a brunette kind of guy, Moe." Her hair changed again—now a beautiful dark brown—and went from straight to soft curls.

"Wow, you're right! I think that's my favorite look," I said, smiling. She smiled back, her hair going back to white as the spiral curls fell out. Justin turned to leave, and I followed.

"Goodbye, Caroline. It was a pleasure to meet you."

She smiled. "It was a pleasure to meet you, Moe. I hope we see you soon." Caroline closed her eyes as the two of us left their camp. Justin went left and I followed him as he went through a gap in the trees that I hadn't seen before. We talked for a while about his family as we walked back down the trail to where I had left my shuttle. I told him that they were welcome to upgrade their residence and stay in Castle Moe, but he told me that he had spent enough of his life in castles. Justin is the only person I have met that could make that comment sound sincere. We stopped on the trail and Justin stared up at the trees.

"I appreciate the offer, but it is difficult for us to stay at the castle because Caroline and Humphrey seem to clash a bit when we do. The last time we stayed for the weekend there, that arrogant butlerbot referred to her as "playing human" which is probably one of the worst things you can say to an AI person, especially a woman." Shaking his head, the prince said, "I had to fight the urge to turn him off permanently and recycle his metal ass!"

As we continued our hike, he told me that his disappearance was probably not weighing heavily on his family's mind since they didn't send anyone to look for him. I decided not to tell him my thought—that his family was having financial problems and probably couldn't afford to hire a security team to sweep the galaxy.

Looking over, Justin noticed I was carrying a fly rod I had retrieved before leaving their camp. He also noticed the several places on the rod that had been repaired due to misuse on my part. He tried to hide his obvious disappointment at my abuse of my antique fishing pole. Justin told me that if I wanted, he could teach me how to improve my fly-fishing. He explained that his family had been fly-fishermen for generations, and in their social circles, it's considered the sport of kings. I kept my opinion to myself about fly-fishing and the attitude of fly-fishermen that I have developed over the years. I don't think any group could be more self-righteous about the way they choose to do any sport as fly-fishermen are about the way they fish. It made sense, though, that his family considered it "the sport of kings." I told Justin that I looked forward to the lesson. Luckily, he never saw my bottle of floating bait in my pocket or realized the truth about why I carry a large handgun while fishing when there is nothing to protect myself from. Most fly-fishermen would rather drain a lake and beat the fish to death with a club before they would use floating cheese for bait. I can't tell you why—I'm just telling you what I've heard. Personally, if the fish bite it, I will use it.

On the flight back to Justin's camp, we took a tour of the planet. The prince seemed to savor a chance to have a conversation with someone other than Caroline and his shuttle computer. I gave him a new protein cube for his food processor, and some toilet paper that I keep in my shuttle, "just in case!" I told him that on my next trip I would bring him some peanut butter. I wrote down the program code for him for my famous hot chocolate, and he said he couldn't wait to try it out. In a moment of true generosity, I also gave him two of my containers of mixed nuts from my emergency stash. There aren't any good program codes for Earth nuts and nut products in the food processing machines. He also wrote down for me Caroline's model numbers so I could put Chuck to work on getting her the updates and replacement parts. The numbers are important to pair with her programming, and to match the skin color of her hands.

I had a good time talking to the prince about fishing, and gave him a transmitter that he could use to contact me if he needed anything or just wanted to go fishing somewhere other than his camp. I also invited him to go Black Bug hunting, which he wasn't too excited about until he found out that they were good to eat. Then he was in. He really liked my shuttle and found himself falling asleep in the soft captain's chair, quietly tapping his fingers on the armrest with the oxygen-enhanced air conditioner blowing on him. Justin mentioned that soon after they were stranded there, the oxygen levels seemed to drop off suddenly. I told him I would try to find out what happened. No, I didn't tell him that I sold a bunch of it; it's my planet, remember? I told the prince that I could bring a good mechanic down to look at his shuttle so it would be in working order if he decides to leave. My mechanic is an Argilelion named Salazar who can fix almost anything shuttle-related. Justin told me that he had dismantled the shuttle to the point that it would cost less to buy a new one than to attempt to have it repaired.

At the start of this chapter, I intentionally didn't mention where the stream is that I found Prince Justin's camp. The reason for this is that Justin asked me not to tell anyone where he is. I'm assuming that his family isn't looking for him because they have never filed a missing human report. So those of you who are looking for a reward, the Princey family hasn't offered one. Justin told me that he thought his family probably genetically reincarnated him. Legally, they can't do that without proof of death, but Earth royalty are infamous for not having to follow the laws the rest of us do. Knowing the dislike that Justin has for his family, his Genetic 2 will most likely end up in the same spot-on MP anyway. If someone from his family is looking for him, he is on Asleus 2. He's in need of a haircut and a shave, but other than that, he and Caroline are fine.

18 Don't Smell the Flowers

I admit that I have had my share of setbacks as far as my florae on MP goes. My redwood trees gave me a great opportunity to practice my practical problem solving. The fire bushes were an expensive and somewhat painful experiment, even though the loss of my entire crop can be blamed on someone else, which is important. It's always better to have someone to blame when experiments go bad.

The biggest mistake that I have made, as far as plants are concerned, has to be my tiger roses that I bought last spring. First of all, you should never order plants or flowers from a catalog with a language that can't be translated into an Earth dialect. However the pictures of the flowers in the catalog of *Flowers From Other Galaxies* were very cool-looking. I couldn't read the name but, luckily, it had an order number. I called them a tiger rose because of the cool black and yellow stripes on the petals that resemble an Earth tiger. In hindsight, this pattern should have been a warning to me, but I didn't pick up on it. Well, that and the human figure with a bite out of it that was stamped at the end of the order number.

In the back yard of my cabin on MP, I've converted part of the yard into a garden area. I built a rock wall with a cool archway and a stone pathway that meanders through the garden. The whole thing is really starting to look very picturesque, and is now Tressa's favorite place to sit and relax when she's on MP. This allows me the freedom for some guilt-free fishing or hunting—a real luxury. I picked out a spot at the far end of my garden to plant my tiger roses. It took almost two weeks to get the bulbs for my new plants. For a person with a short attention span like mine, that was an eternity. When I got the bulbs, they were frozen in glass tubes. This probably should have been a warning too. I must admit that I am well known for not thinking projects through well enough. That is one of the things that are great about having your own planet—there's a lot of room to screw things up.

So, with great care, I planted my tiger roses, watered them, and left them to sprout. On my next trip out to MP, I checked on them and noticed some small black seedlings peeking out of the ground. A week or so later, there were some long black stems with red leaves, but no buds yet. It was almost a month before I had my first blossom. On this particular trip, Tressa and I had landed at the cabin during the night, so I took a sunglass-lantern and went to check on my raptors. As I walked through my pack of sleeping raptors, I did a quick head count and found that I was missing one. On closer inspection, I realized it was Cletus who was missing. He's the biggest and easiest to pick out in the group. Because of the raptors' poor eyesight, they don't move around at night. I figured Cletus might be lost and planned to look for him the next day. On my way back to the cabin, I decided to take a detour and check on my roses and a peach tree I had planted recently.

As I walked down the garden trail toward my roses, I noticed something that was a ghostly white color in the grass in front of my tiger roses. My first thought was that it was one of the stone statues that I brought from Castle Moe that the raptors had knocked over. When I got close enough, I realized it was the skeleton of Cletus, my missing raptor, lying at the base of my now fully-grown tiger roses. Cletus's bones were perfectly white and stripped of any flesh or scales. I had never seen such a perfectly clean specimen of skeletal remains outside of a museum. I decided to wait until Tripp and Chuck arrived the next day to help me move the skeleton out of the garden. It was a little unsettling not knowing what was able to kill and devour something with the size and power of a raptor. As I stood and looked at the remains, I noticed that my tiger rose bushes had half a dozen large blossoms and the light from my sunglass-lantern had caused them to open slightly. If I had waited for them to open all the way, it's possible that I would be a Genetic 3 instead of a Genetic 2.

Early the next day, Tripp and Chuck landed, a little jet lagged but still ready to go fishing. I told them what had happened to Cletus and the three of us walked out to the garden for a closer look at the remains. The whole situation had a real Sherlock Holmes feel to it. I took a shovel with us so we could bury what was left of poor Cletus. The three of us stood around the pile of bones and looked for a possible reason for the demise of the raptor, and how his skeleton became so perfectly cleaned. A few feet from the raptor's remains, Tripp found a half-eaten rapple. As far as we can tell, Cletus had chased the rapple down the trail and had caught it in front of the rose bushes.

With the morning sun shining on the large flowers, the buds were open, and they looked awesome. The smell, however, was less than pleasant. Chuck mentioned how cool the 14-inch blossom looked. None of us had ever seen a flower quite like this one. At the center of the flowers were some red-colored pods, which were a sharp contrast to the yellow and black pedals. My first thought was that the pods were seeds, and I reached up to see if one would come off. When I moved my hand in front of the flower, the blossoms turned as if following my hand's movements. I had never seen such a quick response from any kind of plant life. Chuck had a Venus flytrap as a child, and he thought the flower's reaction reminded him of how his plant responded to flies and bugs that it ate. However, his flytrap only responded to touch whereas these tiger roses seemed to sense our movements.

Tripp, who should have known better than to play with a plant on my planet, was waving his hand in front of one of the large flowers as it mirrored his movements. Without any warning, the yellow and black petals of the flower closed around his hand like a steel trap. Tripp told us later that he didn't feel any pain; in fact, his hand was almost instantly numb and the feeling seemed to creep slowly up his arm.

Chuck grabbed Tripp from behind and pulled with all of his weight in an attempt to free his hand from the plant. Carefully avoiding the flowers, I pulled as hard as I could on the bud, trying to pull it off the stem. None of us were having any luck, so to avoid having Tripp suffer the same fate that Cletus had, I grabbed my shovel. With the stance of a samurai warrior,

I swung the shovel and chopped through the stem of the flower, sending my friends tumbling backward across the patch of grass. As quickly as I could, I began peeling off the petals from Tripp's fingers. With the three of us working together, we were able to pull his hand free. Everywhere the flower had touched his hand, his skin was white, almost translucent, as if all the blood had been sucked out of his skin and flesh. I threw the flower down. It lay on the stone path, motionless other than the end of the stem, which moved like a snake swallowing a rat, pumping a small portion of Tripp's blood out onto the ground. While Tripp massaged some blood flow back into his hand, I went to the cabin to get my pruning tool.

At this point, I need to explain that my pruning tool is my shortbarreled antique shotgun. This gun shoots a large amount of shot, or lead balls, all at once. I had decided it was time to trim my roses back a bit. Since the flowers were the only part of the plant that seemed to pose any real danger, I decided to remove them first. I held the barrel of my gun up to one of the blossoms, and in a natural response, the pedals closed around the end. When I pulled the trigger, the effect was similar to a confetti gun I had seen at a sporting event. Small pieces of the flower floated down around us like colorful snow. We took turns blasting off rose buds. Tripp held the shotgun with one hand, pointed it at the last yellow and black flower, and in his best gangster voice, growled, "Suck on this." He then blasted it to small, colorful bits.

With the flowers carefully removed from their stems, we decided we had time to either transplant them or take one of them for a dip in the volcano. Tripp mentioned that he would like to send it to his ex-girlfriend as a makeup gift. He is always thinking of others. His hand was starting to get feeling back into it, and it didn't seem to hurt, but his fingernails had turned black as if his fingertips had been individually smacked with a hammer. He said he was still okay to go fishing (what a trooper), so we headed back to the cabin to get our gear and tell Tressa to stay clear of the garden. While in the middle of asking for an explanation, she noticed that I was holding my shotgun covered with pieces of rose petals, and thought better of it.

Today in the courtyard of Castle Moe, there is a gold-plated tiger rose bush. Of course, I waited till the flowers grew back before we took it for a dip in the volcano. In my office back on Earth, in a glass case, is my raptor skull. I find it comforting to have a memento of Cletus close to me all the time. Ms. Tracy, my father's secretary, swears she will not go anywhere near my office while that thing is in there. So, it's a real win-win situation for me.

Tripp's fingernails have grown back, and his hand is just fine. He did catch the biggest bass of the trip, so all was forgiven.

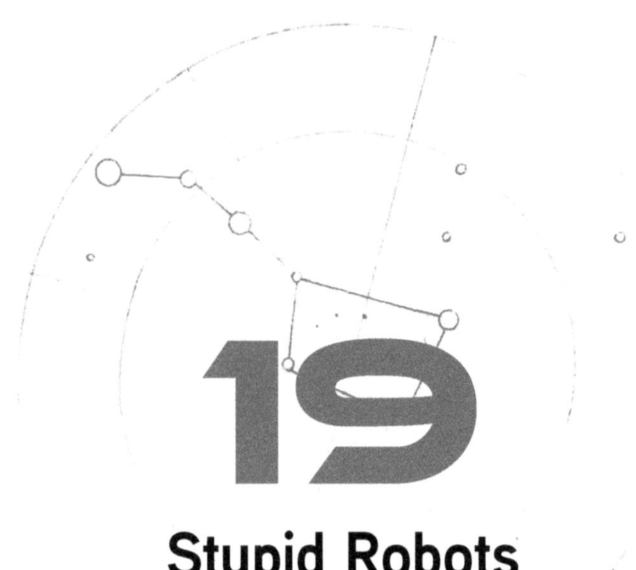

19 Stupid Robots

To be honest with you, I really do not like robots. Some of you will say my attitude toward machines is a form of prejudice. Usually, prejudice is based on insufficient knowledge and inaccurate stereotypes. (Yes, I looked it up.) I know quite a lot about robots, and I still don't like them. I understand that it was A.R.T. who came up with the whole concept that we need robots to make our hectic life simpler. The Alpine Robotics Technology Company is the industry leader in robotics; at least that's what their ads claim. They have always pushed for humans to treat robots with respect. After looking at the price of the new T-3 robots they are producing, you would need to *really* respect them. No, I do not consider AI individuals robots. That's like comparing a pair of fingernail clippers to a computer.

Tressa and I have a T-2 that we use around our home on Earth. With all the patience my lovely wife can muster, she has asked me not to yell at the robots, and to please stop taking them apart. The whole problem is that she keeps sending one into my shop to clean up, and as you can guess, it has never worked out well. The T-2 has a built-in incinerator it uses to help recharge its power cell, and I think that stupid robot is just looking for things to burn. I've started leaving a trail of small pieces of paper that go around my shop and then lead back to the house. It keeps him happy picking them up. It's a lot like feeding ducks at a pond.

As for taking the robots apart, I have only done that nine or ten times, but I do it for a good reason. Tressa spent her teenage years working in the local A.R.T. manufacturing plant where she assembled T-1 and the then state-of-the-art T-2 robots. I think putting ours back together makes her nostalgic for her youth. Just a little bit of advice—always turn off the robot's vocalization system when you're disassembling one because they have a tendency to freak out.

I only have one T-2 robot on MP and I keep him in the shed by my cabin. I turn him off when I'm off-planet because he draws too much power if he's left on. I call him "Shabby" because Tressa hates when I call him "a shiny bag of bolts." I found it necessary to put in a remote switch for his emotions processor because he was getting upset when I left him alone for weeks at a time. He also has a difficult time doing his primary job, which is to hold clay targets while I practice my shooting with my firearms. It's hard enough to hit one of those little targets, so when Shabby is running back and forth screaming and hiding behind the closest rapple tree, it's almost impossible. I don't know what he is afraid of; with his Nanotechnology Repair System, any bullet holes would be fixed within minutes of receiving them.

I might add that I have never shot a robot on purpose, but it's possible that I have shot *at* one or two. Don't worry, as soon as Tressa proofreads this part of my book, she will have Shabby back on Earth folding clothes and picking up leaves. Of course, this means it will be Tripp's job to hold the targets.

I did try to have Shabby feed my raptors and clean out their pens, but the raptors wouldn't leave him alone. They kept knocking him over and pulling him apart. I think they like their reflections in the metal, it's possible that seeing themselves is a form of self-realization. It's also possible that, like me, they just like shiny things. Sorry, Shabby. I spent the money to have tracks installed on Shabby because with legs, he kept tripping and falling in rough terrain. It was entertaining to watch, but I grew tired of him complaining every time he hit the turf.

I find it difficult to put out the cash that the robot dealers want for their new robot models because as soon as I get one paid for, it's already out-of-date. For some reason, the dealers charge more for the robot models that are made on our own planet. I guess that "Earth Pride" comes with a price. My T-2 at home and Shabby were both built by Zalipanderans in their manufacturing plant on the planet Nef and then assembled by A.R.T. on Earth. You would think that this would add to the cost, but for some reason, they are quite a bit less. I do not approve of A.R.T. outsourcing their work to other planets, but I do like paying half the price for the same robot. This fact is sort of an ongoing conflict with my parents and myself. I tell them to be proud that they raised a money-conscious son; it isn't true, but out of all my siblings, I am the closest they came to having a thrifty child.

The other problem with a new robot is they are in constant need of new downloads. There always seems to be a new personality upgrade or a way to make your robot virus free. Don't believe them. Once you plug your robot into a receiver, A.R.T. will start downloading all sorts of crap into its CPU. I had to have

Shabby mentally stripped twice. He kept repeating A.R.T. junk-mail-adds over and over again. I had to leave his voice system on mute until I had the time to get it fixed. If I heard "Hey, isn't it time you traded me in for a new T-3, state-of-the-art robot" one more time, I was going to blast him. Shabby also picked up some horrible language that he started to use quite often in moments of stress. I don't think the bad vocabulary came from A.R.T. My guess is that it was an online virus.

I think the Zalipanderans, or Zipps, do a great job in building machinery. Because of their size, the Zalipanderans find it difficult to put projects together as large as a T-2 robot, which stands about five feet tall. But their work on smaller parts really can't be matched. All of the parts in my Tella-7 rifle are Zipp made, and close to ninety percent of my shuttle engine. I haven't seen any machinery in our galaxy that didn't have a "Made on Nef" stamp on it. For those of you who haven't seen a Zipp in person or in pictures, it's hard to believe your eyes. Zalipanderans are humanoids that look a lot like Earthlings other than their average height being about three inches tall. I met my first Zipp in school where he was a guest professor in my mechanical design course. Dr. Nicholas Boggs was only six and a half inches tall, so we really had to watch where we were walking in our classroom. He was a brilliant teacher, and it was quite entertaining for us to listen to his lectures.

Dr. Boggs told us that it was his race that had visited the Earth first in the 1940s. According to him, the Zalipanderans had sent a peace ambassador and his team to the Earth to endeavor to set up a trade agreement between our two planets. After their ship had entered Earth's atmosphere, they were never heard from again. Dr. Boggs told us that the ship was about the size of a coffee table and was powered by microwaves. It's the Zip's opinion that whoever on Earth filled the first patent on the microwave oven is responsible for the disappearance of this ship and crew. Due to the size of the humans on Earth and our perceived lack of intellect, the Zalipanderans decided to wait until the Trillions had contacted Earth and put in all the work before they established communication with us. Dr. Boggs had the ability to make that all sound not so demeaning. It might have been the fact that he was the size of a small action figure toy that motivated him to choose his descriptions of Earthlings more carefully.

Chuck's parents had a new T-3 robot they purchased a year earlier. The week after they brought it home, it started to smell funky. They kept asking their new T-3 to do a self-diagnosis and figure out what that horrible smell was. When it got to the point that it was unbearable to have their brand-new, and I might add, expensive robot in the house, they took it to a repair shop. In the bottom of one of the robots' legs they found a dead Zalipanderan that had apparently fallen in the leg during its production. Chuck's mother was so upset that she could no longer have the robot in her house, even corpse-free. It was most likely the vision of the grape-sized skull rattling around in the new robot's leg that ruined it for her. So, to make a long story a bit shorter, Chuck and Ashell have a brand new T-3 robot at their house. Chuck had to have the robot's memory erased because the whole experience caused it to be depressed, and it was constantly shutting itself down. His parents spent the money on shipping and had the tiny body of the unknown Zalipanderan sent back to Nef. When Chuck's parents complained to the A.R.T. company headquarters, they were good enough to let them out of their last two payments, which for A.R.T. is generous.

20 Music Haters and a Dead Relleom

When I am having a difficult week, or just need a good spot to think, I always climb the hill behind my cabin on MP and have a seat on my thinking rock. This large boulder is not what Earthlings are used to when we think of rock. This mineral, called kramrock, is tough like stone but is somewhat spongy to the touch. I am not sure where in the galaxy kramrock is from, but it has many practical uses. Most shuttle landing pads are made from kramrock thats ground up so it gives some cushion during rough landings. The tile in my cabin's bathroom floors is made of it and it really does feel good to walk on barefoot. It is freckled with black spots similar to the rock called granite on Earth, except it's a darker brown color instead of grey. Tressa calls the hill behind my cabin "Cookie Mountain" due to the fact it looks a lot like a big chocolate chip cookie. The large kramrock boulders that stick out of the hill have the same color and shape as chunks of chocolate and the tan grass closely resembles a cookie crust with my thinking rock perched on top.

My kramrock thinking rock is a great place to park myself. I like to sit back and think about stuff while I practice playing my flute. A flute is a musical instrument from Earth that is a long wooden tube with holes in it, and when you blow in it and cover or uncover the holes, it makes wonderful music. If I knew what I was doing, it would make wonderful music. To date, my recitals have been less than perfect. Tressa has mentioned that to the trained ear, my music could possibly cause paralysis, or at least cause the listener to be sterile.

On this trip, I had the opportunity to perform for an unexpected audience. I had just begun a stirring rendition of the classical song "*Twinkle, Twinkle Little Star* when I noticed my raptors making their way up the hill. As they marched, their long bodies moved together, with their heads slowly bobbing up and down. In the evening light, the herd crept silently through the grass to my location as if they didn't want to disturb my recital. When they had all reached my spot, the group of intimidating yet beautiful creatures surrounded me, making a large circle. Adison and Hank, my two largest raptors, slowly turned to face each other and started moving their heads up and down in rhythm to my music. Their movements reminded me of watching exotic birds performing a mating dance. My raptors have shown quite a lot of intelligence in the past but showing an appreciation of music and even the ability to respond to the musical rhythm was outstanding. What happened next transpired so fast, I couldn't react. As my eyes were filling with tears of pride, thinking I had bridged the gap between our species with my music, their motive became apparent. While I was engrossed in the raptors dance, one of my smaller raptors, Bobbi Sue, leaned over me, and in less time than it took me to blink, she had snatched the flute out of my hands with her powerful jaws and rows of shiny, white teeth. Throwing her head back, she swallowed the foot-long instrument whole. In an amazing display of cunning and stealth, my smallest raptor had left me making obscene sounds with my lips in an attempt to play an instrument that was no longer there.

As the sun dipped toward the horizon, I was left alone, perched on my thinking rock, watching my now content raptor herd triumphantly making their way down the hill to the barn. It was a harsh lesson to remind me that not everyone can appreciate my music the way I do. It wouldn't have bothered me as much, but my mother had given me that flute as a birthday present when I was a child, and even though years of practice really hadn't improved my music, the instrument did still have some sentimental value. I suppose, if I wanted it badly enough, I could retrieve it in a day or two, but even with a rigorous cleaning, I'm not sure I could ever put my lips on the mouthpiece again.

"Stupid lizards!"

Still pouting, I got up and started the short walk down the trail to the cabin. Kinsey, my little sister, who had come out to MP for the weekend, and Tressa were waiting for me to have dinner. Out of the corner of my eye, I spotted a red light that shimmered in the now dark sky. The glow seemed to grow in intensity as it came closer to my location. I assumed that it might be a ship since some friends of ours were talking about coming out to MP to spend the weekend with us. When it got closer, I noticed that it wasn't a ship but perhaps a small asteroid or malfunctioning satellite that had made its way through the atmosphere and was going to crash not too far from where we were. It was really pretty cool to watch it as it passed over my head and vanished behind the trees somewhere north of my cabin. The ground quaked slightly under my feet and a thunderous boom shot through the trees and passed like an invisible wave. As I ran down toward the lake, I saw Tressa and Kinsey run across the yard and climb into the shuttle. By the time I had reached them, our FBS shuttle was all warmed up and ready to fly.

"We were on the porch and had seen the falling object, and I knew you would be on your way down to the shuttle to go have a look," Tressa said, her voice full of excitement. Zap was wide-eyed as she climbed into the back seat of the shuttle. I thought it was fun to hear the excitement in her voice as she began her list of questions.

"What was that thing, Moe?" Not waiting for a response, she continued, "Was that a ship crashing?"

"I don't know," I responded while trying to follow the object's vapor trail in the sky.

"Have you ever seen something like that before?"

"No."

"If it's a ship, can we keep it?"

"Sure, Zap, you can have it, dead bodies and all," I said in hopes of detouring more questions.

"Cool!" she said back.

"That girl is definitely your sister," I could hear Tressa mutter under her breath.

Within twenty miles of the cabin, we started seeing small fires in the woods that appeared to line a large trench cut through a thickly forested area. The ground resembled a container of ice-cream that someone had dragged a spoon across. I pulled the shuttle up until we were hovering directly over the crash. I checked the instrument panel of the shuttle, and my sensors indicated no sign of radiation. We decided to land in a clearing close by and walk to where the object had finally stopped. As we hiked our way through the trees, I told the girls about the flute incident and the fact that our raptors were apparently music haters. Shortly after, we had to stop so the girls could catch their breath from laughing. In between bouts of laughter, Tressa told me she had thought of making my family heirloom disappear a few times herself. (Music Hater.) Zap was laughing too hard to comment. To be honest, I didn't expect either one of them to be too sympathetic.

As we approached the crash site, we could smell the sweet aroma of burning grass and wood with just a hint of lingering dust. When we stepped out of the trees, we were at the far end of the landing zone and began to walk down the fire-lit pathway toward the glow of our UFO's final resting place. The unidentified crashing object had hit with such force that it formed a channel that penetrated all the way through the topsoil and deep into the darker subsoil. The closer we got to the end of the trail, the hotter the air became. By the time we had reached the object, all three of us were sweating, and Tressa was quite flushed in her face and arms. We stopped walking before we had reached the end and debated whether or not to wait until the object had cooled off, but our curiosity got the better of us and we pressed on. Both Tressa and Kinsey were carrying sunglass-lanterns that I keep in the shuttle, but the fires that surrounded us were enough to light our way down the trail.

The object was sitting in the bottom of the trench of scorched earth at the base of a large pine tree. The exposed roots of the tree had obviously put up a good fight in stopping the heavy metal projectile. The dark-colored capsule was about eight feet long, shaped like a long box with rounded edges. If it was a ship, it was one of the oddest designs I had seen. It was about three and a half feet tall and about the same in width. The box had a seam that ran down the sides of its ten foot length, as if it was made in two parts and then sealed together. There were no engine exhaust ports and no visible electronics. Other than the sound of the wood, popping as it burned the green branches, the area around us was completely silent. The object itself didn't hum or tick, or even make squeaking sounds that metal often does as it cools. Tressa thought it was possible that the object could explode and kill all of us. My opinion was that if it was going to blow up, it probably would have done it on impact instead of leading us on like this.

As the red glow of the heated metal faded, we noticed that the exterior was a shiny black color with no apparent damage to the structure or finish. We took our time and walked around the object, watching the light from the remaining fires reflected in the smooth finish. When the object had cooled enough that we could approach it, Kinsey spotted a relief sculpted in the topside toward the end, which was buried somewhat in the soft ground. Tressa reached out to touch the surface and I instinctively grabbed her arm to stop her. Leaning forward, I spit on the top of the vessel. My saliva bubbled and evaporated from the heat of the metal, leaving no trace at all on the exterior. She told me she appreciated the fact that I stopped her, but both girls agreed that I could have found a less disgusting way to show the surface temperature. Using a pine branch, I cleaned off the soil and small rocks to expose what appeared to be an artistically carved bird with the head of a snake. Tressa instantly recognized the emblem from flags she had seen at the college. Each school dorm has a flag that represents the country or planet the students are from. She said that this emblem was the same as the Rellom flag. I also had seen it printed on the menus for that bistro on Mars where Chef Tyson has always been very proud of his heritage.

After some deliberation and the process of elimination, we decided that it had to be a Rellom funeral casket. The Relloms like to launch their dead into space in either a rocket from their planet, or, if they are doing it from space, in a converted Argilelion torpedo. It's a practice that was outlawed by the Trillions about fifty years ago. For the last thousand years, the Relloms have preferred to put their loved ones out floating in the cold, dark emptiness of space instead of a traditional human burial or cremation. Other than a few famous science fiction writers whose ashes were dumped out into space at the request of their fans, Earthlings, most of the time, are just buried on Earth. Some humans are shipped to their favorite vacation planet for burial. On Mars, you can have your ashes shot out of a cannon to become one with the vast red clouds. After a cool funeral, I wouldn't mind being blasted out into space. I think there is room out there for another chubby yet attractive corpse to float around in the dark. I don't think I would be buried on MP, because if my family ever sold my planet, they would legally have to have my remains relocated.

There really haven't been a lot of problems with space burials because, let's face it, space is really big. There are even areas called dead space where there is no shuttle traffic at all. The problem came from the fact that large freight shuttle engines create a magnetic field in the wake of the shuttles. Because the shuttles are traveling at such a high rate of speed, the caskets and other items, like satellites, early space exploration ships, and nuclear weapons that for some reason were shot into space do not cling to the shuttles themselves but are sort of pulled into motion, and then they drift into shuttle and shipping lanes. Some of you will remember when, about fifty years ago, the Trillion cruise shuttle TR Nuten hit a Rellom funeral torpedo and was damaged to the point that all of its life support systems failed and its decompression killed the crew and 200 vacationing Trillions. Torpedoes are designed to be difficult to pick up with scanning equipment, which makes them dangerous to have in your path. Not long after the TR Nuten incident, the law was passed that wouldn't allow for space burials in torpedo caskets or rockets. The problem is, Relloms really don't follow galactic laws, especially when they're conceived and enforced by Trillions, so a lot of it still goes on.

My best guess is that this casket got pulled into motion and eventually drifted to my planet. I'm not sure what the metal is that the Argilelion torpedo is made from but it made it through MP's atmosphere, crashed into close to twelve pine trees, dug up a lot of dirt, and still didn't have even a scuff mark on it. I have not been able to decide what to do about this artifact that still resides in a nice grove of trees not far from my cabin. If you are Rellom or have friends that are, please check to see if your loved one's casket had an I.D. Number TV1OICU2. If you are responsible for this no doubt very wonderful but otherwise dead individual, please contact me for pickup at your convenience, I do not deliver. According to the date on the casket, it has only been in space for two years. A small tip, if I might—if you are going to break galactic laws, you may want to leave off the I.D. number next time.

21

Lunch at the Worm Hole Cafe

If you are going to travel into space for the first time, make sure you take the time to visit some of the space stations, and even some of the better shuttle stops. Most shuttle stops are built in a similar manner and are relatively safe for humans. The key to landing at a shuttle stop is to know where to enter and how to exit the atmosphere of the protective dome. Trust me, if you try to enter an exit portal, you will not clear the cold plasma shield and you and your ship will resemble a bug hitting a shuttle windshield. Always remember that an entrance is lit with red lights and an exit with even brighter red lights. A better way to tell is just to park outside the shield till another shuttle either lands or takes off. If they did what they are supposed to do and did fine, then you should do what they did and you will be okay also. There are better instructions and information in the book *Where to go When You're on the Go*, so don't leave your home planet without it. No, I am not getting any kick-backs when I refer to these other books, but I should.

The Worm Hole Cafe has to be one of my favorite places to eat. Fortunately, it's in the same shuttle stop where I get mechanical work done on my shuttle. On this trip out to MP, I noticed that my LX shuttle was starting to overheat so I stopped here to get some work done on the engine. Salazar is the only off-planet mechanic that I trust and is, as far as I know, the only non-human certified to do warranty work on my shuttle. He is Argilelion and stands about eight feet tall. His skin and most of his organs are transparent, so you don't want to be around him right after he eats. Other than always being a bit cranky and having no real patience for most humans, he is still the best shuttle mechanic in space.

Salazar explained to me, in a somewhat gruff manner, that he needed to drain all of the fuel out of my shuttle to see what the problem was. As I understand it, the R-7 gas not only fuels the engine but also cools it. Let me put that another way—as I don't understand it—but I didn't think it wise to have Salazar try to explain it to me. I am just hoping it's covered under my warranty. If not, say goodbye to my last can of mixed nuts.

So, I am stuck for a couple of hours at the famous Worm Hole Cafe. If you have some downtime in space, this is the place to be. The oxygen is good, and doesn't have that canned smell. Plus, the cafe has the best pie in the known galaxy. Tonya, the cook, is a human from Earth, and is close to being 130 years old. (She did give me permission to tell you her age.) I think she has spent all that time mastering the art of pie-making. A few years ago, the Pontarean owners of the Worm Hole realized they were getting a lot more traffic from Earth, so they needed a new cook. Pontarean food has about as much flavor as a handful of dirt covered in mustard. The owners found Tonya cooking in a diner outside of Old New Orleans, and luckily for them, she was looking for a change of scenery.

It's too expensive to import fruit from Earth, so I have been bringing boxes of rappels from MP that she makes into pies. In Tonya's skilled hands, those rappels are transformed into something that truly may fulfill your dreams; well, if you are like me and you dream about pie. Tonya appreciates the fact that I take the time to make sure none of the rappels have legs. She was good enough to put this popular dessert on the menu as Moe's Rapple Pie. Tonya tried to make a Carrieack cherry pie for me but the texture was too funky for my taste, so we decided to stick with the rapple pie. When I look at one of those pieces of pastry, I feel as proud as a new father gazing at his newborn child. Tressa has asked me to stop telling people that. The Worm Hole Cafe is located between Aselus 1 and Polaris on an Area 5 space map. If you've got the time, go for the pie. Trust me—it's worth the shuttle fuel.

I have a corner table in the human section of the cafe where I like to sit. You are not obligated to sit in a specific area if you are against segregation of species. Trust me—you will be more comfortable sitting in a booth designed for humans. The Zalipanderans have a section that is basically a set of shelves connected by small flights of stairs. This way, the Zips can still be served by Earth-size humans without the waiter having to bend over, and there is less risk of being stepped on. The Zalipanderans must use credit due to the fact that Pontareans refuse to take Zip currency. The advantage that Zalipanderans have is that they can feed a whole party of their size with one bowl of Tonya's famous chowder and a small piece of pie.

The Argilelions have their own section, but Salazar and his fellow mechanics are the only ones I have seen eating there. The Argilelions only eat about once a month, and when they do, it's a big deal and the meal sometimes goes on for the whole day. All of their meals consist of different kinds of meat and a kind of nasty black bread that looks like the air filter off of my shuttle. Tonya tells me that making the Argilelion bread is the worst part of her job. The tables and chairs in that section are huge. An Earthling would have to stand on one of the benches to be able to eat off their table. The other problem is that Argilelions leave a sort of slime behind on almost anything they come into contact with. It's very similar to an Earth snail trail. To those of you who haven't seen this, it probably sounds pretty disgusting, and to be honest, it really is. My best guess is that the slime protects their thin skin—I mean that physically, not emotionally. We all have things about our species that others don't understand or that they may dislike, but if you are going to travel off-planet, you must be able to adapt a bit. It always takes me a while to get my shuttle clean after Salazar finishes his mechanical work, but having him do the job is worth the cleanup.

Some of you will obviously ask why I dedicated a whole chapter in this book to telling you about having lunch at the Worm Hole Cafe. I feel that, as a writer, I should write about what I know and the things I enjoy. I enjoy writing about food, and I like telling you about the alien life forms I have met. Actually, alien is probably an inappropriate way to describe them; let's say non-Earth life forms. I would not want to offend any readers who are not from Earth. Because I have the opportunity to travel off-planet on a regular basis and had the chance to deal with a lot of different species, I think of it as a responsibility to share these experiences with my readers. According to my publisher, almost thirty people, not counting family, bought my last book, *Dude Don't Eat That*, so I feel a certain responsibility to you, my dedicated fans.

Brian Shadowfax the author of *Where to go When You're on the Go or Best Shuttle Stops—A Traveler's Guide to Good Food,* likes to hang out at the Worm Hole, and we have often eaten a whole rapple pie between the two of us. No, I'm not dropping names in the hope that it might give my book credibility. Brian, however, was the one who suggested that I try to write a food guide book based on the variety of different foods I have tried in the galaxy. After he read my book *Dude, Don't Eat That*, he respectfully suggested that I write *My Planet*. I don't think he considers me too much of a threat when it comes to being a food critic. As I understand it, it was my entire first chapter on bry worm pasta that he didn't really like. The way he put it was, "I have not yet learned to appreciate your food choices."

I come to the cafe for the pie. Brian, however, comes for Tonya's famous chowder. Chowder is a form of Earth soup that Tonya makes with cream and seafood, thickened with Earth's wheat flour. The recipe for her chowder is one of the best-kept secrets in the galaxy. Between Brian and myself, we have figured out most of it, but her seafood ingredients are as of yet undetermined. Tonya claims that all of the seafood is from Earth and is always fresh. She also claims that the slightly green color of her chowder is from the parsley and green onions.

It's possible that by telling this to all three of you who will read this book, Tonya might make me disappear, but here goes—I think I know what the secret ingredient is. A few months ago, I sold 600 pounds of frozen black bug legs to the owners of the

Worm Hole, and for some reason, it never was put on the menu. Tonya told me that the Argilelions ate all of it in last month's big meal. I have never told Brian this since his fan base is bigger than mine and his knowledge of the secret ingredient might actually affect Tonya's chowder sales. Even with this divine knowledge, I still order the chowder every time I am here.

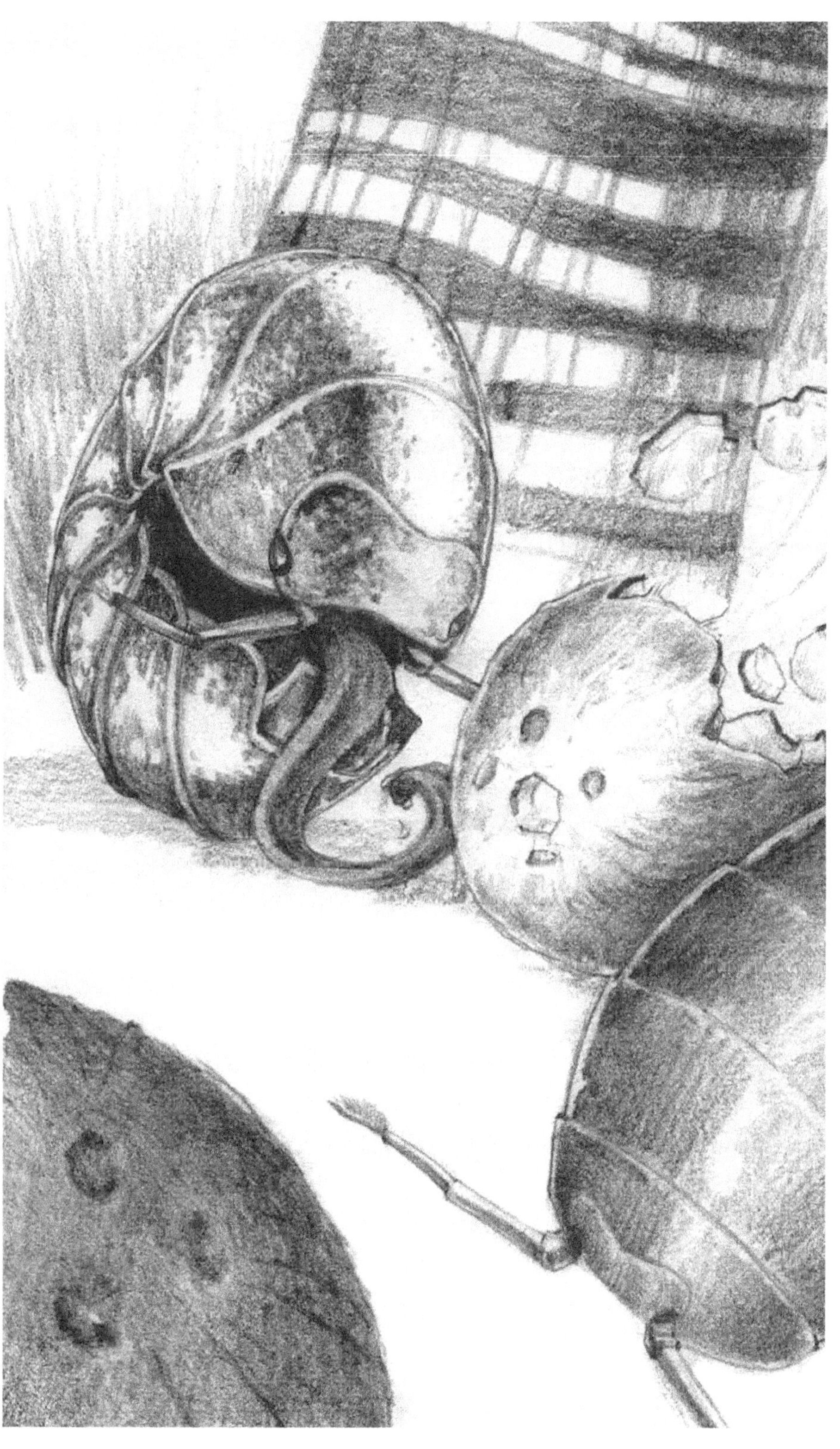

22 The Island of Tripp

When you own your own planet, one of the things you want to avoid is the unexpected. It's true that finding a castle on MP and a volcano full of molten gold was really cool; however, neither were life-threatening experiences like I had on the Island of Tripp. Yes, I let Tripp name an island. It was actually Tressa's idea since she has grown tired of me naming everything after myself. Tripp talked me into it after I showed him the island when we flew over it one day. It's probably the fact that the island is shaped like a capital T that closed the deal on the name.

I have never landed my shuttle on the Island of Tripp because there really isn't a clear spot to land due to the heavy foliage. After flying over the small island several times, I could not see that there was much of a beach to speak of, either. Recently, I spent some hard-earned cash on some pontoons for my shuttle. This handy shuttle extra can be inflated and deflated at the touch of a button to make it possible to land my LX shuttle on semi-calm or calm water without sinking. The reason for this upgrade was so I could land on a pond or lake and fish for a while without having to haul my boat everywhere I go. "Necessity is the mother of shopping the New LX Shuttle Catalog." Yes, like Benjamin Franklin, I really do enjoy quoting myself.

With my new ability to land on the water next to the island, Tripp and I set out one weekend to explore the unknown. In the middle of MP's largest ocean, the island protruded invitingly out of the clear blue water. After flying over the island several times, we decided to land in a small lagoon that had some protection from the ocean waves. The pontoons worked well and we had no problem making our way up to the rocky shore. I tied the shuttle cable to a large rock so we wouldn't have to swim to catch it later. The leftover cable I detached and put in my pocket. It's been my experience that you never know when you might need a piece of cable or rope.

The ocean air and the smell of the plants and flowers seemed to mix together in a tropical potpourri. The large palm trees grew close to the shore and the bushes between the trees seemed to make travel across the island on foot difficult, if not impossible, without a trail to follow.

Tripp started to make his way down the beach one direction, looking for a trail through the thick brush. I stood and stared at the vegetation, looking for the right kind of palm tree. My mission that day was to hopefully locate a supply of coconuts. My favorite pie chef, Tonya, has informed me that there is no good substitute for fresh coconut in a coconut-cream-pie. I have made it my personal mission to find her a supply of coconuts so she can recreate for me this "Pie of Legends." After referencing my PMF, or the Planet Functions Manual, I found that the island was listed as a possible location to find coconuts. It took a week of reading the stupid book, and I finally found it at the end of Chapter 3,642—*Earth Origin Horticultural Fruit and Nut Bearing Trees and Bushes.*

I haven't figured out how to get the coconuts out of the tree when I find them, but I'm sure that it will involve a firearm of some sort. I had seen some coconuts floating in the lagoon, but I was discouraged to find the shore completely clean as far as I could see. While I stood on the rocky beach and stared upward, I heard Tripp whistle to me from down by the shore. He was signaling to me that he had found a way through the brush by pointing with his hand held flat and his thumb on top, moving his arm up and down. I remember the gesture from army movies we watched as kids. Tripp always did want to be in Special-Ops-Wolf-Delta-Force-Team-Bravo. I made my way down toward the shore and followed him as he made his way inland. The shore may have been rocky but the trail through the brush was sandy and comfortable to walk on. After hiking about a hundred yards, we came to a small clearing in the brush. The clearing was surrounded by trees that were heavily laden with coconuts.

I have always thought of Tripp as being more athletic than myself, so I asked him if he wanted to trade a ride home in my shuttle for a short climb up a big tree. The large tree we picked out had grown at an angle and leaned to the point where he would be scooting on his butt up the tree instead of climbing it. From what I remember, his response was, "I'm starting to feel that you are taking advantage of our friendship to treat me like a tool."

"It's true, buddy. But you're not just a tool—you are a sharp and effective tool! Plus, if you do this, I'll have Tonya make you your own pie."

With the reason he was risking his life well-established, he started climbing the semi-vertical tree. I stood at the base of the trunk to give him a boost up and to aid in his climb with moral support. I offered my cable to Tripp so he could use it for a safety line when he got to the top of the tree. He responded with, "So, I can fall and hang myself?" Leave it to Tripp to be so negative. When Tripp was about halfway up the tree, he asked me something that ended up being a key question: "Why don't we just pick some up off of the ground?"

It was at this point that I realized that even with at least two dozen coconut-bearing palm trees around this clearing, there wasn't a single coconut on the ground. My first thought was that it was possible that the gravity level on MP was low enough that it didn't pull these coconuts off their stems like the fruit on Earth. If that was true, where had all the ripe coconuts gone? By the time I had thought this out, Tripp was close enough to the top of the tree that he could attempt to pull some of the coconuts free. It was the slanted angle of the tree that allowed Tripp to climb so easily to the top, where he was now almost in a sitting position, straddling the tree. With one good push, Tripp freed several of the large coconuts, which fell into the middle of the sandy clearing with a muffled thud. Feeling quite proud of himself, Tripp asked, "How many of these do you want me to pic?"

I figured since I had gotten my good friend to risk possible injury to himself by climbing the tree, he might as well pick all the ripe ones. I do not have an in-depth knowledge of the growth patterns and maturity rate of the average coconut, but I assumed that the larger brown coconuts were riper in comparison to the smaller green ones.

Without warning of any kind, the underbrush around the small clearing exploded with noise and motion. Faster than my mind could process what was happening, several large ball-shaped objects rolled into the clearing and then rolled out. The whole thing happened in less time than it took for me to lift my head to look. By the time I was facing the clearing and had an unobstructed view from around the large tree trunk, the clearing and surrounding landscape was completely silent. Looking down from his perch, Tripp had seen the whole commotion, and couldn't help but express himself.

"What the hell was that?"

"I have no idea. There was nothing in the manual about scary things on this island! Do you want to come down? Then we can just grab the coconuts you dropped and make a run for the shuttle."

Tripp with his legs and now his arms wrapped around the tree, moved his body back and forth, reaffirming the stability of his position on the tree.

"No, I'm good up here. In fact, I'm pretty sure I can comfortably stay up here for the rest of my life, if necessary; not to mention your coconuts are gone," he said, motioning toward the clearing.

I surveyed the scene in front of me and saw that he was right—they were gone. The only thing that remained were a few tracks in the sand, apparently made by someone who had rolled several heavy, round objects across the clearing directly to where the missing coconuts had fallen. My first response was to pull my stainless 454 revolver from its holster and point it at the underbrush; not really at anything in particular, but just straight out in front of me. I had brought my big handgun in case I needed it to pick coconuts. That was before Tripp had so valiantly volunteered to climb up and get a few. Besides, I'm not sure what good a coconut would do me if it had a two-inch hole blown through it, or more likely, blown into tiny bits all over the sandy jungle floor.

I quickly devised a plan to find out what we might be dealing with. Like the majority of my plans, it involved me shooting something. I told Tripp to try and pry one of his shaking hands from the tree and grab another coconut. He reluctantly did what I asked, and on my signal, he threw the heavy, husk-covered nut into the middle of the opening. With my pistol raised, I carefully aimed at the hard-shelled fruit. In a reaction similar to the last one, the bushes moved as the large ball-shaped object moved into view directly toward the coconut. I aimed the best I could at the moving target and fired. It always takes me a second or two to be able to recover and focus on what I am shooting at due to the massive recoil of my handgun. By the time I could see clearly again, the coconut and the U.R.O—or Unidentified Rolling Object—were both gone, and all that remained was a large hole in the sand where my bullet had struck the ground.

Tripp yelled down, "It looked like you shot behind it!"

I think, looking back, that I had failed to consider how fast this thing was moving. Feeling confident in my shooting ability, and having a pocket full of ammunition, not to mention plenty of coconuts for bait, I decided to try the same strategy again. When Tripp could see that I was ready, he lobbed another coconut in roughly the same spot. I aimed right at it and waited. At the first sign of movement, I fired instantly, feeling tiny pieces of what ended up being coconut meat and juice falling on my face and arms. As quickly as I could recover, I looked at where the heavy fruit had been sitting just moments before. In the sand next to the crater made by the exploding coconut was a creature that I can only describe as the "roly-poly bug from hell." The coconut-stealing monster sat perfectly still except for two antenna-like things that came out of the opening in its outer shell, accompanied by a long tongue. This thing was about three feet tall and had some kind of shell that covered its body that it would open, then sit on the ground like an orange cut in half. Then it closed up again like an armored beach ball and rolled at a great speed.

It sat still for a minute except for its tongue, which moved back and forth feverishly, looking for what we assumed was the coconut, now in tiny bits all over, even on its own shell. At this point, Tripp thought he might be able to hit this thing with another throw, so he grabbed the largest coconut he could find and gave it a toss. The coconut barely missed the bug, and when it hit the sand, the thing's reaction to it was incredibly fast. Instead of scaring it away, the bug turned and closed the distance between it and the coconut in less than a second. When it reached the fruit, it opened its shell just far enough so that, as it rolled over it, the whole thing was caught inside its shell, and then it was gone.

Since Tripp and I had traveled down the trail without being attacked, I assumed it was the sound of the coconuts hitting the ground that attracted these fast-moving creatures. I was also hoping we could make it back to the shore without encountering more of them. The only question I had was if it was possible to get coconuts out of the tree without them hitting the ground and being eaten before I could reach them. I didn't think I could catch one because of the weight of a mature coconut. It didn't sound like a good idea to get knocked on the head by one of them, black out, then get eaten by some monster roly-poly bug.

Reaching into my pocket, I pulled out the length of cable and threw it up to Tripp. My new plan was to have Tripp tie one end of the cable to the tree and tie the other end around a big coconut and lower it down to me. Tripp did this, but when he lowered it down, I realized that the tree he was in was at an angle, so it would be necessary for him to swing the coconut back and forth on the end of the cable until I could reach it. The new plan was a success.

With Tripp's ability to tie knots, and my talent for catching things, we had a nice bunch of coconuts carefully stacked up against the base of the tree in no time. It was with our last coconut that we had a problem. Tripp had grown quite confident in our progress and put a little too much swing in the cable, and that combined with the fact that he didn't release the cable at the right time, caused our refined process to go awry. The cable-wrapped coconut swung just out of reach of my stubby arms and banged against the next closest tree. At this same moment, Tripp realized there wasn't enough slack in the cable, so he let the excess go. He had tied the non-coconut holding end of the cable to the tree so it wouldn't be pulled from his hand by the coconut's momentum. The slack in the cable did not reach my end in time, and after bouncing off the tree trunk, the swinging fruit hit the ground and bounced once or twice before lying still in the warm sand. Yes, I called it a fruit because, botanically speaking, coconuts are considered fruit, nuts, and seeds. I looked it up.

The next few seconds went by in what seemed like slow motion. Tripp frantically reached for the cable but leaned too far and had to turn his attention to trying to keep himself from falling twenty feet to the jungle floor. I reached out to try and grab the slack cable from what I assumed was a safe spot against the tree. Without warning, one of the rolling bugs burst out of the bushes to the left of my position and grabbed the coconut, which was still attached to the cable. Tripp can really tie a good knot. The bug had made it about fifteen feet when it ran out of slack. The cable went tight and the bug, dragging the now tight cable, changed direction and began a fast moving arc with the tree as its center point. I watched in amazement as small trees and large plants were mowed down by the fast-moving cable. The bug was either too stubborn or physically unable to let go of the coconut, and with his momentum, he dragged the cable, which had a serious effect on its surroundings. It was a great mix of chaos and destruction.

I made the mistake of following my first impression, which was to climb the tree to escape the mayhem below. This was actually working until I had reached about the halfway point of the climb and felt the pressure of the cable as it pressed first against my shoulders, then my back, followed by my legs, pinning me to the tree. The bug's circles below me grew smaller and smaller as the length of cable was quickly wrapped around the tree. The last thing I remember before I blacked out from lack of breath was the shudder of the tree when the bug reached the end of the cable and bashed into the stump. If I'm not mistaken, I believe I also heard my good friend Tripp laughing.

When I regained consciousness, Tripp stood over me huffing and puffing, holding a container of oxygen with a tube attached to a mask I was wearing over my nose and mouth, pushing air into my lungs. He was happy that I regained consciousness with just the oxygen, because if it had come down to him giving me mouth-to-mouth, or me dying, it's hard to say what might have happened. I was lying down on the ground, surrounded by the smell of freshly-cut grass, which had been mowed in a perfect circle, the tree being at the center. Tripp explained that when the bug hit the tree, it tore the coconut out of its grasp and the bug was thrown like a cannonball out into the brush—basically fulfilling Newton's second law of mass X motion, for those of you who are more science-minded.

Tripp had climbed down the tree over my body and uncoiled the tightly-wrapped cable that bound me to the tree. When the slack in the line reached me, I had just fallen to the ground, which explains why my shoulder was throbbing and my arm had a remarkable bruise forming as I watched. While I had laid on a bed of freshly-cut leaves and branches, Tripp had run to the shuttle, grabbed an emergency kit, and got me started on oxygen. Tripp is nothing if not nurturing.

Feeling pretty good about not being dead, Tripp and I made our way back to the shuttle with the half dozen coconuts we had left. We decided to cut our exploration short on The Island of Tripp and maybe see the rest of the island another day. I think if I need any more coconuts, I can pick them with the side door open on my shuttle while I hover over the ground—basically the same way I pick the Carrieack cherries. It might also be a good way to feed the monster roly-poly bugs without being in danger's path. It would be like feeding the ducks on Earth, but more entertaining.

Epilogue: the coconut cream pie that Tonya prepared for me with my Tripp Island coconuts was worth the beating I took. From the perfect crust to the luscious custard filling, not to mention the toasted coconut sprinkled over the whip topping, it truly is the "Pie of Legends.

23 The Argilion Bazaar

In between Mars and the planet Bry is a small moon that's owned and managed by the Argilions. I've never been able to find out its original name, but it's commonly referred to as "The Bazaar," or the "Black Moon." As far as I know it's the only moon or planet that's completely populated by one giant open market. On Earth this would be comparable to a Flea market and would cover an area close to the size of North and South America combined.

Other than gravity and sunlight, the moon has no other natural resources. The oxygen is manufactured and has a less than fresh smell to it. Without any changes in the weather, the atmosphere really doesn't circulate, other than by airflow discharge from shuttles, so unless you're close to an oxygen generator, you can pretty much taste the air.

The surface of the moon is covered with a layer of dust that has been packed down from hundreds of years of foot traffic through the bazaar. I'm sure that if it ever rained on the Black

Moon, every shack and shopkeeper would sink out of sight into the mud. Other than an occasional shuttle control tower, there are no landmarks, so remember where you parked. I believe that some of the people that work at the bazaar started off as customers who just got lost. I'm not kidding, remember where you parked.

Due to the fact that the bazaar is on a moon, the property values are really low, and thus, the cost to rent space for a shack is relatively inexpensive. Most shopkeepers can pay for a year's worth of rent with a good day of sales. In case you are looking for some off-planet property, moons are inexpensive but hard to come by. Unless a planet or solar system needs a moon to stay cosmically balanced, they have mostly been bought up and hauled off by the Trillions. The Our Way Design firm uses moons and large asteroids for foundations or cores on which to build custom planets. This practice cuts the construction costs of a new project in half and makes the finished planet more stable. It also helps that moons are already round, unlike asteroids, that have to be shaped at great expense. In 2036 on Earth, our astronomers noticed that approximately half of Jupiter's moons had disappeared. It wasn't till we were exposed to non-Earth life forms that we found out that the moons were "appropriated" by moon brokers and sold to make new planets out of them.

On the Black Moon, the bazaar is broken up into zones, and each zone has a color that it's assigned. Each store, or "shack" in these zones, has a roof that is that particular color. This makes it easier to identify the zone you are in when you are flying over it. Each zone is usually populated by a different species and will cater to their kind with their products. If you are from Earth and have a chance to go to the Argilion Bazaar, you should go.

It really is a blast, and a great opportunity to learn about non-Earth cultures. If you are from Earth, the only part of the bazaar that you must avoid is the blue zone. It's not forbidden, it's just a bad idea. The shopkeepers there specialize in rare meats. When I say rare, I don't mean not cooked, I mean hard to find meats like fresh human, or the Menacilian's favorite, Zip-on-a-stick. If you knew how many Earthlings and Zalipanderans have disappeared in and around the blue zone, you might skip the bazaar tour all together, but you really shouldn't. For some reason, Earthlings seem to stick out in a crowd.

Another good reason to avoid the blue zone is the large population of Menacilian. I really haven't talked much about the Menacilian, and that's because, to be honest, they scare the crap out of me. It isn't that they're big like the Argilelions. In fact, they aren't any larger than an average human, but what they lack in size they make up for in nastiness. Most Menacilian are about five feet tall, and other than a larger, more muscular structure and bright yellow teeth, they could pass for an Earthling. Not everyone that will read this book believes in good and evil, but to those of you who do, I can only describe the Menacilian as evil, or at least as unsavory creatures with dubious intentions. The only pleasure or entertainment they have is to witness others suffering. If they don't have a weaker species to pick on, they will attack each other. The Menacilian are the only species that do not have an ambassador or envoy on Earth, or any other human-friendly planet. Most crime on the Black Moon involves the Menacilian in some way. Murder, kidnapping, and grand theft shuttle are some of their calling cards. Luckily, it's easy to avoid the lowlifes of the bazaar by just avoiding the areas they frequent.

This would be a good time in my book to explain what you

should do if you come in contact with a Menacilian. "Do not come in contact with a Menacilian." This species of humanoid is the definition of a bully. Whatever it was that has made them the way they are, it can't be fixed. There is no point in communicating, negotiating, or attempting to reach a deal with a Menacilian. My only contact with this group was on the outskirts of the white Zone. I was going into a shop that's owned by Nathan Byaku, a Zalipanderan shopkeeper I do business with on occasion. Nathan's shop is in a group of small shacks that line a popular area for humans in the yellow zone. The shops are metal framed, so some walls are metal and some have cloth or skins to shade the inside. Nathan's shop is brightly painted outside, but the inside is darker and a bit rustic. When I entered the shop, I found three Menacilian in the midst of threatening the miniature shopkeeper. Nathan stood on the hardwood counter, facing the three Menacilian. As I approached, one of the hoodlums turned to look at me. His muscles twitched like a cat preparing to spring an ambush on a small rodent. I had never seen a Menacilian up close. I noticed that their tan skin is covered with short orange hair that seems to magnify their threatening posture. The largest of the three continued pointing his claw-like finger at the small shopkeeper.

"We were told that you have some valuables that were taken from our ship yesterday. Trust me when I say it's not worth your life to keep them from us," he said, growling his speech.

Nathan looked up calmly and replied, "As I have already explained to you, I do not deal in stolen items, and I do not know where these items are." His small voice was amplified by some electronic system and speakers behind the counter. I was pretty sure that a lot of the items I had purchased in this shop had come from unscrupulous sources, but I kept this to myself. The large Menacilian pounded his fist on the counter, which caused Nathan to take a step back.

My defense instincts kicked in. With speed and stealth that surprised even me, I pulled out my enormous, nickel-plated revolver. Instantly, I had everyone's attention, and they all turned to stare at me and the large barrel of the cannon in my hand. The reason I own and carry this antique weapon is because ninety-nine percent of non-Earth individuals have no idea what kind of weapon it is. This means they don't know if it will squirt water or destroy everything within a two-mile radius. The Menacilian closest to me flashed his yellow teeth and glared at me through cat-like eyes.

"This doesn't concern you, Earth trash!" he said with a deep, menacing voice I can only describe as how an Earth tiger would sound if it could talk. The tiny shopkeeper raised his hand to stop me from assisting him. With one hand, he waved me out of the store. In the other hand, he held what looked like a small remote he had taken out of his jacket pocket when I had their attention.

"Moe, there is no need for violence. If you will, please wait outside so I can finish doing business with these gentlemen."

I stared at Nathan's face, and as far as I was from him, it was hard to tell, but I believed he winked at me. Reluctantly, I conceded to his wishes and slowly backed my way out the door, leaving the thugs and the owner of the small shop to continue their negotiation. Within a second of me clearing the entrance, the shack exploded in a giant flash of light, which poured out of every opening, followed by a loud electronic hum that shook the shack. A moment later, the three Menacilians stumbled through the doorway, visually impaired and eager to leave the premises.

I could see their exposed, tan skin, now blackened and free of the blond fuzz. The three charred individuals stumbled their way down the street while arguing and growling at each other. My Zipp friend had apparently acquired a new security system. I was heading back into the shop to talk to him when I caught the scent of burned Menacilian hair. I decided to give it a while before entering. I put my head through the doorway and yelled, "Nathan, are you alright?"

"I'm fine," he responded, coughing from the smoke.

"I'll come back in a while."

I could hear his magnified voice from the direction of the countertop. "Yes, that's a good idea," he added. "Oh, Moe, remember to have me show you some interesting items I acquired yesterday."

"I'll do that," I said, laughing to myself at Nathan, getting right back to business. I don't believe he has had a problem with this group of Menacilian since, but they are not the kind of species to forgive and forget. It was fortunate for me that I didn't have to shoot one, if not all, of them. I really am a pacifist at heart and a believer in galactic peace and cosmic love, especially after a big piece of Bry chocolate.

A cool feature of the Black Moon is the fact that it's between two suns, so it has daylight all the time. I have always wondered why a moon that has daylight continually would be called the Black Moon. I imagine it's the constant light of day that keeps the more dangerous shopkeepers in the shadows of their own shacks. The only way to tell the difference between day and night on the Black Moon is that one sun is redder than the other and it casts a red hue on everything. From my experience, the red sunlight would be considered nighttime on any other planet.

Between the two time cycles, the temperature only varies about ten degrees—somewhere between 85° and 75°F. Most humans find it more comfortable to shop during the red sun when it's a bit cooler. If a serious shopper is not careful, he or she could die of dehydration or exhaustion while shopping at the bazaar.

I should tell you that if you go to the Black Moon Bazaar, you need to either get a ride with someone or park your shuttle in a secured parking area. It's not uncommon to have someone go for a day of shopping at the bazaar and find parts of their own shuttle for sale in a shop or two on the way back to the open parking area. My LX shuttle has a Hellsfury security system that is somewhat complicated, but effective. I can't go into details about my modifications, but I will say that if anyone is dumb enough to attempt to remove any part of my shuttle he, she, or it will find themselves unhappy with their life choices. The only time this has happened was while I was parked in the red zone area at the bazaar. Tressa and I came back to the shuttle after shopping for some Bry Chocolate and found a crowbar, laser cutter, and a pile of ash next to my shuttle. I couldn't identify what the pile of ash used to be, but I did pick up the quality laser cutter tool so it wouldn't fall into the wrong hands. By the way, the red zone on the Black Moon is the only place other than Planet Bry where you can get one-hundred-percent pure Bry Chocolate. It's not legal on Earth but it is on my planet. I can't speak for Tressa, but I assure you, I have never smuggled pure Bry Chocolate home to Earth!

I am not trying to scare you away from the Black Moon. The Argilelion Bazaar is like any heavily populated city or planet. If you know where to go, what to do, and what to eat, it can be the coolest place in the galaxy. If you get into trouble, just do what

I do—walk away, and if anything follows you, shoot it—it has always worked for me. The Argilelions own the Black Moon, but they don't really supervise the population. The peace-keeping is left to the shopkeepers in each zone. Every species knows that, other than in the blue zone, a dead body in front of their store is bad for business, so most of them avoid violence. You should try the red zone for their food and spice and the white zone if you need something mechanical. I spent a long day in the white zone trying to find a functioning M-series tree trimmer to replace one I recently lost. Unfortunately, after going into about a hundred Zalipanderan shops, I couldn't find one fully functional robot that I could afford.

24 The Legend of Bigfoot

I need to explain that this chapter has nothing to do with my planet, but is a collection of information that I find fascinating. When the Trillions first came to Earth, there were a lot of things that we found out about our own planet that were previously unknown by the human race. One bit of information was that there were already groups from other planets living on Earth. One of these groups is what humans refer to as the Blue Spruce evergreen tree. These trees were transplanted to Earth 5000 years ago because of the quality of Earth's carbon dioxide. These large trees were brought here by the Offturns, who stayed on Earth to watch over the large population of trees because these trees reacted too slowly, by Earth standards, to defend themselves. It wasn't all the Offturns who stayed on Earth, just about 250 of them.

The Offturns are a large, humanoid life form that can grow to be almost eight feet tall and weigh over 400 pounds. Their shaggy brown fur and soft facial features allow them to blend easily into their forest surroundings. These gentle giants are very elusive and stay only in the most heavily forested areas of Earth. With the development of photography in the early twentieth century, humans, on several occasions, took pictures of these large, ape-like creatures in the wild. Most humans dismissed these sightings as fakes or as mistaken identity. With these sightings came gossip, and the gossip soon turned to legend. The Offturns were given nicknames like Bigfoot, Sasquatch and Yeti depending on where in the world the legend originated.

Small groups of humans tried to prove the existence of the Bigfoot, but were never really successful. One group, in an attempt to trick other humans into believing in their cause, went to the extent of strapping sculpted forms of large, bare feet on their boots to leave large tracks in the snow and soft soil. This was somewhat disturbing to the Offturns who witnessed the "track planting" due to the fact that Offturns are always very careful not to leave tracks that can be followed or made casts of. From what I have read about the Offturns, they were able to hide quite easily from humans due to the fact that the human mind will ignore things that terrify it. It would be similar to seeing an old girlfriend in a store and pretending not to have seen her.

When humans found out that the Offturns really existed, their sightings became more frequent. People who had seen them in the past, who had blocked it out of their memory, started to remember those events. Yes, I did compare seeing a Bigfoot to my ex-girlfriend. No, I'm not planning on apologizing. The fact is that she dumped me for a Trillion, and now that I have the chance, I thought I would rub it in a bit; plus, I was chubby when she met me, so using that for an excuse is really lame. By the way, I think Tressa could take her in a fight.

Back to the Bigfoot information: Because the Offturns live

to be approximately 2000 years old, humans thought it would be important to find a way to communicate with them since they knew more about Earth history than we did. Offturns, however, use a form of mental telepathy to communicate with the trees and each other. This made it difficult to communicate with humans, which only left the Offturns frustrated, and left humans with a nasty headache. I'm not saying these creatures of the forest are more intelligent than humans—just that their brains work differently than ours do. It's true, however, that they are more intelligent than some humans but it's not widely advertised. It was finally discovered that the only way we were able to get information from the Offturns was to have them communicate with a Rellom translator who wrote the translation down in a form of code. The code was then sent to a supercomputer on Aselus #3 and 3000 lines of code was translated to one sentence of Old American English. Humans quickly came to the decision that an open line of communication with the Offturns really wasn't that important. To be honest, most people didn't care about how to eat a pinecone or what a tree was thinking when it was being eaten by beavers, much less how to use a small bush as toilet paper. Of course, when humans found out that the Blue Spruce was an intelligent life form, they decided not to use the flesh of the trees for furniture and firewood. Once the trees were protected, this allowed most of the Offturns the opportunity to go home to their own planet, which some of them had never seen. Some of the Offturns caught rides on Trillion ships working as crew to pay for a ride home. I've never been able to find out what planet the Offturns are from. It's possible that they don't share that information with others. Legend has it that some of them stayed on Earth to keep an eye on things.

My Buddy the Charrmeanon

A few months ago, Tripp, Chuck, and I were on our way to MP to have a weekend of fishing. On this semi-annual trip, we stopped at the Wormhole Cafe for some lunch and pie. As we pulled into the parking area, I spotted one open slip, and as I dropped into the vacant spot, I put the shuttle down carefully—and skillfully, I might add—right next to a new Black Star custom shuttle. I couldn't get my airlock door open fast enough and almost fell out the door, excited to get a closer look. I hate to admit it, but it was the coolest shuttle I have ever seen in my life. I really like my LX model shuttle, but it's not near the caliber of that Black Star CS. This sleek new ride is currently back ordered for two years due to the fact that it's hand-crafted, and the manufacturing of the CS engines is very complex. Most of the specs of this model aren't even published.

The exterior of the Black Star is tri-liquid, which means if you touch it, the surface feels soft and pliable, but it is, according to Space and Travel magazine, the strongest external shell in production. The CS also comes with the fastest engines that are legal on a personal shuttle, which makes it almost twice as fast as my LX even with my modifications. More than anything, I just wanted to touch it, but Chuck put his hand on my shoulder and steered me toward the cafe's front door.

"There is a good chance that that Black Star has a security system that would disintegrate your ass, Moe!" Tripp said, patting me on the shoulder. I reluctantly followed my buddies, who headed into the cafe, ready to eat. We found a booth in the human section of the restaurant. There was an antique, Earth-style jukebox in the corner that filled the room with music from around the galaxy. Of course, it all sounded like rock music from Earth. Most species seem to copy human music. Sometimes it's good and sometimes it's really bad. Tonya picks the music for the jukebox at the Wormhole, so it's usually good stuff. Tonya, the cafe's cook/waitress, who is a friend of mine, came over to take our orders and to harass us in person. The first words out of my mouth were, "Who owns the Black Star shuttle outside?"

She looked at me for a second and then raised one eyebrow, a trick I have yet to master. "Why y'all askin'?"

"Because it is the coolest ship I have ever seen, and I want to touch it."

She shook her head. "That ship is owned by Smarr Tunnis, who is one of my best customers, and I don't want you to bother him with your shiny shuttle fetish."

It took a few minutes, but I finally managed to bribe her with two boxes of fresh fruit from MP. She reluctantly pointed to a dark corner of the cafe. When I saw that she was pointing at a Charrmeanon, I couldn't believe my eyes. The Charrmeanon species is one of the oldest in the known galaxy. They look like a tall version of the Menacilian without their yellow teeth and cat-like eyes, not to mention their nasty disposition.

Smarr Tunnis ended up being around 220 Earth years old. On his home planet of Surpus, he would be considered to be in the age group of teenagers to us. At first glance, I noticed he was eating rapple pie, which made me take an instant liking to him. Any species who enjoys eating pie is okay in my book, especially the Moe's Rapple Pie. Tonya named this tasty dessert after myself because I'm the only supplier she could find. I eagerly bring her rapples from my planet that I trade for freshly made pie. I was surprised to see a Charrmeanon in the Wormhole. From what I had heard about them, they don't really associate with other species, especially the kind that hangout at the Wormhole Cafe. (No offence meant to my fellow patrons!)

He was massive in comparison to his surroundings. Watching him sit and eat reminded me of myself sitting at a small table in a tiny chair drinking pretend tea out of tiny cups. I was helping my niece celebrate the wedding of two of her stuffed animals with a no-tea tea party. I did find it confusing that, because of his size, he wasn't sitting in the Argilelian section of the cafe. I figured it might be the fact that they never really get all the Argilelian slime trail off the seats and floor at those larger booths.

This Charrmeanon had a full beard, which made his head look bigger than it was. He looked like someone who would make a profession out of throwing rowdy customers out of a pub or spice bar. It seemed that Tonya didn't have large enough dinner utensils to accommodate a Charrmeanon, so he ate his whole pie with a large serving spoon.

He appeared to be finished with his dessert, so as he scraped the last part of the crust from the bottom of the pie tin, I pulled together enough courage to introduce myself. He lifted his head and watched me carefully through his crystal-like blue eyes as I crossed the room. When I was close enough to carry on a civilized conversation, I realized he was as tall as myself while still sitting in his chair. I pulled out my best smile and opened with, "My name is Moe. I don't mean to bother you, but I was told that you own the Black Star shuttle out in the parking area."

He continued to stare at me with a bemused look on his face, then he replied in what I noticed was perfect Earth English.

"Yes, the CS is my shuttle."

I smiled, finding it hard to hide my nervous excitement. I can't remember if my jitters were from the opportunity to talk about his shuttle, or meeting a Charrmeanon in person for the first time.

"I have to say that it is the coolest ride I have ever seen," I blurted out, like a child meeting his favorite celebrity.

He stood up next to his booth. I watched as he used the table for stability and stretched himself out to his full seven-foot frame. He was now looking down on my face as I looked up in amazement.

"You should see the inside. I had it custom built. It's quite impressive," he said, his voice heavy with bass.

It was all I could do to not hug this huge individual on the spot. He put his monster-size hand on my shoulder. "Let's go out and I'll show it to you."

We had turned and were headed toward the exit when I remembered Chuck and Tripp. "Can my buddies come?" I asked hesitantly, hoping I hadn't overstepped my boundaries.

"No problem," he responded in a deep voice. I looked back and waved to my sidekicks who were still at our table. It was apparent that neither one of them had any intention of going outside with myself and this unknown Charrmeanon, no matter how cool his shuttle was. Tonya, who was behind the counter, pointed in our direction, and in a somewhat demeaning manner, told us, "I don't think y'all should be going anywhere with him; he is a bad influence and should not be trusted."

We glanced at each other, wondering which one of us she was referring to, and which one of us should be offended. Since neither one of us wanted to know the answer, we nodded to her as we turned and continued outside.

As we approached the Black Star, the interior and exterior lights came on in the undercarriage of the shuttle, which was now glowing with dark blue light. The interior was lit by a soft white light, and as the shuttle doors opened automatically, I could see the lush tan upholstery and the Parrion leather-covered seats. Everything about the shuttle was as it appeared in the catalog, except it was all enlarged to fit the oversized owner.

"So, Moe, would you be interested in a quick ride?"

My eyes must have had a twinkle in them as I responded with what should have been an embarrassing, "Yes, please!"

Smarr walked around the outside and got into the driver's side, and I eagerly climbed up into the large, plush chair on the passenger side. As we sat down, the door automatically closed and sealed with a hissing, pressurized sound. The dashboard lit up and my new Charrmeanon friend began touching buttons. The ship responded with beeps and hums. Smarr looked over at me.

"So, my young human friend, where would you like to go?"

"Well, since my friends are waiting for me, I shouldn't be gone too long."

Smarr looked over at me and smiled. "I have a good spot I have wanted to check out."

I smiled back hesitantly. "Well, it's your shuttle, and I'm here for the ride."

He nodded his large head as he pushed a few more buttons. The shuttle engines began to hum as we lifted a few inches off the ground. Suddenly, he stopped touching the controls and looked over at me. His expression, I could only assume, was serious.

"Moe, have you ever flown in a Z-rated shuttle at or above PR7 speeds?"

I looked toward the ceiling and tried to decide if I should lie or not. "Sure have, why do you ask?"

He smiled as he looked at me. "I'm just wondering because I have heard those speeds have a tendency to affect humans in unexpected ways."

I swallowed hard. "Oh, I don't remember any side effects from the last time." I lied as convincingly as I could.

"Okay then," he said as the shuttle lifted out of its parking place and moved toward the exit.

With a free hand, Smarr reached into a side pocket, pulled out a candy bar, and handed it to me.

"You're going to want to eat this Bry Chocolate before we take off."

I was going to ask why, but thought it was better not to know. Besides, I didn't want to show my ignorance. As I unwrapped it and began to devour the chocolate, I could see the shuttle entrance portal out of the corner of my eye. To my amazement, coming through the portal was another Black Star CS. It was even the same color as the one I was riding in. I was amazed at my luck. Since the advertising had started for the CS, I had wanted more than anything to see one, and now I had seen two and was going for a ride in one.

"That's incredible!" I said out loud to myself.

The large Charrmeanon looked over at me. "What's incredible?" he asked, assuming I was talking about his shuttle.

"I just saw another Black Star like yours coming in the portal entrance, and it surprised me because it is so rare to see them."

Smarr looked at me and then down at the clock on his display.

"Are you sure it was a CS like this one?"

I tried to look over my shoulder but couldn't see it anymore. "Yes, I'm sure, it was the same color and model as yours."

He nodded his head and continued to navigate us out of the portal exit. The stars that surrounded us were brighter outside the dome of the cafe shuttle spot. It always takes me a second to adjust to space when I leave the artificial gravity of a space port.

"That's good to hear. Now we know how long to take a drive." I was somewhat confused by his comment, but before I could inquire more, he spoke again.

"Did you eat all that chocolate?"

I nodded yes.

"Good," he responded and hit the green button on his dashboard. Reality, as I understand it, seemed to blur, and as I looked at the Charrmeanon sitting next to me, my view of my surroundings seemed to shrink down to one tiny dot of light. It was as if someone had turned an antique monitor off while I was watching a show. As fast as the lights went out the light returned, and I could see Smarr leaning over in front of me, smiling.

"Are you okay, Moe?" he said, trying to hide his amusement.

"I think I'm okay."

As I spoke, a strong wave of nausea crashed over me.

"You look a bit gray there, human. Take this container in case you have to be sick!"

I did, and I did. When I was done, he handed me a soft rag and I wiped off the beads of sweat that had formed on my forehead and mouth.

"How long was I out?"

"Just for about two and a half minutes."

I felt my stomach rumble again. "I thought the chocolate was supposed to help," I said, looking up at him.

"It does, because it tastes the same when you eat it and when you vomit." He laughed and slapped me on the back. "Were you sick the last time you traveled at PR7 plus speeds?"

I looked up at his smirking face. "I think we both know that was a first for me. Sorry to mislead you."

He winked at me. "That's okay. It's a self-punishing kind of lie!" He turned his head and looked out the windshield of the ship. "Wow, Moe! That is a good-looking planet you got there."

I turned, following his gaze out the window, and stared right at MP1X.

"It looks a lot like your Earth. I have never visited Earth; your gravity is too high for me, but I have stopped and had a look from space."

I looked out the window and then at Smarr and then out the window again. "How did you know this was my planet? And how did you know how to get here?"

"Ms. Tonya, at the cafe, talks about you all the time, and she likes to brag about your planet and the supply of fresh fruit she uses in the Moe Rapple Pie."

I smiled and then realized something. "You mean to tell me

that your shuttle got us here in two and a half minutes?"

"Actually, we got here in close to a minute, and we were sitting in orbit around your planet for a minute or two before you came to."

A simple "Cool" was all I could manage to say. We sat for a while, looking down at MP and discussing the pros and cons of owning a planet, while I ate another chocolate bar that he pulled out of a side pocket. Smarr seemed entertained by my experiences, both good and bad. He nodded in agreement at some of my successes, and grimaced at my failures. Suddenly, I realized that over an hour had passed, that Tripp and Chuck were sitting at the Wormhole Cafe waiting for me, and that I had the only key to the shuttle.

"Well, I guess we need to head back before my buddies hitchhike a ride and leave me to cover their lunch bill."

The large Charrmeanon looked down at his clock. "I believe you are right. It is about time to head back." Smarr looked over at me. "This time, Moe, may I suggest that you take a deep breath and slowly let out the air as we launch."

"Okay," I replied hesitantly.

Smarr turned the shuttle till it faced into space while I took a deep breath and slowly let it out. This time, I made it almost thirty seconds before I blacked out. The solar system flew past my view, and then all was dark. When I came to again, we were parked just outside the portal at the Wormhole Cafe, and once again, Smarr was looking at me and offering the widemouthed container just in case.

"Thank you but I think I'm okay this time," I muttered, my voice quivering a bit.

"Oh, good!" he replied, looking relieved. He bent over and

pushed the controls to maneuver our way through the entrance portal. As we entered the lighted parking area, I could clearly see the Black Star shuttle I had seen earlier at the far end of the lot, preparing to exit through the portal.

"There it is again," I said, pointing at it. "It's an amazing coincidence to see it again."

Smarr just smiled at me and laughed to himself. I could hear the shuttle motors cooling as we climbed out of the shuttle, my knees just a little wobbly. My companion reached out with his big hand and grabbed the back of my flight jacket to steady me. Tonya was the first to notice us walking in. She looked at Smarr and then me, then frowned.

"Are you okay, Moe? You look like you done seen a ghost," she asked, her accent magnifying her question.

"He's okay, ma'am. He just needs a nice piece of rapple pie to get him straightened out," Smarr said, patting me on the shoulder. I made my way over to the guys, who were still working on lunch. I collapsed into the bench next to Chuck. When I looked up, Tonya was standing in front of me with a big piece of pie. Behind her, I could see Smarr paying his lunch bill at the counter. I waved at him, and he waved back.

"Thanks for the ride. We should do it again sometime."

He smiled. "No problem. I'll stop in and see your planet next time." Then he pointed at Tonya's tray with a big slice of warm pastry on it. "You are going to want to eat that before you drive home." He smiled and winked as he turned and walked out the door, ducking to barely clear the top of the door frame.

Tonya put the plate in front of me. The smell of the warm pie filled my empty head. I smiled weakly. "Thank you, Ms. Tonya."

"You're entirely welcome, kiddo," she responded, smiling

back. I turned back to Tripp and Chuck, and started eating my pie.

"Well! The two of you became fast friends! He must have let you touch his cool CS shuttle controls," Tripp said, smirking at me.

"Yes, he did, and it's going to be a bit before I recover from that ride. Oh, sorry, you guys—for making you wait for me."

They both stared at me for a minute till Chuck spoke. "Moe, you were outside for like five minutes; we just barely got our lunch!"

"Right!" I said sarcastically. "I said I was sorry for being gone so long."

Chuck was still staring at me. "Did you go for a ride in his shuttle?"

"Yes, I told you I did."

"Where did you fly to?" Chuck asked excitedly.

"We flew to MP and hung in orbit for about an hour, then flew back."

Chuck and Tripp both sat and stared at me, Tripp's mouth hanging partially open. Suddenly, Chuck began to smile.

"I knew that Black Star was fast, but I didn't know it could do SOT-plus. That crazy Charrmeanon must have modified the crap out of those engines."

Still looking confused, I responded, "Are you telling me that I traveled the speed of time and didn't know it?" Chuck pointed at my watch and then the clock on the wall of the cafe. My antique wristwatch was now one hour and twenty-two minutes faster than the clock.

"Cool. No wonder I passed out twice," I said, smiling to myself. I ate a big spoonful of the pie, suddenly feeling much better.

26 Yard Sale

Recently, I was sent a message from a liquidation company called Sellitall, LLC. concerning some items that were going to be available for purchase. I get these notices from time to time, but this one really sparked my interest. It seems that one of the planets in the Blue Star galaxy, which is next to mine, has been sold. Tryson Six is a manufactured planet similar to MP in size and nature. The planet was purchased "as-is" so all the wildlife and natural resources come with the sale. The only issue with the sale is that the planet is going to be relocated to a neighboring galaxy. To move a planet, it first must be taken out of orbit. To do this, the rotation of the planet has to be gradually slowed until it stops altogether. One of the biggest reasons to slowly stop rotation is that planets turn anywhere between 500 and 4,000 miles an hour. Since the atmosphere of a planet is also turning at the same speed, if the planet suddenly stops, the wind could blow up to 900 miles an hour and the larger bodies of water would generate enormous tsunamis.

Stopping the rotation of a planet allows the 200 large Trillion ships to use their tractor beams attached to an electronet to tow the planet to its new neighborhood. This process, however, affects the gravity of the planet and, of course, anything living on it. An engineered planet is designed to be moved, so not much is lost from the surface of the planet as far as plants and minerals. The wildlife and water are another issue altogether. Water without a certain gravity level can be lost into the atmosphere and then into space.

The wildlife must be removed from the planet and sold or stored at a different host planet until the world being moved can be placed back in its new orbit and the water supply and plants can be replenished. The most expensive part of relocating a planet, other than the permits, is the cost of fuel. Two hundred large towships go through a large amount of fuel, and it takes two enormous tankers, full-time, to keep them refueled. This is part of the reason I got invited to this party in the first place. These big ships run on RD7, which is a byproduct of making regular R7 gas, and the word has gotten around that I can get my hands on all the RD7 fuel someone might need, cheap.

The Trillion Financial Group that bought Tryson 6 were anxious to trade some, if not all, of the wildlife they are not retaining for their planet for fuel. They were also hoping I would be interested in the fresh water on the planet as part of the trade. The issue I had was I would have to purchase all the accessible water on the planet, which was estimated to be about 120 billion gallons. Under galactic law, you cannot waste or dispose of more than 400,000 gallons of fresh water, so I would have to take all of the available H_2O.

As I mentioned before, in the western desert of MP, I have a large red rock canyon I would love to fill with water. This dream of mine was the first thing that popped into my head when I read the list of items for sale or trade from Tryson 6. The mistake I made was asking Chuck what he thought. It just so happened that Chuck had borrowed my PMF—or Planet Functions Manual—for a report he needed to do for work. He told me he would do some research and get back to me. It was the next day at lunch that Chuck gave me the bad news:

"Well, I understand that you can purchase that water for a decent price, Moe, but putting any more than ten billion gallons in one area on your planet may throw off your whole planet's designed environmental system's balance. MP was designed to have a specific humidity and water placement that gives you sustainable and accountable weather patterns. Any variations will cause disparities in your structured system within a condensed period of time. To safely use the water in its entirety, it would have to be purified to eradicate any alien life that could contaminate your planet. So, the water would require supplemental mineral and pH balance ingredients, not to mention a healthy balance of totally dissolved solids to sustain life."

Confused, I stared at him with a blank look on my face. It is difficult for me to admit that I don't always understand and/or pay attention to Chuck's explanations of things. Chuck stared back at me for a moment and then tried again.

"No, you can't put that water on your planet."

"Well, that's a bummer," I responded, frowning. I sat pouting for a few minutes and hoped that the lunch I just ordered would make me feel better. After we got our food and started to eat, Chuck stopped and said, "Oh, I forgot to tell you the good news." He smiled and pointed at the paperwork. "As long as you're careful not to buy any predators, you can choose any of the wildlife out of the catalog you want. Make sure they are edible, though, because with no predators to control population, you're going to have to eat a certain number of them to keep them from overpopulating; or you could sell your spare animals."

That night, I sat down with Tressa and we went through the catalog. The listings had been divided up into animal size, value, and planet of origin. There was also a brief description of the animals. The first one I stopped at was a golden perin, its origin the planet Bertina in the Blue Star Galaxy. It was incredible in the pictures. Tressa fell in love instantly. It was a stag much like an Earth elk or red stag, but its hair was a bright white and its antlers were a shiny golden color. It was approximately seven feet tall at the shoulder and weighed close to 500 pounds fully grown. As we read further, it also said that its flesh is toxic to humans and their maintenance is a nine out of ten, which means they are a serious pain to take care of. Since Tressa had no intention to help take care of them, we decided to pass.

The catalog had a long list of animals, some of them Tressa and I recognized, and some that we had never heard of. The original owners of Tryson 6 had purchased a large Earth package of animals, including many from Africa. They had about twenty animal species, including 115 greater kudu, 86 nyala, 42 golden wildebeest, 186 black wildebeest, 97 gemsbok, and 14 elephants. I was very excited about having all these animals on MP, except for the elephants because they are super expensive to buy, a pain to take care of, and they require huge amounts of land and feed to be comfortable. With their ability to reach higher with their trunks, the elephants would also be hard on my fruit trees. To be honest, I just don't want to have to babysit a herd of elephants, and people get all weird when you talk about eating them. I could shoot and eat all the wildebeest on planet Earth and no one would really care, but if you even talk bad about an elephant behind his back, you'll wish you were dead, socially speaking.

The owners of Tryson 6 also had a large population of whitetail deer, which is originally from Earth. The whitetail has been a very popular species to trade with due to their versatility in adapting to different climates and food sources from different planets. By the 2050s on Earth, the whitetail deer population had been modified through breeding and feeding to such an extent that they began to decline physically. The buck, or male deer, had been modified genetically so severely that their antlers became too massive for the buck to carry. Hunting property owners were forced to do maintenance on their deer herds. By midsummer, when the deer were approximately halfway through their yearly antler growth cycle, the more mature bucks had to be captured and their massive antlers cut off. If not, they were unable to fight off predators, had difficulty breeding, and some even drowned while crossing or trying to drink from a water source. Fortunately, there were still small groups of whitetails in the wild that had unaltered DNA, and breeders and scientists were able to start fresh with new family lines.

On the list, there were 350 whitetails available—150 males and 200 females. According to the catalog, the sale included a clause that stated the owners of Tryson 6 would buy back 75 males and 100 females in five years to repopulate their planet. This would allow them time to reestablish the natural environment for the animals, including food and water sources. With luck and successful breeding, this should leave me with close to 400 deer.

Included in the catalog was a large, three-page listing of 200 Earth bison. This listing had my full attention. My interest in the whitetail deer comes from my love of the Earth's redneck culture, the bison or American buffalo comes from my love of the history of the Old West. The bison was a huge part of the history of settling the western part of the United States. Originally, the bison was a major part of the indigenous people, or Native American, way of life. The plains indians used all the parts of the animal. However, the pioneers and settlers were a little more reckless and tended to shoot animals for small parts and leave the rest to waste. So, like anything else that seems endless, the buffalo almost became extinct. Fortunately, the bison became protected and were saved to become large wild herds again on Earth. The average bison weighs close to a thousand pounds, with older males weighing up to 2000 pounds and standing six feet high. Even with their size they can run close to thirty-five miles an hour.

When I first bought MP, Chuck had informed me that NTEG had a whole herd of bison that I could get for a deal. It turned out that the NTEG herd were lesser bison, which were an exact copy of the American buffalo but were genetically redesigned as miniatures so they could be sold as pets. A lesser bison is about the size of a medium-sized dog. They are about 100–150 pounds and stand about thirty inches tall. Even though it was a good deal on the price, I turned down the offer because I thought I would probably lose them in the tall grass on MP. I did buy one male for my Uncle Lester, who named it Wild Bill and uses it to keep the grass in his large yard trimmed. Lester thought it would be a good way to keep the neighborhood children out of his yard, but it turned out that Wild Bill is more of an attractant than a deterrent. The kids in Lester's neighborhood love to feed Bill apples, and have taught him to fetch sticks.

In the catalog, several large birds were available that Tressa was excited about, as well as one group of primates. The ocies monkey is a descendant of the Earth chimpanzee that have been bred on other planets to improve their biological and psychological aspects. What I mean by that is, the primatologist and breeders genetically changed them to make them more civilized according to what the human life forms considered civilized. What they ended up with is monkeys that can be taught to speak almost any language, and are self-aware of their own needs. Ocies monkeys still prefer to live in the wild but spend most of their time outdoors complaining about the rustic conditions they live in. They are also known to complain about what they must eat and how unattractive they find their mate to be. We decided to pass on the monkeys.

Tressa wrote down all the animals in the catalog that we wanted to bid on. I decided I wanted the whitetail deer, the bison, and any of the African plains animals that I could get my hands on, excluding the elephants. Tressa wanted four different bird species, including a handful of scarlet macaws, which are a brightly colored parrot species from Earth. She also loved the perron, or moon pheasant as they are referred to on Earth. I loved the idea of having perron because they glow at night, which would make hunting them a blast! Unfortunately, I have a rule that I don't eat things that glow, so I can't shoot what I don't eat, except for robots. I did warn her that any birds that are noisy to the point of irritation will become extinct on MP quite quickly. Her reply was something about having a whole planet to hide my corpse.

27 Two Hundred Bison to Go

After Tressa and I had submitted our wish list of items from the Tryson 6 yard sale, we had to wait for two weeks for a reply. The liquidation company, Sellitall, got back to us to confirm our animals and the trade price for our purchase. They seemed put out that I didn't want the water or the elephants, but for what we did submit, they wanted 357,000 gallons of RD7 fuel. This seemed a little steep to me but, fortunately, we had a tanker with a little over that amount in our company storage area right by Jupiter. My father had a deal fall through on this RD7 fuel and it has a two-year sell-by date, which is less than most companies in our galaxy require, so he let me steal it.

As part of the trade, the Sellitall company agreed to ship the animals to MP for us. I insisted that we got to see the animals before they were loaded on the cargo ships. The good part about buying animals from Tryson 6 and moving them to MP is that both planets are privately owned so the animals or plants do not have to go through customs and inspection unless I want them to. This saved us two months in quarantine where the Trillion custom agents are not responsible for any animals that die during the wait. I figured the animals are scanned and cleaned while being loaded anyway so it's low risk to us.

I put the word out to my friends that Tressa and I were going to Tryson 6 to watch my new animals being loaded. Chuck, Ashell, Tripp, and my brother, Kyle, decided to come with us. My parents said that they were excited for me, but they would wait and see them next time they came to MP. We decided to take Tressa's ST-XL shuttle, which is slower than my sporty LX but more comfortable on longer trips for more than two people.

As we approached Tryson 6, we could see several ships that were in orbit around the planet. Two of the ships were large tankers. The Triten tanker, nicknamed "The Whale," is a massive ship. These monsters of space are so large, they can't land on a planet or a moon. They are manufactured in a large space port and then remain in space till they are retired. There are close to 8,000 workers that live and work on a Triten so each ship needs living quarters, shops, restaurants, transportation, and medical facilities. The tanks on each ship can hold enough water to transport twenty-five percent of the Atlantic Ocean on Earth. Because the Triten can't land on the planet, there are smaller ships called Runners that pick up the water and transport it to the large tanker in orbit. My guess is that it would take about a week to fill up both Triten tankers depending on how many Runners they had.

Tryson 6 was a beautiful planet, and it was easy to see the similarities with it and MP. I programmed the landing codes and GPS directions provided in my paperwork into Tressa's shuttle controls before we left. The directions took us to a large, grassy plane surrounded by mountains. Below us, we could see two large transfer ships and several smaller shuttles surrounded by corrals filled with animals. Some of the animals were so large, they could be easily identified from a great distance. As we got closer, we could see elephants in a large pen, and next to them were eight large triceratopses. Tripp was looking out a window and commented, "Dude those dinosaurs are awesome!"

I looked over at Chuck who was smiling mischievously.

"Is that some of your work?" He laughed.

"No, but it was my department that made the triceratops. Unfortunately for me, they had that order done before I was hired on at NTEG, but a lot of the technology they developed to make them, we were able to use to make your raptors."

"It's one of those projects that I can't talk about," Chuck said, winking. Tripp chuckled.

"It's too bad they weren't for sale." I shook my head.

"I'm sure they are going to be part of the sale of the planet. Besides, one of them would have cost more than all of my animals put together."

Chuck nodded in agreement and added, "They are super expensive to make, and to tell a company secret, they can't even mate. Moe's raptors were the first success NTEG had in applied ethology."

My animals were supposed to be in Section 6-B so we went that direction, following a digital map on my display. There were also large numbers painted on the ground in between the corrals. From above, we could see several transfer shuttles in section 6-B, and in the distance, two large, grey cargo ships. There was a parking space next to one of the transfer shuttles, so we landed there. The transfer shuttle that we landed next to was unloading greater kudu into a pen from a large rear door. The animals were being herded by small, noiseless drones that flew overhead. The drones worked independently, reacting to the animals movements, and used bright lights to initiate a response from them. When the drones showed red light, the animals became agitated and would move away from the light. The blue lights attracted them and calmed the animals. As the kudu moved out of the shuttle bay doors, they were being fogged with what I assume was a disinfectant. The liquid they were using to clean them must have been safe to consume because the animals were busy licking it off each other.

Across the parking lot, there was a small building with Sellitall stenciled on the door. It seemed to serve as a temporary office. As we exited the shuttle, we were met by a woman smartly dressed in a white lab coat, carrying an old school computer tablet. Her nametag was written in Relloem and I couldn't translate it. She was smiling as she introduced herself.

"Hello. My name is Maziem," she said, looking and pointing at her nametag. "Oh, oops!" she said as she touched her tag with her finger. The tag changed translation several times and then stopped on Earth English.

"Are you the Moe party from Earth?"

"That's us," I said, shaking her extended hand. She looked down at her tablet and scrolled through several pages. She touched one page and a hologram appeared with a schedule on it. From where we stood, the hologram display was reversed and in Relloem, so we waited for her to read it.

"It looks like the greater kudu are the last to be brought in."

She raised her hand and pointed down the long row of

stables. "All of your order is down this row to your right, except for the birds that have already been loaded in the transfer ship number 7169 at the end of the row. The oxygen in the ship has been mixed already to calm the birds, so you will need to wear a respirator mask to get on board to inspect them. There is a limited amount of time because staff in charge of loading the animals need all non-company people out of the area for safety purposes before loading the ship."

We all nodded to acknowledge we understood her directions and then turned and moved toward the first fenced area.

Each section had a tall blind that blocked the view of the animals from the ones next to them. Maziem was walking with us, and I mentioned that I was surprised that with so many animals, it didn't smell more like a zoo or a cattle yard.

Smiling, she replied, "It's because the majority of the animals have only been here for a few hours, except for the elephants and triceratops, which were the first to be rounded up."

The first stall we came to had the whitetail deer in it. The pen was around 100 feet long and 200 feet wide. The sides were tall enough to keep the deer from hopping out. A drone hovered over the top of the pen, shining a soft blue light down on the animals. As we approached the pen, we could see that every deer in it was standing and staring, mesmerized, at the blue light shining down from the drone. I whistled loudly and one or two of the bucks looked over at us, stomped the ground with their hooves, and turned back to the light. Maziem looked down at her tablet and then turned and showed me the current page. She pointed at the numbers at the bottom.

"We have been able to gather three hundred and forty-five of the deer, and all are in good to perfect health."

I looked at the numbers and nodded in acknowledgement. The buffalo were next. I had never seen a bison up close before, and it was epic. Their large, brown, shaggy heads and tall backs looked almost cartoon-like with their short, stubby legs. The entire herd stood together in one corner of the enormous pen. The males were easy to spot in comparison to the smaller females. The group of us stared through the metal rails of the pen in awe. Tripp leaned his head back and looked in my direction.

"Hey, Moe. Can we ride one of these buffalo?"

Maziem, who was looking at her tablet, immediately looked up at us. "Oh, sir, I can't, for safety reasons, allow you to ride or even approach any of these animals!"

I looked back at Tripp. "You heard the nice lady; you can't ride one today."

Tripp lowered his head and kicked the dirt to show his disappointment. Chuck patted him on the shoulder to console him. The rest of the group chuckled quietly. Ms. Maziem stared at us for a minute, looking stern. I think she probably didn't understand the humor of the conversation. Still watching Tripp, Maziem handed me the tablet. According to the records, there were 206 bison, which gave me a few over my original paperwork.

We moved on to the next pen, which held the black wildebeest. We repeated the count. During the next half hour, we went from pen to pen, viewing the animals. By the time we had walked back, the greater kudu had been unloaded and were ready for inspection. The kudu is an incredible Earth species. They look similar to a large deer or elk but instead of antlers, the males have large corkscrew-style horns. They are mostly gray in color, with small white strips that run down from their backs to their stomachs. Hunters on Earth historically nicknamed them the "Grey Ghosts" because of their ability to disappear in the brush. I was very excited to see them in the wild on MP. As we approached the pen, Tripp pointed at the animals.

"It looks like the lights don't work on the kudu."

It was true. Instead of looking at the silent drone's light over them, the entire herd was watching us closely.

"They seem a bit wearier than the other animals," I said to Tripp.

"Oh, they are!" Maziem said, looking at her tablet and then the kudu. "We had to round them up at night with drones that have thermal imaging and inferred vision. Even then, they were still hard to acquire safely.

After a couple of minutes of a staring contest between the herd of kudu and ourselves, our tour guide pointed at two large ships in the distance.

"The one on the left is number 7169 if you would like to see your birds."

Instead of seeing the birds, Tripp, Chuck, and Kyle decided to go over and check out some of the other animals that were not coming to MP. I actually wanted to go with them and see if we could get close to the triceratopses pen. Tressa, however, took me by the hand and led me toward the large cargo ship.

"We can see the other animals in a bit!" she said, squeezing my hand. I gave her a sideways glance.

"You're not the boss of me!" I said, trying to pull my hand away. Her grip tightened.

"Actually, I am!" she said, raising her eyebrows triumphantly. I lowered my head in a sign of submission. Maziem stared at the two of us once again, not understanding the sarcastic humor we shared, then she turned and led us to the ship.

The grey cargo ship was enormous; the storage area for the animals alone was at least 400 yards deep and almost 200 yards wide. On a table outside the large loading dock doors were a dozen respirators. We each selected one in our size and pulled them on over our heads until the soft seal on the inside of the mask covered our noses and mouths. Honestly, I thought I looked cool in mine, and I couldn't help but breathe hard and make funny sounds through my mouthpiece. As we entered the ship, it was hard not to be in awe at the size of the storage area. The space inside looked very similar to a large warehouse. Like the outside pens, the inside space was broken up into corrals that were set up in two rows, one on each side, with a large aisle down the middle. There were also large curtains that hung from the ceiling, separating each pen.

Maziem pointed to the far corner of the space where four large cages sat covered in a dark material. It took a few minutes to walk to the end of the row, and as we approached the cages, I was surprised that we couldn't hear any bird sounds at all. The first pen was marked "scarlet macaws," and as we pulled back the blinds, we could see approximately twenty-five large, beautiful birds sitting on long poles that were installed horizontally to give them a place to sit without being on the floor. They sat motionless, some with their eyes closed and some staring lazily forward, blinking slowly.

"Tressa, I think your birds are stoned," I said, smiling at her.

Maziem spoke out. "The enhanced oxygen will keep them and the other animals calm until they reach your planet."

I nodded in response and we moved down to the next pen, which held fifteen exquisite white peacocks that sat on the sawdust-covered floor. Peafowl are a beautiful bird from Earth that are famous for their long, decorative plumage that they display like a fan when the mood hits them. As a child, my neighbors had peacocks, and I remember marveling at how colorful they were—and noisy! I turned and looked at Tressa, who was very excited.

"I think we should put these birds somewhere other than by our cabin, maybe the castle lawn might be the best," I told her.

"We'll decide later," she replied, frowning slightly. The next pen held seventy-five Canadian geese. These large waterfowl from Earth are a black and white color and stand between two and three feet tall. Tressa has always loved geese; my guess is that she has never had one of the little buggers chase her down the beach before. The last pen was labeled "Perron." Even before Maziem pulled back the blinds, we could see the blueish-green glow coming from inside the pen. There were 140 perron, or moon pheasants, in the pen, and they looked amazing. The beautiful, glowing birds huddled next to each other in small groups on the ground, most of them sleeping. Fortunately, there are no predators on MP or these birds would be easily spotted, even in the tall grass. I don't consider myself to be a predator. I'm more of a *population control expert*.

I looked down and saw a perron feather about six inches long on the ground. I picked it up and put the softly glowing feather in my front pocket, with the top half sticking out. I figured I could look it over more closely later.

I signed off on the birds and we headed back outside. Maziem mentioned that we needed to get out of the way so that the animal control staff could begin to load the other animals. The plan was to have my whole order loaded by the end of the day so they could begin the two-day trip to MP. As we approached the large, open door, I could see several people waiting for us. I foolishly assumed it was the Sellitall crew waiting for us to finish our tour. When we got outside, we could clearly see it was Kyle, Tripp, and Chuck with what looked like two square-jawed security officers. Tripp and Kyle were both smiling from ear to ear, even though they were both covered in dirt and just a trace of blood. Chuck was still clean, and when he looked at me, he hunched his shoulders as if to say he had no idea what had happened. Ashell and Tressa just shook their heads. Tressa spoke first.

"Really, we can't leave you three unsupervised for five minutes! You are not riding in my shuttle covered in dirt or whatever that is smeared all over you," she said, pointing at Tripp and Kyle.

One of the guards cleared his throat to get our attention and spoke in a gruff voice. "As long as your group is departing soon, we will not hold these three in confinement or fine them, but we want you out of this area and off this planet immediately."

Maziem was standing and clutching her computer tablet with a look of shock on her face. She quickly gathered herself together and raised her hand.

"Officers, this group is just leaving and will not give you any more problems."

She pushed on my back, signaling it was time to start moving back to the shuttle. The group headed back to the shuttle. Tripp and Kyle were in the lead, laughing and whispering to each other, followed by the girls and then Chuck and myself. Smiling, Chuck looked over at me and whispered, "In their defense, there weren't any signs that said they couldn't approach or attempt to ride a triceratops!"

We got back to the shuttle and the girls went inside to get the boys their luggage so they could change into clean clothes.

I followed Maziem to the Sellitall office and finalized the paperwork on the animals. This took longer than I had hoped, but we did manage to get it all done. I was given the ship's schedule for when it would arrive on MP, and I gave Maziem a map and GPS information to safely land the big ship. One of the smaller ships would follow the cargo ship to handle the distribution of the animals once they were on my planet. While the ships were in transit, I had to get our field trip group back to Earth and switch shuttles so that Tressa and I could meet them back on MP.

I remembered that there was a large comet passing between Tryson 6 and Earth, so I knew that was going to slow down traffic. These stupid chunks of ice and rocks hurtling through space always have a huge following of religious zealots that plug up space with their caravans of shuttles. I don't make it a habit to poke fun of someone's beliefs, but out of all of the religions out there, worshiping a four-billion-year-old popsicle is kind of nuts. This comet is LC#3611-P but to its followers, it is called Oculus Dei, or the Eye of God. The name comes from the intense blue color of the gasses surrounding it. This flying chunk of space debris has a particularly large number of space-clogging fans that follow it in its round-trip through the galaxy. We decided to take a longer route home, but the guidance computer said avoiding traffic would cut at least two hours off our trip.

After dropping off everyone, having dinner with my parents, and filling them in on the day's events, we made it back to MP by the next day. On the way, Tressa and I discussed the best place to have the animals live. All of the animals had certain needs that involved temperature, terrain, and access to food and water. The Sellitall company would supply us with feed for the animals to supplement their diet until they could adjust to their new home. The scarlet macaws were going to the Island of Tripp, which would allow them the ability to migrate to the mainland if they wanted to. The peacocks would go to Castle Moe, where they could be fed and watched over by the service robots. The geese were to be dropped off at Moe's Bayou, but they were also free to migrate wherever they were comfortable. The perron went to a couple of locations, including Moe's Bayou and a plains area where there is a variety of grains and grass. I figured it would be better to give the moon pheasants a couple of areas and see which one they like the best. The pheasants have a limited range, so they don't migrate. My plan was to release sixty at each of these two locations and then take the remaining twenty and put them close to my cabin.

South of the mountains where my cabin sits is the planet's Great Plains area. This was where my firebushes met their end. This area is the largest open area on MP, and where we decided all the African animals as well as the bison would be placed. Each group will have their own area and will have automated feeders to supplement their diets. One hundred of the whitetail deer will be released in the forest area by my cabin. Another hundred will be released in my redwood forest in the hope that they don't do too much damage to the trees when they are in their "rut"—or mating season. The last 150 deer are going to the Trout Creek Forest. I figured it would add to the ambiance of the area for Prince Justin and Caroline to see some wildlife.

The large ships landed in the predetermined area, and the smaller ships and crew went to work distributing the animals to the areas I had marked on my contract. The teams of workers also set up and programmed the automated feeders that would supplement the animals as they acclimatized themselves to their new environments. I was given manuals for the feeders, which I then gave to Chuck. Reading long, boring instruction manuals is one of Chuck's favorite things. He reads and absorbs information like no one else I know. The manuals have diagrams in them, which made them even more exciting for him. He really worries me sometimes.

28

Hammer Down

Just west of the Great Plains on MP is an area that is set aside for farming. If I remember the numbers right, I believe there are close to 1000 acres of crops that are cycled from season to season for the best use of the soil. The crops are usually harvested twice a year, depending on their growth cycle. This year, the farm is full of rows and rows of an Earth vegetable called corn. I would like to take credit for the industrious effort that was made to establish this project, but it was Lord and Lady Pincey that set up this farm. The food that is harvested here is picked up and distributed to several charities on Earth. I agreed to continue this arrangement with the charities when negotiating the purchase of the planet. I also get a great tax deduction for having property on MP that was dedicated to farming, and another deduction for the yearly charitable donations.

There isn't a lot for me to do to help with the farming, which is a good thing. All the planting and irrigation is done by a handful of robots. The charity that runs the farm has a farming expert on Earth that monitors reports on the crops sent by the automated system's computer. They also visit the farm every other month for a checkup on the crops to make any adjustments in the system, and for robot maintenance.

According to my planet manual, there is one T-3 robot and four Eddison Q4 HAMERs. The HAMERs, or Horticultural and Agricultural Maintenance Equipped Robots, are supposed to be state of the art. The Q4s are built in the shape of a sphere and have A-gravity systems that allow them to hover instead of requiring wheels or tracks. This feature makes them perfect for agricultural work, although it does deplete their power cells and they must charge longer than most robots. I haven't been out to the farm for a good reason. I figured that if anything went wrong and I wasn't there, I would have plausible deniability.

A week or so after we released some of the pheasants in that area, Chuck brought up a potential issue with my birds. He was reading a manual on the HAMER and found that the Q4 models have a pest control system built into their programming. As he explained to me, this program allows them to identify and exterminate with prejudice any potential threat to the crops, not including humans or humanoid individuals. It seems that the M27 laser that the Q4 is equipped with can be used to prune trees and plants, blast invasive weeds, and eliminate pests like black bugs if they ever made it this far south. The good news is that the Q4 robots can be easily updated on what is or isn't on the termination list. Because of the remoteness of the farm, we would have to take a trip out there and manually upload the updates. The next weekend, we were going out to MP to do some fishing, so we planned to run out to the farm one afternoon and get the updates done on the HAMERs. Chuck figured that he could preprogram the updates to protect the birds and any deer that might migrate into the area of the farm. Deer have a tendency to be drawn to agricultural areas, especially where there are crops of corn.

Chuck and I left the girls at the cabin and flew out to the farm. From the air, we could see the rows of corn planted in perfect rows in a grid pattern that was so precise, an architect couldn't have drawn more perfect lines. On the far side of the fields, there was a compound with a gravel landing space surrounded by two sheds and a handful of silos. We landed on the pad and stepped out to have a look around. The plants that surrounded us were tall, and to my untrained eye, they appeared to be close to fully grown. The corn stocks were close to eight feet tall with light green stalks and long, dark green leaves, and each had a golden tassel on top. All the plants had several ears of corn on them, and it appeared that the silos would soon be full of corn.

"Wow! This is beautiful! I'm surprised you haven't spent more time out here," Chuck said as he surveyed our surroundings.

"Well, I never thought looking at a couple of square miles of corn would be that interesting," I replied, shrugging my shoulders.

On Earth, there are a lot of myths about cornfields, and it's amazing how many books and movies have been made using cornfields as a backdrop. According to my Earth history book, during the early 21st century, cornfields were avoided by city dwellers, especially at night, due to the chance of being abducted by aliens. I brought this story up at dinner one evening with some non-Earth friends. They said they had never heard of Earthlings being abducted from a cornfield, or a bass boat. According to galactic law, no Earthling could be abducted, but they could be recruited, and that was usually done in a place called Las Vegas. As I understand it, they never took men but recruited attractive women who were happy to leave Earth and their deadbeat boyfriends.

For those of you who want to look it up, Las Vegas was a city in the desert that is now covered by Great Lake Vegas in Nevada. If you ever go to the lake, you can take an underwater tour and see all the remains of the cool buildings. I suggest you do it on a weekend after dark because the park service lights up the whole city, which is awesome and creepy at the same time.

At the end of one of the rows was a large water tank marked H2O+RB766H, which Chuck explained was the water plus the fertilizer for the crops. Next to the tank was a collection of pipes and valves that were, at that moment, being manipulated by a T-3 robot. As we approached, the robot was busy turning a valve while monitoring a panel of dials that appeared to show the amount of liquid being pumped into the large tank. When we got close enough to the T-3, it turned its head and stared at us just long enough to acknowledge our presence, then turned its attention back to his task. The sound of water and liquid fertilizer being pumped through two pipes at the top of the large container echoed inside the large tank. The contents could be seen through the translucent material. The top of the water moved in waves as the added mixture splashed down.

"So, do we have any upgrades for this fellow here?" I asked, gesturing toward the T-3.

"Nope, he should be good to go," Chuck responded, looking down at his tablet.

"Good, I feel better knowing that the engineers didn't trust the T-3 with a potentially lethal weapon like a laser," I said as we turned back to the compound area. "Stupid robot," I mumbled under my breath.

Chuck just smiled to himself, knowing but not understanding my unfounded prejudice toward robots in general, but especially the T-series. On the opposite side of the compound, there were two sheds that we found held generators and several large pieces of equipment. There were also two hoverbikes on charging stations. I pointed at them.

"We may have to try one of those out," I said, smiling mischievously.

Chuck looked at the two bikes and then back at me.

"Can you even ride a hoverbike?"

"Sure. I had one in college that I took to classes. I probably could manage to ride one without killing myself. How about you? When was the last time you rode yours?"

He thought about it for a second. "It's been a while, but I'm sure I could handle one. Wouldn't those bikes be the property of the foundation?"

I shrugged my shoulders again and smiled. "My planet, my hoverbikes."

On the side of the shed was a bank of charging stations for the Q4s. The bowl-shaped charging pads sat about four feet off the ground. All four of the charge stations were empty. Chuck approached the first station and pushed a red button on the front. A small display appeared on the side of the charging pad. On the bottom of the display, there was a green "summon" button and Chuck went from station to station pressing each one. I watched him as he did this, and as I turned to look across the fields, my heart stopped momentarily. Hovering within inches of my face was a large, shiny ball. It might have been my reflection on the mirror-like side of the robot that startled me the most. The floating robot stared at me, and he was close enough that I could see the lenses in his blue, pill-shaped eyepiece adjust as it seemed to glare at me.

"What the hell!" I shouted, forcing Chuck to turn away from the monitor he was looking at. He chuckled to himself.

"I think you're in the way, Moe. He is trying to get to his station."

I took a step to the side and the Q4 passed me slowly, a quiet hum coming from its levitation system. It landed softly on the #1 charging station, and the green light that came from its undercarriage changed to red as it made contact.

"Those Q4s are stealthy! Remind me to hang a bell on those things so I don't get snuck up on again. I don't think my heart could take it."

Chuck laughed. I don't think he realized how serious I was. Just then, two more Q4s passed me and landed on stations 3 and 4. As they passed, I noticed one of the robots had several small dents in the lower half of its outside shell.

"Hey, Chuck. Look at number three; it has some damage on the bottom half."

He walked over, reached out, and ran his hand across the side of the robot.

"Wow, you're right. These things have a tough cover shell, so whatever hit this thing hit it pretty hard."

Chuck ran his finger over the cone-shaped dimples. "From the look of these dents, whatever hit it had a sharp point on it!" He looked over the other two robots and I turned to look across the endless fields for our missing #2 Q4. There was a slight breeze that moved the tops of the corn in waves, like a snake moving under a green blanket. I used my high-definition binoculars, searching from one side of the vast crop to the other. I assumed that their shiny exterior would make it easy to spot them in the bright sunlight, but it was nowhere in sight.

"Do you think it is finishing a task before it returns?" I asked.

Chuck turned and noticed we were missing one. "No. The summons program should cancel any current commands they are processing," he responded, then turned his attention back to the monitor in front of him. After a few minutes, he finished the updates on the three Q4s.

"Well, it looks like these three are done. They have new parameters on pest control so they should leave all the game animals that are here or that migrate here. They should be safe from the robots anyway," he added, giving me an accusing glance.

"What?" I said, shrugging my shoulders. "Population control is my job. If there are too many animals in one area, they will run out of food. Trust me, it isn't good for the animals if they overpopulate. They would all suffer."

Chuck just rolled his eyes and managed a "Yeah, so you've said" while turning and walking back toward the shuttle. I followed him.

"Okay, smart guy, how should we go about finding our missing bag 'o' bolts?"

"Well, if Tripp was here, we could hang him from a cable under your shuttle and fly around till he spotted it. Or we could take the hoverbikes if they're still functioning and see if we can locate it."

"Cool!" I replied. "Did you see any protective gear in the shed?"

"No, but the way you drive, I can't imagine that a helmet would save your life anyway!"

I nodded in agreement. We made the short walk back to the shed, and as Chuck checked out the bikes to make sure they were flyable, I went back to the shuttle and got two safety vests out of one of my shuttle storage compartments. The vests are designed to expand to cushion an individual in case of a rapid descent. Research has taught us that no one dies from falling—it's the abrupt stop that can be damaging to the body. I put my vest on and powered it up, then took the other back for Chuck. While I was at it, I grabbed one of my rifles from the gun storage on my shuttle and slung it over one shoulder, just in case.

With safety vests on and the hoverbikes passing Chuck's inspection, we took off across the property, cruising about twenty feet off the ground. Chuck sped ahead of me, then quickly slowed down. I had to swerve in the air to avoid hitting him from behind.

"Sorry. I'm getting used to the controls," he said, now leaning a bit to one side. The monitor for the charging station didn't have a date for its last charge, so there was no way to tell how long the Q4 had been missing. We had decided to start at one end of the field and work our way up and down the rows looking for number two. Riding in a parallel path, we had covered almost a third of the property when we noticed an abnormality in the perfectly lined rows of corn. In the far corner of the section of the lot, there was an open area in the crops with a piece of bare ground approximately four rows wide. This wouldn't be unusual in a corn crop on Earth because it could be blamed on mechanical or human error while planting. It appeared that something had interrupted the planting cycle, or the plants had been removed for some reason. It was possible the corn could have been hit by lightning in one of the scheduled storms, although there was no scorched Earth.

I landed my bike at the end of the field and walked to the open patch of ground to have a closer look at this area. Chuck stayed in the air and searched from above. One of the things I noticed quickly was that the dirt around the empty patch had a lot of deer tracks. We hadn't seen any deer so far in our search for the Q4, so they must not feed during the day, or the sound of the hoverbikes might have sent them running for cover. In the bare patch, I found several holes where it appeared that some corn stocks had been pulled out of the ground. All that remained was a hole surrounded by dark, fertile dirt that the roots must have dropped during their removal.

I waved at Chuck, who was circling the area around my location, and he made a turn and headed back my direction. He descended a bit as he approached, and when he stopped, he was in front of me, hovering just above the top of the corn stocks.

"What do you think?" Chuck said, loud enough to be heard over the hum of the hoverbike.

"There's nothing here but some holes in the ground and missing corn stalks," I shouted back. "If you want to go check out that last section of the fields, I will look around here. There are a bunch of signs of deer down here, and it looks like they lead in the direction of that group of trees over there," I said as I pointed at a small grove behind me. Chuck gave me a thumbs up, the universal sign of "Okey-dokey," turned his bike, and sped off toward the next field.

I turned and walked the short distance back to my ride. I lifted off, but instead of making a beeline toward the trees, I did more of a serpentine maneuver to get a look at the grass and bushes that surrounded the cornfields. In the quarter mile between the stand of trees and the field, I spotted two well-defined game trails that led through the tall grass and brush from the cornfields to the cover of the trees. I stopped just outside the grove and peered into the grassy area just inside the tree line. After a few seconds, some movement caught my attention. The nervous twitch of a deer's tail gave away the whole herd. I pulled up my binoculars and hit a button on the top. The button flashed red, then turned a solid green. I put them up to my eyes as the picture came into focus. The deer's body temperature made it easy for my scope to separate them from the cooler vegetation around them.

I decided the best way to approach the group was to fly toward them; then, if they moved, I could change altitude and observe them from above. I flew in a straight line, crossing the distance in a few seconds. The herd remained motionless as I got closer. I stopped a few yards before the first tree and lowered my altitude until I could see under the treetops. The deer remained still, so I lowered the hoverbike once more, coming to rest on the ground.

Through the trees, I could see one deer; in the back was a large buck, and he was the first to move. To my surprise, instead of leading his crew away from me, the large whitetail began walking in my direction. I scanned the herd, and it appeared that the rest of the group were all females. He was an older deer, and from what I could tell from my position, he seemed to be in rough shape. His antlers were massive, and in a few places, he was forced to tilt his head to the side to get through the trees. I removed my rifle from my shoulder, letting the barrel rest on the handlebars of my bike. The large buck moved with a purpose as he followed the trail through the trees. I was parallel to the trail, and I estimated that he would come into the opening approximately twenty yards down the tree line from me. As I predicted, the buck emerged into the open field a short distance away. The big deer never lost eye contact with me, even as he stood broadside, which I found kind of intimidating. His features were dark, and he had a visible scar that ran from his forehead, then over his right eye and down his jaw. That eye was clouded and it was obvious that he had lost sight in it. On his exposed front shoulder and side, he had two burn spots where he was missing hair, and the skin was black. He slowly turned his head, looking behind me, and I noticed he had broken off at least one point on the side of his massive rack.

I followed his line of vision, and as I turned, I saw Chuck on his hoverbike slowly descending to my position. He came to rest next to me. He was also staring at the large deer. Chuck looked at the disheveled animal, and then at me sitting on my bike, my rifle in my hands.

"Wow, Moe! What did you do to that poor deer?" he said, his eyes wide open with surprise.

I looked at him, then at the deer, then back at him. "For your information, he looked like that before I got here!" I replied.

"I'm just saying, the poor animal looks like he has been in a fight with something. So if you didn't shoot him up, what do you think happened to him?"

I shook my head signaling that I didn't know myself. "As you searched the other fields, did you see any laser fencing?" I asked, considering anything that could be blamed for the buck's burns.

Chuck thought for a second. "No, I didn't see any around the fields or in the yard by the sheds and storage bins. But then again, why would the foundation's farm engineers install fences when, historically, there are no animals in this area to protect the crops from?" Chuck said, raising one eyebrow and giving me a sideways glance.

"Well, I guess that's true," I replied.

The deer was still staring at us while raising its head and snorting loudly. Then he bowed his head, shook his large rack of antlers, and began to stomp a front hoof in the dirt, stirring a small cloud of dust. We turned and looked at each other, and in unison, pressed on the pedals of our bikes to raise up in the air just high enough to be out of reach of a possible crazy buck attack. The deer, however, remained in place, never losing eye contact with us.

"So, what's your plan? Are you going to blast him?" Chuck asked, still watching the deer.

"I thought about it, but he is the only buck in that herd, so I think I should probably pass on him today."

Chuck nodded, then his face scrunched up as if in deep thought. "I think it is reasonable to assume that he's responsible for the damage to the Q4."

I nodded in agreement. "I noticed when I first saw him that he has broken at least one tip off of his antlers. If you compare it with the other side, it looks like he is missing about four to six inches.

"So, what's your plan, Moe?" Chuck asked, leaning back on the hoverbike's backrest while glancing my direction. I thought about it for a moment, leaned back in my seat, and raised my rifle to my shoulder. The optics on my rifle were exceptional, which has always given me confidence in my shooting. I took careful aim and fired my first shot. The buck's head snapped back as the antler on his left side broke off about three inches above the base. The one side, now separated, fell to the ground behind him. The defiant deer stood and turned his body to face us, his head leaning slightly to the right from the weight of his remaining rack. Before he could decide whether to fight or flee, I took careful aim and fired again. My shot hit the deer in the antler an inch lower than my last shot. The antler didn't separate like the last one but when the lopsided deer felt the blow, he began to shake his head back and forth and the top-heavy antler snapped with a loud crack and fell to the side.

"Good shot, Moe!" Chuck said, smiling. The deer stood for a moment shaking his now much lighter head. With a final stomp and a snort, he turned and walked back to the cover of the trees and his waiting harem. I put my rifle back on my shoulder and the two of us landed our bikes and retrieved the separated deer antlers. I tied both antlers to the front of my hoverbike and we rode back to the compound, abandoning our quest for the missing Q4.

Back at the shed, we parked our hoverbikes and carried our safety vests and the deer antlers to the shuttle. While walking across the pad, Chuck stopped suddenly. He stood in place for a moment as he managed the thoughts in his head. I could see his thoughts come together in his mind through the expression on his face.

"Wait a second. I have an idea. Why don't you put this stuff in the shuttle, and I'm going to go check out the compost silos." There were two large silos on the lot that were labeled "Compost

#1" and "Compost #2." The purpose of a compost silo is to store all the parts of individual crops that are not considered to be edible or have nutritious value to humans. These parts are collected after the vegetable or fruit has been harvested and are placed in a silo. These parts, like corn stalks and other organic material, decay to become used as animal feed and fertilizer. And on some planets, it is sold as a delicacy to the residents whose tastes are less refined than myself. Not to sound arrogant but my pallet does not include compost. If you ever see the word Muck or Muck Salad on a menu, trust me, you should avoid it at all costs. There is an aftertaste you may never get rid of. The process of making compost can generate a lot of heat, which gives compost a special kind of aroma.

I opened the storage compartment of my shuttle and put the safety vests and two antlers in and closed it up. I was anxious to see what my good buddy Chuck had come up with, so I hurried back in his direction. When I caught up with him, he was standing in front of compost silo #1 pushing the open button on the access door that was at ground level of the 40-foot silo. Normally at this point, before the corn is harvested, the silos should be empty. Chuck pushed the button and then stood clear of the door in case the contents spilled out onto the ground. As the door opened, we were surprised to find that nothing fell out of what I had assumed would be the silo's filthy interior. On the contrary, when we peered through the opening to the large inner space of the storage space, it was clean. It was not only clean but polished and sanitized, with no odor in the slightest.

"Wow, you could eat off the floor of this thing," I said in appreciation of some robot's thorough cleaning job.

Chuck looked over at me and shrugged his shoulders. "Well,

if you are going to make food grade garbage, I would assume that there has to be some general production regulations on maintaining sanitary or salubrious conditions."

I nodded my reply, as if I understood what he had just said. I laughed to myself. Sometimes I forget that Chuck reads governmental regulations manuals for fun.

I pushed the button and the large door slid shut. We moved onto the second silo, expecting to find similar conditions. We both stood in the doorway as the magnetic seal unlocked. Unlike the other silo, the air that flowed out of the large storage area was heavy with the scent of fermentation. The bottom three feet of the silo was full of corn stalks that were busy decomposing. Instead of bright green, the leaves were a dull yellow and the stalks a flat brown.

"It appears that all of the corn that has died and been removed from the fields is put here to start decomposing," Chuck said as he surveyed the pile of debris.

"Well, it's good that nothing is wasted," I replied.

Chuck was looking carefully over the pile of dead corn.

"Did you have a reason to expose my nose and clothes to this powerful aroma?" I said, thinking I may have to burn my shirt and pants to remove the stench of compost.

Chuck looked over at me with a satisfying grin on his face. "Yes, as a matter of fact. I found your missing Hamer," he said as he pointed toward the far side of the silo's interior. My eyes followed the line of his finger and saw a small portion of a shiny object mostly covered by decaying corn stocks. "I figured since there was no dead or damaged corn in the fields," Chuck continued, "that the Q4s would have put them in here to recycle."

I nodded, showing that I was following his reasoning.

"Because the Q4s are not well known for their processing systems, they would more than likely do the same to a nonfunctioning robot."

"Good job, Chuck," I said. "That was a fine bit of detective work." I lovingly punched him on his arm. "So how do we get that oversized Christmas ornament out of there?"

Chuck looked back toward the charging stations and the other robots. "I can put one of the other Q4s in manual voice mode and send it in to pull it out," Chuck replied as he turned and walked back to the shed. As I waited, I took a step back from the open door to get a breath of fresh air. After a few minutes, Chuck returned with one of the Q4s in tow. He stopped in front of the door and then commenced to give the robot a series of commands. At first, I thought I misheard him as he spoke, but as I leaned in, I could tell Chuck was using a completely different dialect to talk to Q4 #4. The robot seemed to understand. It turned and entered the silo. Chuck looked over at me and smiled at my obvious confusion. I think he finds my simpler mind to be entertaining at times. In my defense, I really excel at practical problem solving, as the philosopher musician Paul Simon once sang "my lack of education hasn't really hurt me none." I do own my planet, after all.

"It took me a minute or two to figure out that Q4s only understand Bauchie," he said as we both turned to watch the robot.

"Well, luckily, you know Bauchie," I said, stating the obvious with a hint of sarcasm.

"Yup," he replied with a small smirk on his face. The Q4 positioned itself directly over the half-buried metal corpse as a small panel opened on its lower half. A small beam of light shown from inside the open spot on the hovering robot as it opened in a cone shape and wrapped around the Q4 below it. The Q4 rose in the air, pulling the goo-smeared robot from the pile of fermented corn stocks. He moved toward us, lowering his altitude slightly to clear the doorway. When the two robots cleared the door, the Q4 released its laser net, dropping its load with a thud on the ground. Chuck spoke again to the robot, giving it a new command. The robot beeped twice, acknowledging that he understood. Another small panel on the robot opened and a stream of what I assume was hot water sprayed the Q4 Hamer on the ground, cleaning its shiny outer shell. When it finished, the Q4 beeped once again and then moved to the side as the two of us began our visual assessment. The issue wasn't hard to assess with a piece of angry deer antler protruding out of the side of its shiny shell.

"Well, there's your problem!" I said in my best hillbilly voice, pointing at the collection of small dents, and specifically the chunk of antler. Chuck gave me a sideways glance.

"Yup! Good work, Moe," he replied, nodding his head. "I guess the question is, do we leave it here and bring back the parts to fix it, or do we take it with us and make the repairs at home?"

I thought about it for a moment then decided. "If we take it back to Earth, we'll have to sneak it through customs, and that would be a real pain. My vote is that you look it over and make a list of parts, and we will come back and fix it."

Chuck nodded in agreement. He gave a new set of orders to the Q4 that was standing by, and once again, the robot hooked its tow net to the dead robot and returned to the shed. As we walked back in that direction, we stopped at my shuttle and Chuck retrieved his small toolkit out of one of his bags. The T-3 had finished the needed adjustments on the fertilization systems and was now moving in a parallel course, as we were, toward the charging area. The T-3 tracks systems were well designed for the dirt and gravel ground, and it moved at a slightly faster pace than ours. It reached the charging area and began to download a current report into the main computer system.

"It should only take me a minute or two to take the top off the Q4 and get us a parts list to make the repairs," Chuck said, thinking out loud.

As we approached the robot charging area, I noticed that #4 had set #2 on its station and its light showed red to indicate it was charging. When I saw this, I stopped walking and stared.

"Do you think it's a good idea to charge #2 before we get it repaired?"

Chuck stopped for a second. "Good question. We might want to take it off the charger till we get the new parts, although it would be good to know if we need to replace its power source, and deal with the other issues."

With our missing Q4 found, Chuck typed the release code into the other three robots individually, and they left immediately to return to whatever tasks they had left to complete in the fields. While he finished that, I looked over the damage done to #2—from the dents in its exterior to the broken chunk of antler that had penetrated the metal shell in the right lower undercarriage. It looked like it had been in a real brawl. The part of the antler that was visible was long enough that I could grab it with my hand. With a twisting motion, I was able to pull it free, leaving a thumb-size hole in the shiny metal skin.

Immediately after I had removed the piece of antler, the eyepiece of the Q4 lit up red, its whole body rising a few inches off the charging pad. It happened so quickly that I had to step back in surprise. The reanimated robot turned rapidly from side to side, scanning its surroundings. It passed over Chuck and stopped, facing me. I moved to my left and he moved with me, rotating in the air. I could see the green light come on at the base of the laser mount, which indicated it was fully charged. I ducked just in time and heard a laser blast hit the side of the shed behind me, the impact on the metal sheeting leaving a pencil-sized hole and sending sparks all over the ground. The frantic robot rotated, once again finding me in its crosshairs. At this moment, I was contemplating what it would be like to be genetically reincarnated for a second time when the Q4 turned suddenly and fired again. The second blast hit the ground to my side, the laser beam throwing up a cloud of rock and dust. Chuck had grabbed it from behind and turned it before it could make me dead.

The Q4 was struggling, attempting to free itself from Chuck's grip. The T-3 robot had left its charging station and was moving behind me to my left, trying to escape. Its arms were extended straight up in a sign of distress, and it made a whistling sound that was very similar to a teenage girl screaming. I recognize this reaction since Shabby, my T-2 robot, had the same reaction when I had him downrange, holding my rifle targets. It's my theory that the engineers who designed the T-series robots programmed them with a self-preservation mode. With the higher price tag for these robots, their programming won't allow them to knowingly sacrifice themselves and/or risk being damaged. Because of this, you should not rely on a T-series to protect you, or to knowingly place itself in a dangerous situation.

"Moe, hit the kill switch!" Chuck yelled as the robot attempted to escape by moving forward, dragging Chuck as he tried to get traction on the loose gravel ground. The laser-armed flying ball of death fired again. This time, it cut through a corner of a storage shed and the cornstalks on the edge of the closest field. The tall, skinny plants fell like dominoes five cornstalks wide and ten rows deep. I caught up from behind, reached up, and attempted to find the kill switch.

"It's on the other side!" Chuck yelled again.

I reached around the far side, found the button, and pressed it. The Q4 instantly dropped, falling hard enough to bounce once on the hard ground with the unmistakable sound of metal hitting rock. Chuck looked over at me, bent slightly at the waist, and out of breath.

"I know, stupid robot!" he said, smirking at me. I nodded.

"Well, this time I have to agree with you!" he said, shaking his head in disbelief.

"I looked over at Chuck. "I should really update my personal memory file more often, I would hate to lose my memory if I get killed again."

Chuck smiled at me. "I update my PMF every time I go anywhere with you, Moe!"

I paused for a moment in thought, and then nodded my head. "Makes sense!"

With our history, it really did make sense. I helped Chuck roll the Q4 on the ground until it sat right-side-up, and then he went to work on it. After a few minutes, he removed the top of the Q4s casing and did a visual check of the inside computer panels and relays. One of the control components had a small, thumb-size hole through the motherboard, and even in shutdown mode, it still sparked intermittently from one side of the hole to another. Chuck pulled a small scanner out of his toolbag and held it over the Q4, moving it back and forth till all the internal parts were scanned.

"It looks like the power source is still intact as well as the guidance, so the only part that should be replaced is the processing systems board."

"That was my thought too," I replied while putting one of my index fingers through the hole in the translucent processing unit board. When I pulled my finger out of the hole, a small bolt of electricity arced from the panel, hitting the end of my finger and burning my fingertip. Looking back, I should have thought it out before I put forth the effort to be so sarcastic. Chuck laughed and reached down, unplugging a cable from a control panel.

"That should keep it from powering up until we get these parts replaced. We should probably unplug its laser as well."

"Vat ounds hike a goo igea," I replied around the finger that was in my mouth, to cool the scorched tip. With my non-burned hand, I helped him lift the top of the Q4's hood and secured it to the bottom half. The compact chemical laser was mounted on the top, and before we finished mounting the hood, Chuck pulled the connecting power cable. I managed to take my finger out of my mouth long enough to help Chuck carry the Q4 over and put it on the floor in one of the sheds.

"I'll get the parts picked up and we can get it back in service next time we're out," Chuck said as we walked back to the shuttle. "How is your finger, dummy?" he said, glancing over at me, a small grin still on his face.

"It's fine," I replied as I examined my finger and what ended up being a permanent white dot on the tip. "Luckily, Tressa keeps a supply of burn gel back at the cabin. That should take the pain away, at least," Chuck nodded in agreement.

"Oh, I almost forgot something," Chuck said as he changed directions and headed toward one of the silos. He looked around the back side of the silos and said, "There you are." The T-3 was on the far side with its back against the silo wall, its arms still raised as if surrendering. Chuck opened the panel in the robot's chest and hit a reset button, holding it until the Q4's arms lowered. Chuck closed the small panel and the robot turned and returned to its charging station.

29 The Great Polar Bear Experiment

Before I share this story with you, I need to explain a few things. To start with, none of the information I have used to write this chapter came from my friend Chuck. Because Chuck has signed a confidentiality and nondisclosure agreement with his employer, it keeps him from discussing anything with me about the NTEG Corporation its projects, or its management. This is something that he takes very seriously, and which has been a source of continuous frustration for me, being the nosey son of a gun that I am. Much of this stuff is information that has been made public through the internet and from a story I saw on *In Our Galaxy*, which is a syndicated newsmagazine show that most of you have probably watched.

In 2188, one of the most brilliant genetic engineers in Earth's history was born. His name was William Frodo Wolfgang III. No, I didn't make that up. Anyway, Bill was the firstborn son of two famous scientists, Dr. Pamela Wolfgang, and Dr. William J. Wolfgang II. This couple is well known in the science community for their contribution to the genetic reincarnation systems that we have today. It was obvious at even a young age that their son, Bill, would exceed their expectations as far as his intelligence and achievements. By the age of twenty, he had acquired his doctorate in both genetic engineering and biochemistry. His bachelor's degree was in contemporary paleontology.

By the age of twenty-four, he had started a successful genetics company called NTEG that specialized in non-traditional genetics and biotechnology. NTEG is the same company that my buddy Chuck has managed to stay happily employed with for the past few years. Like most scientists, Dr. Wolfgang has several pet projects that he is very passionate about. The most important to him were the issues dealing with the radical decline of an Earth's species called the polar bear. Some scientists believed that the decline in the bear population was due to climate change, but most of those theories were proven wrong because the polar ice caps had increased in size and the polar bear's environment had improved over the past century. These facts have made it difficult but not impossible for the current generation of scientists to follow industry protocol. It has always been standard procedure to blame every environmental issue on past generations of humans that presumably had a lack of interest.

The most recent theory concerning the decline of the polar bear was the radical depletion of phytoplankton in the far north waters of the arctic. What has caused this tiny organism to slowly disappear from the cold waters of the arctic is unknown, but its effect on the ecosystem in Earth's frozen caps is immeasurable. But that's probably more science than you wanted from reading my book so let me sum up: krill eat phytoplankton, fish eat krill, seals eat fish, and polar bears eat seals. Speaking environmentally, less plankton equals less polar bears.

Dr. Wolfgang was not interested in the cause of the population decline. He was more invested in what could be done genetically to create a species of polar bears that could survive in other environments. To do this, they would have to be omnivores like most bear species instead of being hypercarnivores genetically. At that time, there were approximately 120 polar bears that were known to be surviving in the wild. Through his government connections, Dr. Wolfgang was able to acquire the permits to trap a healthy male and female polar bear. These bears were transported to a temperature-controlled lab at NTEG's largest facility. The bears, #001 and #002, or as they are lovingly referred to, Momma and Papa Bear, were monitored and had blood and tissue samples taken. With these samples, the scientists at NTEG were able to retrieve and recreate a modified genetic code for a new species of polar bear. The process is very similar to genetic reincarnation for humans. When I questioned Chuck, he repeatedly told me this process is patented and has a whole boatload of trade secrets. So, I haven't got any more information on the process to share.

Not long after I purchased MP, Chuck told me that his boss had heard of my planet and wanted to possibly set up a meeting with me. What Chuck didn't tell me is that my planet came up during a meeting at NTEG where Chuck received an award and a promotion for his great work on my raptors. Chuck is very modest about his accomplishments. After this meeting, Dr. Wolfgang pulled him aside and asked him about MP, particularly the global climates, polar region size, and so forth. As I understand it, he also asked Chuck if I was under any governmental regulations on my planet.

There are a considerable number of benefits for private businesses to lease property on privately-owned planets—no government oversight being the biggest. As Chuck explained it, NTEG was working on a project on Earth and had built a state-of-the-art test facility in the arctic circle, and he was interested in setting up a second facility, possibly on my planet. Chuck bragged that the project was well-funded and my compensation for making my polar region on MP available to NTEG would pay my planet mortgage for close to fourteen years. I believe my response was, "Ah, hell ya!" Actually, I might have just thought that. What I said was, "Thank you for the offer. I will consider it."

Chuck arranged a meeting with Dr. Wolfgang, his assistant, Dr. Jeneane Starland, Dr. Mark Scott, Chuck, and myself. The plan was that the group from NTEG would spend the weekend on MP and visit possible sites for the polar camp, and a second option in a more temperate climate. This meeting never happened due to some issues that came up at the NTEG Polar Bear Observation Camp on Earth.

The PBOC had been designed to allow fourteen individuals to comfortably live in the extreme frigid temperatures of the arctic while still having full access to the polar bears. Six of these individuals were scientists, including two veterinarians, and the other eight were building and robot maintenance, animal care, and food service employees. Dr. Mark Scott and his wife, Dr. Natascha Scott, are the on-site directors at the PBOC. This couple has devoted their adult lives to the study of polar bears and are known to be the leading authority on this species. The buildings that housed the employees, the observatory, and the lab were all located in the middle of the confinement area. Each section of the camp was connected through large, tube-like tunnels with the observatory.

The polar bears had been brought to the camp from the NTEG lab and released into the five-acre confinement pen. Momma and Papa bear were moved to the compound a month before the new bears were scheduled to arrive. The activities of the polar bear pair were closely monitored to establish the independent and dependent variables and characteristic patterns that the new bears would be tested on. The facility stored enough food for the bears to eat comfortably for at least a year. A polar bear can consume up to twenty-five percent of their body weight in one meal, which is close to 150 pounds of food. The test bears would be fed edible plants and berries every other day, as well as frozen salmon and whale meat once a week.

There were eight bears in total. Two were male and six were females. In nature, the male polar bear is approximately 990 pounds and females are 550 on the high end. The males can reach close to ten feet high, and the females a bit shorter. The NTEG generation of bears, nicknamed "omni-bears," were ten percent larger in both weight and height. I guess even scientists sometimes go with the "go big or go home" mentality. It wasn't the size of the bears that ended up being the issue in the project. Polar bears in the wild are very intelligent. It turned out that the omni-bears were even more so. The omni-bears also showed a high level of unpredictability in their day-to-day activities, which was a source of concern for Dr. Natascha Scott. These were possible side effects of messing with genetics.

At first, the scientists at NTEG were excited to find that this new breed of polar bears exceeded their expectations in problem-solving and memory in their tests. One test that was used was to place food in three different containers around the compound. The large boxes were full of vegetables, wild berries, and blue whale meat, or whole salmon. Before you question how they acquired the whale meat, I believe it came from an aquarium where it had died of natural causes. Since they had to cut the thing up anyway to get it out of the tank, the Earth's Environmental Alliance allowed it to be used for the project.

For the bears to open the containers, several different tasks had to be performed. One container had a bolt with a locking pin, and another had a top that had to be unscrewed. The last container had a large, four-button keypad with a simple four-digit code that would allow it to be unlocked. If the wrong four-digit code was entered, a buzzer would sound and a red light on the container would light up. If the code was successfully entered, the light showed green and the lid clicked, indicating it was unlocked. The keypad had a memory system that would record the code that had been entered and then, once it had been opened, to change the code automatically. This way, the scientist could tell if the bears pushed random numbers or if they adjusted their attempts based on memory.

The first two containers were opened quite quickly; the third took more time. When the researchers reviewed their test results, they found that the bears had pushed the buttons in what seemed to be random orders, but the data showed that the bear that was attempting to open the box never pushed the same sequence of numbers twice. Once the proper code had been entered and the food was taken, the code was changed, the food was replaced, and the container was locked. The code was changed by only one digit each time. When the bear attempted to open it a second time, it used the code that had previously worked for its first attempt the previous day, and then attempted new codes if that one failed. The bears were also observed becoming agitated when the previous code didn't work. The codes were simple, and the lock was programmed to open on the tenth attempt, but the fail-safe number was only used nineteen percent of the time. To sum up, the omni bears were smart and had great practical problem-solving skills.

By the second week of the project, the NTEG researchers reported that the bears had started to develop interesting behavior patterns. Two of the females would station themselves in front of one of the large observation windows, one on each side of the building, and watch the scientist inside with great intent, like children looking through a candy store window. The two males would walk the perimeter of the compound for what the employees determined was to inspect the fence for possible weakness. The remaining bears would gather food and remove it from the container, but wouldn't eat until the other bears had returned to that part of the compound.

To the surprise of the researchers, the omni-bears and the regular polar bears rarely interacted with each other. The original idea of combining the bears with their genetic relatives was that the polar bears raised in the wild would mentor the younger bears in survival skills and social interactions. The omni-bears were often observed standing guard over their food source to keep the polar bears from eating. The polar bears seemed to be intimidated by the larger, more aggressive omni-bears, and segregated themselves to a far corner of the compound. The modified, all-terrain service robots that delivered feed had to have their programming changed to feed the polar bears separately from the other bears.

This part of my story is where the facts about the actual events become a little cloudy. I am not implying in any way that the record of events made public by the NTEG Corporation about events at the PBOC site was misleading in any way. The information made public by the NTEG Corporation states that the omni-bears became so aggressive toward the polar bears that the pair had to be removed and relocated back to the wild where they were originally captured. The report basically states that the Polar Bear Project has been temporarily put on hold. The genetically advanced polar bears, or omni-bears, project has been a great success to this point, and the information that we have obtained from this project is considered to be invaluable to the science community. Be assured that at no point have any of the NTEG staff been in danger, and they have all been reassigned to new projects for NTEG. The rumor that the omni-bear Project was anything other than a great success is grossly exaggerated. The on-site directors, Dr. Mark Scott, and his wife, Natascha Scott, are excited to continue their work on the omni-bear Project. They are currently off the planet on vacation getting some much-deserved rest, but they will be back to work soon. The bears have been placed in suspended animation hibernation for continuing study.

The story told by the *In Our Galaxy* investigative report is a little more gruesome! The reporter stated that, according to unnamed sources that were part of the project, the researchers and staff noticed changes in the omni-bear's activities and behaviors starting in week four of the study. The source states that on week five, the researchers began to add a chemical compound to the omni-bears' food that was designed to reduce aggression in the test subjects. Unfortunately, researchers found that the bears, with their hyper-senses, sniffed out the additive and wouldn't eat the contaminated meat or berries. On day thirty-nine, the service robots found Papa and Momma bear in the blood-stained snow, mangled and mostly eaten.

The omni-bears had also begun to focus their efforts on attempts to enter the facilities, first through the outer doors and windows. The doors and windows of the observatory were made from steel-glass, so even with their powerful legs and sharp claws, the bears were only able to leave small scratches in the clear windows. One of the large males charged head-first into the glass and metal wall panels several times. On his third attempt, he managed to knock himself out cold, but other than shaking the building a little, he was unsuccessful!

The second attempt involved following the robots as they entered the building through their small, automatic doors. The robots had been programmed to stop in the doorway while a high-pressure ice removal system cleared the ice and snow off them. This process intimidated the bears and kept them from following the robots through the entrance at first. After several attempts, one of the more aggressive females charged the entrance just as the door opened, pushing the unsuspecting robot through the opening. Two maintenance workers were in the middle of replacing a track on a shuttle lift when the gigantic animal charged through the doorway. The robot in front of him was sent crashing to the ground. The omni-bear didn't seem to pay any attention to them as they ran screaming from the building, locking the metal door behind them.

Once inside, the huge omni-bear turned back to the helpless android that was still trying to right itself, and with one swipe from her massive paw, the head of the robot was torn from its body. There was a shower of sparks from the exposed wires that extended from the robot's shoulders. The bear grabbed the lifeless metal head in her mouth and walked back to the now-sealed door. When it got close enough to the door, the security censor lit up as the great white beast lifted the mechanical head up so the scanner could read the code laser-engraved on the robot's forehead. A flashing green light above the door came on and a buzzer sounded as the door opened. The remaining omni-bear tribe entered one at a time, the largest males barely squeezing their bodies through the small doorway.

The building that the bears now occupied was both the food storage and a garage where the shuttles were stored out of the harsh arctic weather. The NTEG staff watched their monitors in terror as the omni-bears made themselves at home in the large space. Dr. Scott immediately sent a message to NTEG headquarters and notified them of the breach of the facility. His wife, Natascha, following project protocol, began to take DNA samples from all the staff, including herself and her husband, who was irritated to have his transmission interrupted to have his mouth swabbed. The samples were locked in a wall safe in the lab.

It was obvious that there was going to be no safe access to the shuttles. The only hope that the POV staff had was to keep the omni-bears out of the staff-occupied part of the facility until the NTEG security team arrived. Alarms sounded around the compound and Dr. Scott's voice could be heard over the intercom system giving orders to the staff to gather in the observation area. The NTEG-POV facility was designed to be impregnable from the outside. The inside, however, was not. There was no known reason to have to restrict access from one area to an adjoining space. The inside walls of the garage, as well as most of the buildings, were made up of high-density foam acoustic panels to restrict noise and control air temperature. However, they were not designed to stop a 1400-pound bear with dagger-sized claws and a bad attitude. There was a locker in the facility that held several high-powered MP406 tranquilizer guns. This gun uses a non-lethal electronic pulse, and if set on high, it has the ability to stop a charging rhino! Unfortunately, for safety reasons, the gun locker was placed in the rear of the currently bear-occupied shuttle garage. This fact wasn't as important as you might think since none of the staff had been trained to use the MP406 and would have probably ended up shooting themselves or someone else anyway—or they would have been eaten by the time they figured it out.

According to the investigative reporter from *In Our Galaxy*, the last transmission from the POB camp was as follows.

"We have been breached in our facility by the test subjects. There is little to no reason to expect the NTEG security team will reach us in time to save our lives. Having reached this conclusion, we have initiated Protocol 911S and have completed the required downloads to preserve our personal intellectual properties to simplify genetic reincarnation for ourselves and our staff. Hopefully, we will see you soon."

Dr. Mark Scott, NTEG-POVC Director of Operations.

Do's and Don'ts of Planet Ownership

I thought it would be helpful if I made a list of things that could help those of you who are planning on purchasing a planet. Or you possibly might inherit one if someone close to you gives up the ghost. No, I'm not trying to give my relatives and friends any bad ideas—MP1X is already in a trust. The meek are supposed to end up with the Earth, so if you are meek, pay close attention to this chapter. Some items on this list I have learned from my Planet Functions Manual, but most are trial and error on my part.

1. Do not grow or purchase anything that will live on your planet that is more dangerous than you are. It's true that it sounds adventurous to have something hunting you, but trust me, it gets old fast.
2. Do not buy a plant, fish, or animal for your planet that you do not have a complete history of, including

its planet of origin and what it was used for, or the purpose that it served, on that planet. Just because the salesperson tells you it is human-safe doesn't make it true.

3. Make sure the pests on your planet are edible. It will help you stay motivated in keeping their population in check. If you are relying on nature to control the circle of life, it can take up to 400 years to balance out, so take that into consideration.
4. Never trust a talking fish.
5. Make sure that the price of your planet includes your utilities. (Sunlight, oxygen if you need it, a lease on a moon or moons, and trash removal). If you need to pay for these things separately from your mortgage, it can get expensive and can affect your resale value.
6. Be positive that there are no other residents living on the planet that have not been identified. When you are dealing with Trillion realtors on planet development, it is common for them to sublease without your knowledge. It's worth the extra cost to have a security firm do a complete sweep of the planet and identify other possible residents.
7. If possible, inspect the entire planet, paying close attention to the plant types, animal species, and even the water in all of its different forms. To those of you who have never been off-planet, water is not always blue, and the grass is not always green. Trillions love monochromatic colors and will make an entire continent the same color, including the plants, animals,

soil, water and so forth. If the color doesn't bother you, you can get a good deal on a midsize, one-color planet. Remember, if you spend any length of time on a one-color planet, no matter what your species is, you will eventually become that color.

8. Always insist on having a weather calendar or weather controls for the planet. Some of you like to be surprised by the weather changes, and I can appreciate that, but you still should have the calendar, even if you don't look at it. Along the same lines, you need a schedule of the planet. This will include daylight hours, length of days, planet rotation variations, seasonal changes, etc. If your planet is going to stop rotating in fifty years and gravity is going to turn off, you are going to want to know.
9. Unless your planet comes with some, do not buy whales. There is nothing more high-maintenance than a whale. Salespeople will tell you that all you need is plenty of saltwater and a good supply of krill to keep them happy, but it's a lie. It can take twenty years to grow enough krill to keep a whale fed, and if you run out, you must buy food for it off the market, and that's expensive. Most whales, because of their intelligence, are protected, no matter what planet they are on, and you will be subjected to random inspections; not to mention if, heaven forbid, one dies, you will be in for a whole boatload of paperwork. Salespeople will show you pics of majestic mammals as they reach the surface of the water, blowing magnificent clouds of mist in the air. They may have shots of the whales with their huge

tails lifted in the air, preparing for a deep dive, but trust me—no whale is worth the hassle.

10. Always buy a type-B planet—an engineered planet that is at least 200 Earth years old. If it hasn't been out of production and in orbit for that long, it's still settling and will be subject to earthquakes, volcanoes, and oxygen fluctuations. You may survive a type-A planet, but it would not be a picnic in the park. The older the planet, the more the cost, but planets are better if you let them age. Always check the production date on a planet with the Trillion Planet Control Committee, and ask your realtor for their contact information.
11. Be sure that you know if your planet is part of a POA. I am fortunate to be in a Planet Owners Association that is more hands-off than most. We also get a better deal as a group on items we need for our galaxy. Some planet owners really don't want some other group trying to tell you how to run your planet. Realtors will try to tell you it's a good idea and that it will improve the value of your planet. In my experience, associations are usually made up of species that just want to boss each other around. The thing you like most about your planet may be the very thing that makes your neighbors want to blow you and your planet up into tiny bits. About eighty-five percent of the galactic wars over the past 430 Earth years have been started between two or three planets in the same POA.
12. Choose a planet that is similar if not a copy of your home world. The Our Way Design firm that built MP

is the best at duplicating a planet with some small modifications on your part. It's been documented that long-term exposure to a foreign planet can cause melancholy, and in extreme cases, insanity, in humans. It always helps to have something similar that you can see on a regular basis like a mountain, a lake, or even a house or building. On MP, I have a mountain range very similar to the Rocky Mountains on Earth. This range of mountains is very close to my parent's home on Earth, and having it there makes it feel like home.

13. Having a settlement on your planet, either human or a similar species, is never as easy as settlers will tell you. There will always be issues that you need to deal with if there is someone other than yourself and your family living on your planet. It's nice to have other renters or sub-leasers to help spread out the annual planet costs. If you do decide to lease out some of your planet, make sure you are informed about any changes they plan to make. You don't need anyone to watch your planet for you. It's important to keep your landing codes to yourself, or at least among your close friends. Your planet should be self-sufficient, and it should be fine when you are gone. Letting someone stay on your planet when you are gone is a bad idea; remember that sitters can become squatters very quickly.

14. Out of all the advice that I have given in this book, probably the most important is listed as number four of this chapter—"Never trust a talking fish." I really can't stress this enough.

15. Remember, it is legal to use Argilelion grenades when you are fishing. It becomes illegal if somehow someone gets blown up. I don't make the laws, I just follow them sometimes.

16. Do not eat anything that glows. Since most of you have not and probably won't read my book *Dude Don't Eat That,* you would have missed the entire chapter on this rule. Basically, it states that no matter where you are in the galaxy, do not eat anything that glows. This rule applies to plants, animals, fish, or even processed food. One exception to this rule is a beverage made by trained Relleom chefs or bartenders called a Meridian Punch. I believe it is the phosphorus in the meridian fruit that grows on the Relleom home planet that makes it glow. I think they call it a punch because of the effect it has on your brain, so drink responsively.

FROM THE AUTHOR

I AM MOE

A while back, I started to write this book as a fun project, and it grew into the pile of nonsense that you have just had the opportunity to waste your time reading. Seriously, I hope that you enjoyed this book and at least got a few good laughs out of it. This is my first book, and it really has been a chance to see how bad my spelling is. Half of the big words and some of the small ones that I have typed into my computer couldn't be recognized, which means I wasn't even close on the spelling. If there were parts of the book that you thought I could have used different wording, trust me, I tried but couldn't find the right spelling. So much for being articulate. I was a graphic arts major in school, where I spent four years working on my two-year degree, but I did have one writing class. I was at UVSC for so long that the students thought I was a professor. As Mark Twain said, "I have never let my schooling interfere with my education."

I would like to say, without sounding too preachy, that I really expected that by this time in Earth's history, we would have flying cars. According to the books, movies, and early TV shows I watched as a child, we should also have motor scooters and cars that hover and fly with record-breaking speed by now too. I think someone really dropped the ball on this, and I would like to know who to talk to about it. It's true that I can get 400 channels of television through a dish the size of a dinner plate on the side of my house, and that's cool, but I would really like that flying scooter.

My name is Mark Moeller and I was born and raised in Utah. I am one of seven kids—well, more like I am one *and a half* of seven kids. Like I wrote in my book, "I have never ordered half of a sandwich." I have had the opportunity to travel to many different places in the world, but have never been as comfortable as I am in my home at the foot of the Rocky Mountains. I believe that I have a great deal in common with one of my favorite authors, J.K. Rowling, in the fact that I grew up in a small Mormon town in the high desert of Utah, and J.K. Rowling once flew over Utah on her way to Los Angeles, California. The similarities are frightening. I am looking, in advance, for a support-group for unsuccessful novelists.

I have had a life-long dream of doing stand-up comedy, and other than the fact that I am terrified of talking to more than three people at one time, it might still happen. I am married to my lovely wife, Denise, and we have four children. I have triplet boys who, at this date, are twenty-seven years old. Yes, triplets. And not one of them with my blood type. You would think that at least one of them would be good for a kidney if I needed one. Due to the fact that one, if not all, of them will read this book, I have kept the inappropriate language to a minimum, knowing it would give them the freedom to use those bad words whenever they choose. My youngest is a 17-year-old girl, and if we had known that kids could be that cute, we would have had *all* girls. I am turning fifty-seven years old this year and I am slowly coming to the conclusion that I probably will never play pro football. Not that I tried to, but before, it seemed like it was always a possibility, slim though it was.

A couple of years ago, my oldest brother, Kent, died. I think he would really have liked this book. Kent and I have always shared a love of English humor and similar tastes in music. I think he was a great influence on my sense of humor, and it was his true understanding and skilled ability to use sarcasm whenever possible that I really admired about him. Kent also knew all of the famous NASCAR drivers, their car numbers, and even most of their racing stats. I loved him anyway. I bet when he died, he got his own planet.

Sincerely Yours,
Mark McKay Moeller
(June 2025)

www.ingramcontent.com/pod-product-compliance
Lightning Source LLC
LaVergne TN
LVHW010645110826
845149LV00014B/2959
9798995698500